DREAMSCAPE

ANTONIA RACHEL WARD

DreamScape

ISBN (paperback): 978-1-7392348-7-4

ISBN (e-book): 978-1-7392348-8-1

Cover image © Sergiy Katyshkin via Shutterstock

Cover design and book formatting by Claire Saag

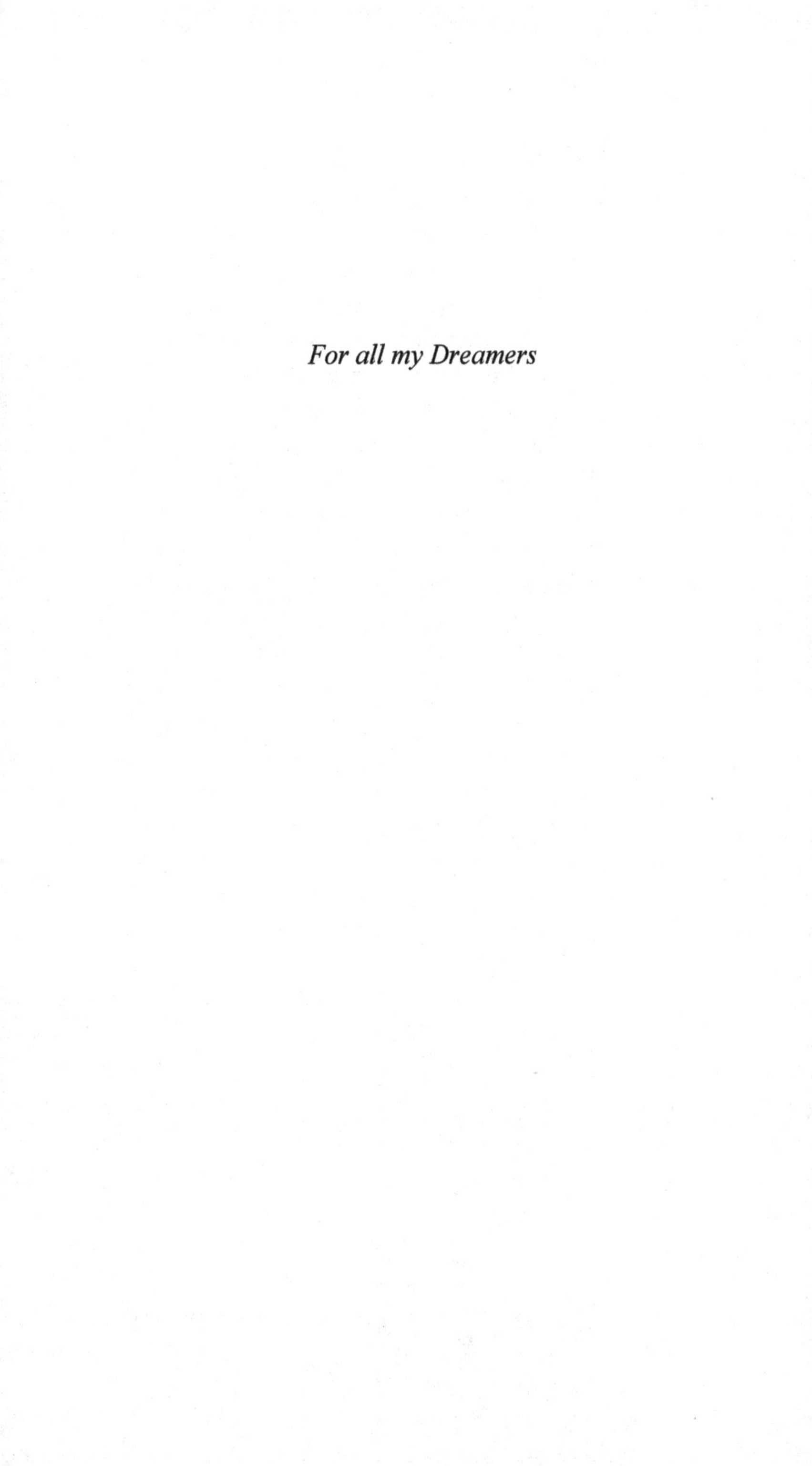

For all my Dreamers

1

When Wren Silver wanted to escape her life, she had to run a long way. San Francisco. Five thousand miles from home and it still didn't feel far enough. Weeks after her arrival, Wren's old life still clung to her like cobwebs. Even the blistering San Francisco wind couldn't shake the memories off.

Sunday morning meant time out from her schedule of classes at the prestigious art college she'd come so far to attend. While her housemates were asleep with hangovers, Wren slipped out of their rickety old bay-style house in North Beach and rode one of the antique cable-cars down to the sea. It had become something of a ritual to her over the last three weeks, this anachronistic journey through the city, the wooden car with its Victorian-style advertisements rumbling down San Francisco's hills on its hissing underground cable.

Wren didn't mind clinging to the poles on the outside of the cab as tourists took all the available seats inside. She didn't mind the patter of the grip man as he joked about losing control on the steep slopes. She didn't even mind the frequent breakdowns that left them stranded in the road while they waited for the next working car to turn up. She could have caught a driverless taxi-cab, avoiding all the fuss and jostling, but she travelled for the journey, not the destination.

That said, she loved the destination, too. She hopped off the cable car at its terminus near the old Ghirardelli chocolate factory, now host to a dozen or so shops and restaurants, and headed to the white bleachers of the aquatic park, where she sat overlooking the foggy bay. Opening her sketchbook, she began drafting the outline of the Golden Gate Bridge, which rose from the fog in the distance.

The weather had been a shock to Wren when she first arrived in San Francisco. California, she'd assumed from her home in chilly northern England, was hot. That was how it looked on TV. She hadn't been prepared for the freezing ocean winds, and had spent the first payment from her college hardship grant on hooded jumpers, gloves, and a woolly hat. On the other hand, she'd also managed to get sunburnt during her first two days in the city, thanks to the intense California sun.

Her sketch completed, she slipped her miniature paintbox from her bag and mixed some colours. She'd never seen anything like the pin-sharp azure blue of the sky here, nor the endlessly deep turquoise of the ocean, and she was determined to reproduce those colours in a painting, just as she saw them. In the weeks since she'd arrived, she kept revisiting this view, trying again and again to capture just the right shades.

Art had always been more than a hobby to Wren. It was a little world of her own that she could take with her wherever she went; somewhere she could escape to whenever things in her real life got too rough. Only when she was working on a painting did she feel truly calm, her tangled emotions blossoming out across the canvas, somehow creating something beautiful out of all the anger and sadness she'd dragged here with her.

"You're coming out tonight, right?"

Wren wasn't sure how long she'd been painting when her friend Delphi announced her arrival by dropping down to sit beside her and throwing an arm around her neck. They'd arranged to meet for lunch, but it was hard to imagine so much time had passed already.

"I haven't decided yet."

"C'mon, Silver. Live a little."

Delphi Morgan was Wren's first and best friend so far in San Francisco, even though she made Wren—with her boring brown bob and freckles—feel mousy and plain. Today, Delphi had swept her waist-length blonde hair casually to one side of her head to show off a single silver skull earring, while her t-shirt featured her favourite band—and number one passion—the Sacred Ravens.

"How's your sculpture going?" Wren asked.

"Ugh." Delphi rolled her eyes. "It's not. I've got, like, sculptor's block or something. Honestly, I don't know what I'm supposed to be doing at all. I don't know why my mom sent me here, I really don't."

"Don't be daft. I've seen your work. You're really good."

"I was in high school, maybe, but not here. Not like you. You get it, you know? You know what you're supposed to be doing, keeping sketchbooks and all that. I'm just muddling around until they realise I can't do shit and throw me out."

Wren laughed. "They're not going to throw you out."

"Sure they are. I've been thrown out of every school I've been to so far. I'm just gonna have as much fun as I can while I'm here. Which is why," she jabbed a finger at Wren, "you have to come to the Masquerade tonight."

"I can't. I've got a project due in tomorrow." Wren gestured towards her sketchbook.

Delphi snorted. "Bullshit. You work too hard, Silver. They say the Masquerade is the best party in the whole of Northern California. You're coming with us. No excuses."

Later that day, Wren and Delphi took the bus back through the fading evening light to their scruffy student house. Beneath its flaking grey paint and rotten wooden cladding, the building had traces of faded glamour: flecks of gold still nestled in the crevices of the carved pillars surrounding the door. Now, though, the place was little more than a ruin, a run-down eyesore with a heavy steel gate across the front door and a pile of black bin bags at the bottom of the steps. Wren and Delphi hopped over the rubbish, the gate clanking shut behind them as they headed inside.

Somebody had stuck a cheap holo-projector onto the ceiling in the dingy hallway, and the beige walls danced with animations, videos, and scrolling messages the house-mates had uploaded. Bikini-clad girls jostled for wall space with comic-book sketches and funny dog videos. Wren rolled her eyes and waved her hand in front of the projector's lens. The images shivered and vanished.

"We're starting over," she called, heading into the

cramped kitchen where her other housemates were gathered. "You guys are supposed to be artists."

"You blanked our hallway." Sitting at the kitchen table, Kazuo groaned, shaking his head and running a hand through his shock of fluorescent green hair. "It's gonna take ages to fill it up again."

Wren pushed herself up to sit on the grubby counter and kicked off her Converse. The smell of Bolognese rose from a cooking pot on the stove, stirred by a dark-haired girl named Ramona.

"What are you guys drinking?" Delphi rummaged in the refrigerator and pulled out a bottle of cheap wine, just as Wren's phone began buzzing. "Wren?"

Wren hopped down off the counter and held up the phone. "Sorry Delph, I'll be right back."

She darted out of the room and took the stairs two at a time, closing the door of her tiny room before answering the call.

"Wren!" Wren's mother, Harper, appeared on the screen. She had a strained look about her, her eyes wide and nervous. Her poker-straight black hair was pulled into a harsh ponytail, and her usually immaculate make-up looked smudged, as though she'd been crying.

"What do you want?" Wren sat cross-legged on the bed, looking down at her phone.

"You have to come home."

"No, I don't."

"Please, Wren. I don't have long to talk. Jared's out, but he'll be back soon."

"Let me guess, you're not allowed to talk to me?"

Harper lowered her voice as though she was afraid to be overheard. "He says you've lost your right to be part of the family by leaving us."

Wren leant against the wall and rested her phone on her legs. "I'm betting he's more upset at losing the two hundred a month I was paying him in rent."

Behind her mother, her brother, Alfie, ran around in his pyjamas with his arms outstretched, making a *brrr* sound, like a plane.

"What time is it over there?" Wren asked.

Harper glanced at Alfie guiltily. "Past midnight."

"What the hell are you all doing up?"

"I just need you to come home. Please. As soon as you can."

Wren sighed. "I'm not coming home. I told you that already. What's going on?"

Harper rubbed her eyes, smudging mascara over her face. "Bethany. She's gone missing."

At the mention of her sister, Wren sat up straighter. "Since when? When did you last see her?"

"Friday. Friday morning she went to school, and she didn't come back."

"So, she's been gone two nights?"

"I assumed she was with that boyfriend of hers Friday night. Then she didn't turn up on Saturday, so I tried to call her and got no answer. I've left so many messages. I looked in her room and her clothes are gone." Harper grimaced, close to tears. "Have you heard from her?"

"No, nothing."

"I already lost you! I can't lose Bethany, too! Please come back, Wren. If she hears you're back I'm sure she'll come home. She misses you. She doesn't like being here without you."

"Did you call the police?" Wren asked.

Harper shook her head. "Jared's out looking for her himself. He doesn't want …"

"… interference. I know." Wren sighed. "Look, you know Bethany," she said, trying to sound more confident than she felt. "This isn't the first time she's disappeared. She's probably just sulking somewhere."

"No, no, this time I'm sure she's gone. I'm sure of it. I'm going to call the police. I will."

"Harper!" Wren heard Jared's voice in the background, then the sound of a door slamming. "Who's that you're talking to?"

Harper gasped. "I have to go. Tell me if she gets in touch."

"I will, Mum. Keep me posted."

Her stepfather's shadow appeared over her mother's shoulder, and then the screen went blank.

Wren lay face down on the bed and pressed her face into her pillow, closing her eyes and letting the blackness engulf her as she listened to her own breath. It was this that she had run away to San Francisco to escape—this chaos, this constant turmoil. Bethany went missing every other week. Every time, Harper said that she would call the police, and every time, Jared talked her out of it. He didn't want anybody poking their nose into the reasons why Bethany kept running away. She always turned up after a few days, hungry but unharmed, but that didn't make it any less worrying. Being halfway across the world was supposed to make it easier to deal with, but Wren found it only made her feel worse. Perhaps Harper was right: perhaps if she had only been at home, Bethany wouldn't have run away in the first place.

She sat up again and tried to call her sister, but there was no answer. Wren sent her a message instead: Please call. Mum's worried. Where are you?

"Wren?" Delphi knocked on the door and then opened it a crack, peering round. "Are you coming down? Your food is getting cold. Hey," she added, noticing the look on Wren's face, "are you okay?"

Wren shook her head. She didn't trust herself to speak, afraid that she might start crying. Delphi sat down beside her and rubbed her back.

"Did something happen? What was that phone call about?"

"My sister's gone missing again." Wren swallowed. "I should be there."

"Oh, honey, I'm sorry. I'm sure she'll turn up safe soon."

"She always does," Wren said. "But one day she won't. What if today's that day?"

"It won't be." Delphi sounded so confident that Wren had to smile. "Come and have some dinner, and then we'll go out, okay?"

"How can I go out knowing that Bethany's out there somewhere? She could be hurt, or worse."

"It's much more likely that she's lying on her friend's sofa with a raging hangover and can't be bothered to pick up her phone," Delphi pointed out. "Trust me, I used to be that girl. That's why my parents packed me off and sent me here. It was supposed to keep me out of trouble." She laughed. "No chance of that."

Wren smiled faintly. "I bet you could find trouble anywhere."

"Damn straight. But I'm still here, aren't I? Bethany will be fine. Sitting in your room won't do her any good, and you've got your phone in case she calls. I'm sure your mom will be in touch if anything happens. Come out and take your mind off things."

Wren sighed. "All right. If you insist."

Delphi grinned. "I absolutely do."

2

The Masquerade was legendary thanks to its ever-changing secret location, wild atmosphere, and frequent police raids. By the time Wren and her housemates reached the water-front where that night's rave was taking place, the party was already buzzing.

It was a dry night, and the DJ had set up his booth on the flat roof of a ferry terminal overlooking the Bay Bridge. Ravers swarmed the street below, dancing, drinking, and pairing off as the heavy pulse of music throbbed through the ground beneath them. A holographic projector threw an array of dazzling colours and three-dimensional shapes over the heads of the dancers, while at the sidelines, men with cooler boxes hawked bottled beers and mysterious foil wraps. Ramona bought some drinks, handing them out to the others as they wove their way through the crowd, looking for space to stand.

Once they'd found a spot, Wren took a swig of her beer and looked around. The atmosphere was electric and infectious, the ear-splitting beats helping to shake away her anxieties. Cool wind blew across from the sea, but in the midst of the crowd they were shielded from it by the heat of bodies undulating to the music like waves breaking on a beach. All manner of subcultures were on display: Neo-Geisha in towering, black-lacquered platforms and elaborate headdresses danced alongside Cyborgs, who scanned the crowd with swivelling laser eyes, and Wraiths, whose veins glowed blue beneath artificially de-pigmented skin and bone-white hair.

"Look up there!" Delphi pointed to a group of black-clad girls who were clambering up the drainpipe onto the roof where the DJ was playing. "Dravens."

"Dravens?"

"They're like, elite Sacred Ravens fans. See their tattoos?"

The girls reached the roof, and Wren realised they each had a pair of tattooed black wings stretching across their shoulder blades.

"They call themselves Erik Dacre's ravens," Delphi explained. "So, Dravens. Erik is the lead singer," she added.

"Even I know that," Wren protested. "I come from England, not the dark side of the moon."

"You're so pale, who'd know the difference? Anyway, I entered a competition earlier, to win tickets and backstage passes for the gig in New York City." Delphi gazed at the Dravens enviously. "I gotta get me one of those tattoos. Imagine if I got to meet Erik Dacre and I didn't have one."

"You wouldn't seriously tattoo yourself because of a band? That's nuts."

"Shut up, they're playing a Ravens song. Come and dance." Delphi pulled Wren into the beating heart of the crowd, and Wren allowed herself to be carried away by the music—dark, heavy, and fast, with a beat that mirrored her pulse.

One of the Dravens let out a loud shriek and threw herself from the roof into the waiting hands of the dancers, who pushed her across their heads and then dragged her down into the depths. Wren hoped she was okay, but there was no way to reach her to find out. The music had everybody hypnotised, unable to do anything but sway.

After a few more songs, Wren left Delphi to dance and stumbled out of the crowd into the cool night air, wandering away from the party to check her phone. She was hoping for a message from Bethany, or at least her mother, but there was nothing. It would have been morning in England, and she could only pray her sister had already turned up safe and sound.

As she walked around the back of the terminal building, looking for a spot quiet enough to make a call, she passed the Draven who'd jumped off the roof, sitting on the ground nursing her ankle with a flock of friends around her. A little further on, Ramona and Kazuo were locked in an embrace beneath a fire escape. Wren smiled to herself and moved away so they wouldn't notice her.

Just as she was about to call her mother, she noticed the oddest sight. A few feet away, on the pier overlooking the water, several dozen people lay flat on the floor, their heads encircled with bands of tiny blinking lights that glittered like a mirror of the starry sky above.

Curious, Wren approached the group. All but one of them seemed to be fast asleep, the lights from their headbands shining directly into their closed eyes. Watching over them was a girl about Wren's age, with pastel-pink hair and a long, Grecian-style dress. Her own band of lights was pushed back atop her head, and she sat with her legs curled beneath her, leaning against a wooden post as she gazed into the water. On seeing Wren, she unfolded herself lazily and stood.

"Hey," she drawled, taking Wren's arm and drawing her toward the group. "We're having a dream party. Why don't you join us?"

The girl gazed into Wren's face with a hazy half-smile. Her eyes were unfocused, clouded with a greyish mist. Wren understood at once what she was seeing.

"You're Scapers," she said.

The girl and her sleeping friends were addicts, connected to an online virtual world known as the DreamScape through a direct neural feed that came from the headbands, or 'Coronas', that they wore. The DreamScape had been outlawed long ago, and Wren had only ever seen a handful of users in her small town, where Scaping was almost as frowned upon as Class A drugs. Indeed, the fog in the girl's eyes was caused by the drugs she and the other Scapers used to enhance their experience.

"We prefer to be called Dreamers, but sure." The girl's fingers lingered, cool pinpricks on Wren's wrist. "We're trying to organize the biggest dream party there's ever been. It's incredible. And," she added, in a hushed voice, "they say the Dream God himself might even appear."

"The Dream God?"

The girl raised her eyebrows. "The Dream God! Hypnos! Can you imagine? I would die to meet him. Here," she pointed at a small pile of spare headbands. "Put one on and see for yourself."

"I … don't think so." Wren tried to back off, but the girl gripped her arm.

"You've never been in the DreamScape, have you?"

"It's illegal."

The girl sighed softly, almost sadly. "Ah, it's harmless. You can't hurt anyone in there. They try to stop us because they don't want us to know true freedom. Imagine! A place with no rules or restrictions. That's what the DreamScape is. The government want you to think it's dangerous, immoral, but what they really fear is that we do not need them there. We Dreamers govern ourselves."

"From what I hear, you don't do a very good job of it."

It was well-known that the DreamScape was wild and unruly, a hotbed for organised crime, and a place where the most degraded people could get whatever experiences they wanted, as long as they could pay the price. At first, the virtual world had been perfectly legal, but order had quickly disintegrated. Not only was the network notoriously difficult to police, but there had been a rash of news stories about people who'd spent too long Scaping and lost their grip on reality.

After a particularly bloody school massacre perpetrated by a hardcore Scaper who was later certified insane, the world's governments had collaborated in order to get the DreamScape shut down, barely ten years after its creation. Wren had only been a child at the time, but traces of the Scape still remained, for those who knew where to look.

The girl smiled. "Before you judge us, you should at least experience things from our point of view. Here." She picked up a Corona and tried to pass it to Wren. "My name is Andromeda. I'll look after you."

"Leave her alone!" Wren heard Delphi's voice behind her and turned around. "Come on, Wren. Ignore her."

Andromeda shrugged and drifted back to her post beside the sleeping bodies. Wren gave her one last glance, then followed Delphi back down the pier.

"Those Scapers are crazy," Delphi said. "You don't want to listen to them."

"She was babbling about something—someone—called Hypnos. Have you ever heard of that?"

"Oh, Jeez," Delphi rolled her eyes. "Some kind of cult, I think. I used to hang with a bunch of them at school. They act like it's a full-on religion."

"Wow," said Wren. "They have gods now?"

"That shit gets into their brains. If you ask me, I think they just made the whole thing up. A Scaper fairy tale. Promise me, Wren—never go in there. I tried it once. I've tried a lot of things, but Christ, that was a mind fuck, and not the fun kind."

Wren and her housemates headed home in the early hours of the morning. It was still dark, but the streets of San Francisco were alive with light, the city a glowing, pulsating entity filled with promise. Wren and Delphi walked side by side up the steep hill towards their house, Ramona and Kazuo trailing behind, and Wren felt strangely calm and happy, despite her worries about Bethany.

She took the steps up to the house two at a time, giggling as she tried to scan her entry card. It took several clumsy attempts, but eventually the lock opened, and she and Delphi tumbled inside, laughing, holding onto each other's waists. Wren was surprised to see a light coming from behind the kitchen door, and a moment later, another of her housemates, Jon, stepped out, his face solemn and tired.

"Wren," he said. "There's somebody here to see you."

Wren went into the kitchen, blinking beneath the stark artificial light. A girl sat at the table, head down, hunched amongst the dirty dishes and discarded artworks. Her hands, with their black-painted, bitten fingernails, were wrapped around a steaming mug, but she didn't look interested in drinking from it. Her long black hair fell across her face, and the hood of her pink top obscured everything but her small, snub nose, but even so, Wren knew her better than she would have known herself.

It was her sister. It was Bethany.

3

Lia Céline sat in a corner of the ballet studio, legs curled beneath her, shoulders hunched as she drew a needle and thread through the ribbons on her brand-new pointe shoes. Once they were securely fastened, she took a lighter and singed their ends to stop them from fraying, the flame dancing just above her fingers. As she worked, the room filled with dancers arriving for their first class after summer break. Amongst them was Lia's friend Marianne, already dressed in her leotard and legwarmers. She dropped her bag down beside Lia's and sat on the floor, stretching her legs out in front of her.

"First day of term, huh? Damn, I am so stiff."

"It's so strange. So much like being back at school." Lia shook her head in amazement, looking around at the all-too-familiar studio where she'd taken daily classes as a student of London's Royal Ballet School.

"Like being at school, except now you're star pupil," Marianne whispered, nodding towards a group of young dancers who kept glancing in Lia's direction. "Everybody's dying to see you dance."

"I used to dream of this. Coming back here, dancing principal roles. I've been doing Sleeping Beauty for years in America, but on this stage ..."

"I'll bet that feels special. I felt the same when I did my first solo role in Los Angeles. Not quite Sleeping Beauty, sure, but it was good to have the spotlight on my home stage."

"You'll get your chance at the principal roles."

"Me? Nah. That ship has sailed." Marianne shifted position, stretching one leg out and leaning forward to rest her head on her knee. "I'm nearly thirty. At my age, I know a soloist is all I'm ever gonna be."

"Well, it's nice to be working with you again," Lia said. "Thanks for convincing the directors to let me dance here this year."

Marianne laughed, switching legs. "They didn't take much convincing. I only had to say the name Lia Céline and they were all over you."

Lia got to her feet, put down her shoes and stood firmly on each toe in turn, pressing down with her whole weight to loosen the stiff glue blocks a little more. Amidst the low hum of conversation, she caught her own name: "Lia Céline? ... Wasn't she the one who used to go out with Erik Dacre?"

"That's all I'll ever be, isn't it?" she whispered. "The one who used to go out with Erik Dacre?"

Marianne lifted her head, shaking a few dark curls out of her face. "Maybe now you'll be the one who married Scott Lincoln. You got a problem with that, perhaps you should stop dating these famous men." She grinned. "How was the honeymoon, anyway?"

"It was wonderful." Lia slipped on her shoes and knotted

the ribbons around her ankles. "Hawaii really is stunning."

"I sure hope you didn't spend too much time dancing?"

"Are you kidding? I practised for two hours a day." Lia turned to the mirror above the barre, catching sight of her reflection's honey-blonde hair and blue eyes as she stretched. "There was a balcony with a gorgeous view, and a railing just the right height to use as a barre. As if I was going to let myself get out of shape just before coming back here."

Marianne got to her feet. "And that's why you're a principal and I'm not. I like my rest too much. Besides, shouldn't you have been spending that time with Scott?"

"I let things slide for a man once before," Lia replied. "And it almost ruined my career. I'm not going to let that happen again, even if he is my husband."

"Scott'll never drain you dry the way Erik did. He's a good egg, as you Brits say."

The two of them stood at the barre, settling into silence as the pianist struck up. Lia melted into the familiar repeated movements, Marianne's solemn words still ringing in her mind. But soon the sequence calmed her thoughts, as it always did, and she began to focus only on the details. Was she arching her foot too much on the *tendu*? Lifting her shoulders as she moved her arms? Were her fingers as soft as they ought to be? When dancing, there was never any room to focus on anything else, and Lia was glad of the break.

Of course she had wanted to stay in shape during her holiday, but that wasn't the only reason she'd spent so much time practising. Ever since her wedding she'd felt ill at ease, frustrated with herself and everything around her, as if she was wearing a life that fit her awkwardly, and she didn't know how to move within it. Dancing was a rest from all of that, but a dancer's career is short, and at twenty-nine Lia was already wondering what she would do when it was all over, when she had nothing left but the gilded prison she had built herself.

She knew what Scott wanted from her. He would have liked her to quit dancing and have some babies, and for her to stay behind and take care of them while he travelled around the world making movies. Lia wanted that too, she thought. Children, and a comfortable home, and the time to enjoy watching them grow up. So far, her whole life had been consumed by the need to keep working, keep practising, stay in shape. At times the thought of saying goodbye to all that for good was inviting. Yet there were days, like today, when she wondered if that was really all life had in store for her. Sure, she would be a wife and a mother, and hopefully a very good one, but when her career was over, what would be left of Lia Céline herself?

It was growing dark by the time Lia took the elevator up to Scott's penthouse apartment. Of course, the Chelsea flat belonged to her too now, but it still felt like Scott's alone, bare and bachelor pad-like, with the same minimalist furniture he'd bought with the apartment five years ago. It was unusually quiet when she entered, although she could tell that Scott was home by the glow of light from within. She put her bag and coat away in the cupboard and headed down the steps into the open-plan sitting room. Opposite her, a vast window looked out onto the glittering London skyline, while in the centre of the room Scott sat on his white leather sofa, hunched over his tablet, his figure small beneath the high ceiling. He looked up as Lia entered, but did not return her smile.

"Hey ..." Lia's greeting faded on her lips. Scott had the kind of face that seemed open, warm, and vulnerable all at once—it was one of the things that made him such a sought-after actor—but tonight his expression seemed unusually guarded, his dark eyes strangely cold. "Everything all right?"

"Why didn't you tell me?"

"Tell you?" Lia was startled to see a flash of suppressed fury cross Scott's chiselled features. Wordlessly, he handed her the tablet, and Lia looked down with a sinking heart at the photograph on the screen.

It was her, outside the village chapel where she and Scott had been married, the white tulle of her wedding dress billowing in the wind. She gazed up at a dark-haired man in a leather jacket, her hand outstretched to meet his. His hair covered his face, but there was no mistaking who he was, and just in case there had been any doubt, the caption—written by some heartless hack on a gossip website, Lia guessed—described 'Ballerina Lia Céline sharing an intimate moment with her ex, Sacred Ravens front-man Erik Dacre just moments before her wedding to *Code Red* actor Scott Lincoln'. *Intimate moment.* They didn't like to mince their words, these gossip columnists. Lia took a deep breath.

"They made it look a lot worse than it was," she said, her voice quiet. "You know what they're like. It was hardly an 'intimate moment'. We were in the middle of the street! I was only trying to get rid of him."

"Yeah, looks like you were really trying."

Lia looked again at the expression on her own face and wanted to cry. They'd chosen to photograph her at the worst possible instant. At that precise moment in time, the last thing she had wanted was for Erik to go, and it showed. Still, it had been a fleeting second, she told herself, and she had nothing to feel guilty about.

"You can ask anyone who was there," she said. "My parents, Esmé, Marianne ... Even Mike. They all saw that I only went over to stop him from causing trouble."

"All those people, huh? You, your parents, your sister ... my own goddamn brother. Every single one of you knew that this bastard turned up on our wedding day and not a single one of you thought to tell me?"

"Scott," Lia reached out to him, but he pulled away. "I didn't want to spoil your day. Our day. Honestly, it just didn't seem important."

"I'll be the judge of what's important," Scott snapped. "This is not how it goes, Lia. You do not get to decide what you do and don't tell me about. This," he jabbed his finger at the picture on the tablet, "this makes me look like a damn fool. Do you know how I found out about this? My manager sent it to me. I had to find out that my wife was meeting her ex not from her, or even from any of our family or friends, but from my goddamn manager!"

"I wasn't meeting him!" Lia protested. "He turned up. I hadn't even spoken to him for three years."

"Please, spare me the damned technicalities. I know what I see here. I know what everybody else sees here. I see you and him making a fool of me in the international press. You don't get to do that, Lia. You understand me? You do not get to do that."

Lia opened her mouth to speak, but her words caught in

her throat, stifled by the tears that threatened to flow. She hurried into the hallway, grabbed her bag and coat, and went back out.

At first, Lia didn't know where she intended to go. She took the elevator back to the lobby, leaning against the wall as it descended and trying to compose herself enough to pass the night porter without letting on that anything was wrong. When she'd dated Erik, she'd learnt the hard way that people noticed every little detail when it came to the famous, and the last thing she needed now was to start rumours of a rift between her and Scott. She'd forgotten that lesson once already, and look how much damage it had done.

How could she have been so stupid? She shook her head and took a deep breath, trying to drive the tears away. How could she have stood there in the middle of the street like that, and not noticed all the tourists with their cameras? The only justification she could offer herself was that Erik hadn't seemed to care, so she had forgotten to care herself, but of course Erik hadn't cared. Why would he? He had nothing to lose from being seen trying to interfere with her wedding—if anything the story would only add to the romantic legend that he built around himself.

The Dravens would love it, Lia thought scornfully, twisting her wedding ring around on her finger. They were probably bitching about her on their web feeds at that very moment, swooning over poor, lovelorn Erik. All of it worked in his favour, whether he meant it that way or not, and no wonder he hadn't given a damn what he did to her in the process.

The lift reached the ground floor, and Lia hurried across the foyer with a cursory nod to the porter, walking as though she had somewhere particular to be. The moment she got outside, though, her steps slowed, and for a while she simply followed her feet, soon finding herself at South Kensington tube station. She considered going to Marianne's, but that would mean explaining what had happened, and she knew her friend would ignore everything else in her haste to blame Erik.

Marianne had been alongside Lia when she was dancing with the Los Angeles Ballet, and had seen her through all of her darkest times with Erik. Because of that, Marianne could see no good in him and—as if the two were somehow mutually exclusive—no bad in Scott. Lia knew exactly what she would say, and she didn't want to hear it. She got on the Piccadilly line and headed towards the only other place she could think of to go.

The performance at the Royal Opera House that night had already begun, and the staff entrance was quiet. Lia slipped inside and up to the cloakroom unnoticed by all except the security guard, who recognised her and passed her a key-card for the studio. He was no doubt used to workaholic dancers turning up out of hours. Almost without thinking, she changed back into her practice leotard and sweats, and pulled her long hair up into a scruffy ponytail before entering the deserted studio.

Outside the window, faraway skyscrapers glittered over the rooftops of Covent Garden. A blimp drifted high overhead, bathing the studio in a wash of blue neon as it projected a holo-advertisement across the city. Lia closed the door quietly and sat on the floor without switching on the lights, finding peace in the darkness. She remained there for some time, ignoring the call from Scott that flashed up on her phone. She considered working on her solo for Sleeping Beauty, but she didn't have the will. Instead, she scanned through her music collection until she found a Sacred Ravens song.

Lia had never particularly enjoyed Erik's music. It was dark and bleak and difficult to listen to, not to mention the fact that so many of his songs were about her. At first, it had seemed romantic—as a girl she'd dreamed of having songs written about her—but the novelty had worn off the very first time Lia heard one on the radio. It was like having her diary shared all over the internet, and it left her feeling exposed and ashamed, sure everyone else could read into Erik's lyrics exactly what she understood from them. From then on she'd tried to block out what he did, treating it as a job and nothing more, even though she knew for him it was his life-blood.

The thought made her feel a little guilty. Sometimes she wondered if she'd really tried hard enough to understand Erik, but then she remembered how selfish he had been—how cruel, at times. If anyone hadn't tried hard enough, it was surely him. And now here he was ruining her life all over again, his presence already casting a dark shadow over her new marriage. She was angry with him, and herself, and Scott most of all, just for being so damn irreproachable. Of course he had done nothing wrong. He never did. How could she expect him to understand a fleeting mistake, a moment of weakness? The worst of it was that she could understand exactly why he was so upset about the photograph, and she knew she would feel just the same in his shoes. Somehow that made her even more furious.

Holding on to her anger, Lia put on the Sacred Ravens song, turned it up loud and got to her feet. Barefoot, she traced a few of the steps from her Sleeping Beauty solo, but soon, buffeted along by the music, the dance started to evolve into something different, something more fitting to the stark, edgy beats. She felt it in the soles of her feet, pushing her into new contortions, twisting her leaps in mid-air, drawing out a desire to create that she had never even known was there.

When the music ended, she raced back to the player, breathing heavily, and set the song to repeat, trying to re-trace and memorise what she'd just invented. It was as though the dance had always been there, somewhere inside of her, and all of a sudden everything had just clicked into place so that it came to her with perfect clarity: a raised arm here, a jump there, a few small adjustments ... And there it was, sharp and bright as a freshly cut diamond. Something entirely her own.

Finally satisfied that she remembered the dance by heart, Lia switched off the music and fell against the barre with an exultant laugh. A few short minutes ago she'd felt desolate—now she was elated, shivering with excitement. She'd never thought of herself as a creative person, but that dance had changed her mind. It was a revelation, and she was desperate to tell somebody—somebody who would understand exactly what it meant. Almost without thinking, she reached for her phone and dialled Erik's number.

It had hardly rung twice before she came to her senses. Aside from his appearance at the wedding, she hadn't spoken to him for years, and there was no way she ought to be contacting him now, after what had just happened with Scott. Still, she let the phone ring on, unsure whether she would really tell him about the dance, or scream at him for not realising how much damage he had done, or lose her nerve and hang up at the last moment.

Just as she was about to give up, it rang out and she heard that all-too-familiar lazy drawl: "Hey, it's Erik. Leave a message."

Lia swiped her finger hurriedly across the screen to cancel the call and packed up her things, feeling rattled. She made her way back to the cloakroom, where she showered and changed, intending to head home and do whatever grovelling was necessary to make things up to Scott. Just as she was drying her hair, she heard a buzzing from her phone and picked it up, assuming it was her husband again. She was about to answer and apologise for disappearing when she saw the caller ID and froze—it was Erik, returning her call.

Lia stood with her finger hovering above the answer button, feeling that to pick up the call would mean crossing a line she was no longer willing to step over. The elation from a few moments ago had worn off, and she cursed herself for calling him, realising how easily her intentions could be misconstrued. Perhaps she ought to answer and explain herself. But what could she possibly say? Perhaps it was better left alone.

Before she had a chance to decide, the phone rang out again, and she hit speaker just in time to hear Erik begin his message.

"Hey Li," he said, sounding uncharacteristically hesitant. "You called me? I, uh, just wanted to check that everything was okay … Are you there?" As he paused, Lia bit her lip, staring at the featureless black screen, too torn to know whether to answer or hang up.

"Look," Erik went on, in his warm, abrasive tone, "just

let me know everything's okay. You don't have to call me, just send me a message, or whatever, all right? Bye, Lia."

Wincing, Lia tossed her phone into her bag, slung it over her shoulder, and hurried home as quickly as she could.

4

"What the hell are you doing here?"

Wren stormed across the kitchen and slammed her hands down on the table, leaning into her sister's face like an interrogator. Bethany glared from beneath her pink hood, her black-lined eyes narrow and suspicious.

"Thought I'd see the nice life you got now."

"Oh, right," Wren raised her hands. "So you thought you'd get on a shuttle and come halfway across the world without telling anybody, just like that?"

Bethany shrugged. "You did." She looked down, started picking at the holes she'd pushed into her cuffs with her thumbs.

"Where did you even get the money?" Wren was acutely aware of her housemates standing clustered in the doorway. At that moment, she hated Bethany for dragging her drama across the ocean and shattering the peace of her new life. "Well? Where did you get the money?"

"Borrowed it."

"From who?"

Bethany looked slyly to one side, avoiding her sister's

eye. "Jared," she muttered, barely audibly.

"You did not fucking borrow money from Jared. You stole it from Jared. How stupid are you, Bethany? Jesus Christ."

"It doesn't matter. I'm not going back."

"Oh, really?" Wren flung herself into the nearest chair, eyeing her sister from across the table. "Well, you're not staying here."

"Why the hell not?"

"For one, what am I supposed to do with you? I hardly have enough money to feed myself, let alone you as well. There's not even enough space for you to sleep on my floor. Two, you're fifteen, for God's sake. You can't just leave home like that. If you stop going to school, mum'll get arrested. Is that what you want?"

"I don't even go to school anyway," Bethany protested. "And ..."

"Shut up! I'm not finished. Three, you're a fucking illegal immigrant, Bethany. You don't have a visa; you don't have a job. The Americans are not going to let you stay here just because you feel like it."

Bethany folded her arms, sullenly. "You don't have to tell anyone, though."

"Ugh! You are out of this world." Wren pushed her chair back, rattling its legs across the tiled floor. "Well, I bloody hope you nicked enough money to get you home, because you're not staying here."

She got to her feet, reaching for her phone, and Bethany jumped up, panicked. "You can't make me go back! He'll kill me! Are you gonna send me back to my death? Because that's what's gonna happen."

"You should've thought of that before you stole from

him and ran away."

"Oh, so running away's all right for you, but not for me? You just abandoned me. You left me to deal with all that shit on my own. You didn't even tell me you were going! You're such a fucking bitch."

"I'm a bitch for wanting to make something of my life, am I?" Wren snapped back. "Well sorry I worked hard at school instead of dossing about all day in the park, drinking."

"Yeah, 'cos I do that 'cos my life's so fucking great." Bethany rolled her eyes. "Stupid cow."

"If I'm such a cow, what are you even doing here?" Wren knew she was going too far, but she couldn't stop. It was as though all the bad memories she'd tried to run from were coming flooding back, all at once. "You just want to wreck everything for me, don't you? You know what? Jared'll come after you. You stole money from him. He's going to come get you. If he comes over here because of you, I'm going to …"

"Go on then. What're you gonna do?" Bethany howled. "What are you gonna do that he hasn't already done to me? You left me. You fucking left me." She swiped her hand across the worktop behind her, grabbed a glass and hurled it at Wren's head. Wren ducked, and the glass smashed against the wall, shattering into a thousand tiny shards.

"You're fucking mental," Wren said, her voice low and trembling. "Get out. Get the hell out."

"Don't worry, I'm going." Bethany shoved past the housemates. "Enjoy your cushy life, Wren. You'll be sorry when I'm dead."

"More like relieved," Wren muttered, but Bethany was already gone. A final slam of the door rattled the windowpanes, and then the house fell silent.

Wren stared at the glass shattered all over the floor, suddenly numb. She'd thought she was safe here, so far away, and now this … It was like an old nightmare coming back to haunt her. She put a hand to her head and turned back to her friends. "I'm so sorry guys."

"Oh my God, Wren, are you all right?" Ramona rushed to take Wren's face in her hands, checking her forehead and beneath her hair. "Did any of the glass get you?"

"No, I don't think so."

"Sit down. You look so pale."

Feeling wobbly, Wren took a seat as Delphi picked her way through the glass to the window. "I can't see your sister."

"She just needs a bit of time to cool down," Wren said. "So do I, I guess. She won't go far. At least, I hope not."

"Don't worry about it." Ramona went to put on the kettle. "Are you going to tell your mom?"

Wren shook her head. "If I tell her, my stepdad will realise it was Bethany who took his money. He'll be furious. He's sure to come after her, and then I don't know what he'll do. Maybe he really would kill her. Jared doesn't care about anything as much as he cares about his money."

"So we have to find a way to get Bethany back to England, without letting on to your mom and Jared that she's been here?" Delphi said.

"Yes. No. I don't know. How can I send her back there? You guys don't know what he's like." Wren held up her right hand, showing a palm that was silvery with scars. "One time he held my hand over the stove. Another time he hit my mum so hard she blacked out. I always tried to protect Bethany from the worst of it, but now that I'm not there …"

"Wren …" Ramona rubbed her back. "Maybe we should all get some sleep. Things will look better in the morning."

"What about Bethany?"

"I'll stay up," Kazuo volunteered. "In case she comes back. And she can call you, right?"

Wren nodded. "I'll keep my phone on loud. Thanks, Kaz. Thanks, all of you."

"Shh," Ramona shooed her out of the room. "Get to bed."

Wren went upstairs, but she didn't sleep. She tried calling Bethany, and when her sister didn't answer, sent a message apologising and asking her to come back as soon as possible. She lay down and closed her eyes, but she couldn't rest when her sister was out there in a strange city, alone. She could only hope Bethany wouldn't stray too far and get lost.

The next morning, though, there was still no sign of Bethany. The police took her description, listened to Wren describe their last conversation with great interest, then insisted on speaking to their mother. Wren sat uselessly by as a keen young detective named Reeves quizzed Harper over video link. She could see the cogs in the officer's mind turning, filling in the gaps that Wren and her mother were leaving in their stories.

"Why do you think your daughter would want to run away?"

"Probably jealous." Harper was choosing her words carefully. Wren recognised her mother's brittle, defensive demeanour from all the other times they'd encountered the police. Even when Harper herself had been the one to call them, she would still put up walls as soon as they came asking questions. "She kept talking about wanting to see where Wren was living now. She missed her sister, didn't she?"

Wren had avoided mentioning her stepfather when she spoke to the detective. She wasn't even entirely sure why, apart from out of deep-seated habit and some niggling conviction that explaining everything would only make things worse for Bethany when they did find her. But now Jared lurked like a shadow in the background of the video call, and Wren could see the concealed fury glittering in his black, button-like eyes.

"What about the shuttle fare? How could she afford it?" the detective asked.

Harper glanced nervously back at her husband. "I have no idea."

"Costs a few hundred dollars, crossing the Atlantic on a supersonic shuttle. You don't know where she might have come across that much money? Did she have a job?"

Harper shook her head, her jaw so tense that Wren could see the tendons in her neck.

"And you haven't noticed any money going missing?"

"No." Another tell-tale glance back at Jared. Detective Reeves leaned forward.

"Has your husband?"

"No."

There was a long pause. Wren folded her arms to keep from fidgeting. When the detective looked at her, she tried to stare back with an innocent, hopeful expression, but she could tell he suspected them of hiding something.

"Well." He unfolded his tall frame and stood. "If you

think of anything, ma'am, be sure to let me know. Will you be coming to San Francisco?"

Wren held her breath. Harper bent her head, pulling her dark hair out of its ponytail and brushing it back from her face with her fingers before looping the elastic around it once more and pulling it tight against her scalp. She was waiting for some kind of signal from Jared, Wren knew, because she didn't dare make a decision that he might not approve of. In the end he answered for her, coming towards the camera, all charm.

"I hope that won't be necessary, officer." He smiled, his gold tooth glinting. "I'm sure you'll find our girl in no time. We just want her back, safe and sound, don't we, sweetheart." He put a hand on Harper's shoulder and his eyes met Wren's. "We'd hate for any harm to come to our Bethany."

Wren glared back at Jared, right into those button eyes. *One day*, she thought, burning all the hate she could muster into her stare, *one day you'll get what you deserve.*

She hoped he understood. Detective Reeves assured them he would do his best, closed the call, and turned to Wren.

"I'm sending you my contact details," he said, tapping his phone. "If you think of anything that might help us build a picture of what your sister was thinking when she left here, let me know. Anything, no matter how small or insignificant. The better we understand her motivations, the easier it will be for us to work out where she went next, okay?"

"Okay." Wren nodded.

"Thank you for your time, Ms Silver."

5

Three days went by with no sign of Bethany. Wren tried to carry on as normal, even as worry clawed at her insides. She went to class, worked on her painting, hung out with her friends, just as if nothing had happened, her stomach knotted all the while. She knew she was damaging the investigation by not explaining the real situation to the police, yet she was afraid of the harm she might do if she told them the truth. She doubted that they could arrest Jared for anything, and if they did it would be the sisters' word against his. Harper would never stand up for them. Most likely it would just make him more angry, and he would take it out on Bethany when she got home.

Even from thousands of miles away, Wren could still feel Jared's clammy fingers around her wrist, pushing her hand into the hot gas flame. *You'll not be doing any more painting for a good while now, will you?* Her scar still ached when she thought about it. Perhaps Bethany was better off, wherever she was now.

Then, one afternoon, Wren was interrupted by a phone call just as she put the finishing touches to her canvas. It was Detective Reeves: they had found Bethany.

"Oh, thank God." Wren's knees went weak with relief. "Is she okay?" Across the room, Delphi caught her eye and darted over, leaning in to listen to the officer's response.

"We need you to come to the hospital, ma'am."

Wren sat down heavily on the nearest chair. "She's alive, isn't she? Please, just tell me!"

"She's alive, yes, but unconscious. You'd better come to the hospital."

Her voice shaking, Wren dictated the police officer's directions to Delphi, who called a driverless cab. Detective Reeves greeted them on their arrival, ushering them briskly inside. He walked through the maze of white corridors with his hands thrust into the pockets of his black coat, his long-legged strides putting Wren in mind of a preying mantis.

"What's going on?" she said, hurrying to keep up.

The detective slowed his pace slightly. "I know you're worried ma'am, but I think it's best that the doctor explains everything."

"But is Bethany okay? Is she hurt?"

"Here we are." Reeves came to a halt beside a viewing window looking into a private ward. "You can ask the doctor for yourself."

The glass was run through with wire mesh. Wren looked through the pattern of tiny diamonds at her sister. Bethany lay on the bed in a white hospital gown, her dark hair loose around her shoulders, her expression soft and relaxed, a drip fixed into one bare arm. She looked for all the world as if she was sleeping, except that around her head was a band of blinking lights, like a halo.

Wren put her hands on the window and leaned in closer, her nose almost touching the glass. "She's hooked up to a

Corona. Why?"

"That's how she was found, I'm afraid." A neatly dressed doctor with a bright English accent approached them, smiling sympathetically, and held out her hand. "You must be Wren. My name is Doctor Nandra, but you can call me Naveen. Would you like to go in and see your sister?"

Wren nodded dumbly. Naveen led her into the dimly lit room, Delphi following close behind. Detective Reeves remained in the corridor. In the semi-darkness, the lights around Bethany's head twinkled like tiny stars. Wren approached her sister and touched her hand. She was relieved to find that it felt warm and alive.

"Where was she found?" she asked, in a hushed voice.

"In Golden Gate Park. Somebody stumbled over her while he was walking his dog. We don't know how she got there, but the detective suspects she was abandoned by whomever she'd been associating with."

Wren reached for the Corona. "Can we take this off?"

"I'm afraid not." Naveen put a hand on her shoulder. "It's dangerous to disconnect somebody from the Dream-Scape too suddenly. Rather like waking a sleepwalker. Bethany's brain activity is so closely entwined with the network right now that breaking the connection could damage her neural pathways."

"So, we have to wait until she comes out of it on her own?"

"That's right. Only, we think Bethany's been asleep for quite a while. At least for a couple of days. We've tried to gently coax her awake, but so far nothing has worked."

"Oh no," Delphi whispered, coming forward. "She's not … lost, is she?"

Naveen frowned. "I'm afraid it's starting to look that

way."

"What does that mean?" Wren asked. "Lost?"

"In the DreamScape," Delphi explained. "I've heard about this. People go into the Scape and they just … don't come out. It's like they're so deep asleep that nothing can wake them."

Naveen nodded. "There's been a spate of cases like this recently. It's one of the reasons the government tries so hard to discourage people from using the DreamScape. The network is unregulated and dangerous, and the drugs people use to help enhance the experience are very powerful, forcing the body into a state of paralysis. Sometimes, a user connected to the network simply drops into a coma and becomes unresponsive. We don't fully understand how it happens, or why, but, like your friend said, they seem to become 'lost' in there."

Wren looked at her little sister. She seemed so young still, despite everything she'd been through. Small, delicate, and vulnerable. It was agonising to think of her lying there, so close, and yet a million miles away, trapped somewhere where Wren could not protect her. She wanted to reach into the DreamScape and pull her out somehow.

"But … she's only sleeping," she said. "She'll wake up eventually, right?"

"Honestly, we don't know," Naveen said, gently. "In our experience, the longer somebody stays in the DreamScape, the less likely it is for them to wake."

"And people like Bethany? Who've been there for days?"

Naveen took a deep breath and sighed. "So far, we don't know of any case where a lost person has ever regained consciousness. I'm very sorry, Wren."

6

"You did not call Erik!" Marianne folded her arms and leaned across the table towards Lia, glaring at her as if simply saying the words would make them true.

"It was a mistake. I was upset. He didn't even pick up, so …"

"So what? That makes it not matter? I knew it. The minute I saw him at your wedding I knew he was going to start messing with your head again."

Lia looked down at her bowl of tagliatelle, twisting a strand around on her fork until it slipped off, back into the creamy sauce she shouldn't have been eating in the first place.

"It's not his fault. It was all me. Scott and I had a fight and I …"

"Had a fight about what?" Marianne reached over to refill Lia's wine glass. Scott was away filming in Italy for the week, and Marianne had turned up at the penthouse uninvited, bearing takeaway from Lia's favourite restaurant. At first, Lia had been glad of the distraction—Scott had left that morning still barely speaking to her, and she knew that without Marianne there she would only have spent the evening brooding—but now she was beginning to wish for solitude, or at least not to have to explain the whole situation to her friend.

"It's nothing. It doesn't matter."

"Come on, girl. You've been looking down all day. Get it all out. You'll feel better."

Lia took a sip of her wine. "There was just some rubbish on a gossip site about Erik turning up at the wedding, and Scott took it too seriously. You know how those people make things look so much worse than they are. I apologised. It's all sorted now. He just needs a day or two to cool down."

"Li …"

"You don't need to give me that look. I know what you're going to say."

"Can't you see that Erik's getting exactly what he wants here? He's poisoning your marriage."

"It's not like that."

"It's exactly like that. I mean, he doesn't even have to try, does he? All he had to do was show his face at the right moment and BAM!" Marianne slammed her hand down hard on the table, making Lia jump. "He's wrecking your life again and what do you do? Call him up. Sometimes I think you're a lost cause, Li, I really do."

Lia bit her lip. "I think you're being really unfair."

"To you or to him?"

"Both of us. Erik's hardly a saint but he would never ruin things for me deliberately. That's just not the kind of person he is."

Marianne spread her hands, her pizza entirely forgotten. "I can't believe you're defending him."

"I'm not defending him. I hate him for turning up like

that. I'm just saying that he's not a bad person. He's just …"

"Just what? Selfish? Thoughtless? A cheat and a liar and an addict who thinks he can do whatever he wants just because a bunch of dumb little girls treat him like he's some sort of god? Let them have him, Li. Delete his number—which, by the way, you should've done years ago. Take a day off rehearsals and go out to Italy to make things up with Scott. I'll tell them you're sick or something."

Lia sighed. "I can't just bunk off work."

"Why not? It's not as if you've got a performance tonight."

"Just … leave it, will you?" Lia wiped her tears away impatiently, frustrated with herself. Marianne gave her a sympathetic smile, which was even worse than her anger. "Maybe you're right. Maybe I am a lost cause."

"Oh, girl, you know you shouldn't listen to me when I'm angry. You've got a good thing with Scott. Just promise me you'll put Erik out of your mind. Don't let him get to you. Okay?"

Lia nodded, smiling weakly. "Erik who?"

"That's my girl."

After Marianne left, Lia curled up on Scott's white leather sofa with her favourite pashmina wrapped around her shoulders, switched on the large screen above the fireplace and dialled her husband's number. He answered almost immediately, appearing on her screen sitting on a bed in a fluffy hotel robe, pink-faced with wet hair, obviously fresh from the shower.

"Hey, Li." He rubbed a towel over his hair and smiled his perfect, American smile, and Lia knew right away that she was forgiven. "I'm sorry I left so abruptly this morning."

"I'm sorry. For everything."

"You don't need to keep apologising. I overreacted. Let's just try to forget about it, hey?" His gaze moved to the dining table behind her, still strewn with empty dishes and wine glasses. "You had somebody over tonight?"

"Just Marianne. She surprised me with a takeaway."

"Yeah? What did you have?"

"Italian. From that place around the corner. Because I couldn't come to Italy, she thought she'd bring Italy to me."

Scott laughed. "She's okay, you know. Makes me feel better to know you've got someone to keep you company. Tell you what, why don't you catch the shuttle out to Venice on Friday when you're done at work? I'll book my room for an extra night, and we can get some real Italian food."

Lia smiled. "That sounds wonderful. How is Venice?"

"I'll bet it's swell, but I spent most of my day jumping out of a window onto a crash mat, so I didn't have a whole lot of time for sightseeing. Naw, it's a beautiful place. You'll love it."

Lia hugged her knees to her chest. "I can't wait. But I should let you get some sleep. You must have an early start tomorrow."

"Yeah, we gotta get some shots of St Mark's Square before the tourists turn up. I'll call you tomorrow. Love you."

"You too."

The screen went dark. Lia sat looking at her own reflection in the black glass. Marianne was right. She had a good thing going with Scott. It was nice to be married. Settled. She never would've had that with Erik. She got up and padded over to the floor-length window to look out at the glittering city below. Her feet were bare and the floor beneath her was made of wood, and she could never resist that feeling. She took a few steps, toes pointed, and sprang up into an arabesque, one leg lifted high behind her, examining the line of her reflection in the window. Last night, dancing to the Sacred Ravens song, she had curved her back just so, and her arms … they had been crossed in front of her chest, and then she had dropped down onto her left foot … Lia completed the movement, still watching herself, and before she knew it, she was retracing the entire dance once again.

The moment she realised what she was doing, she stopped abruptly, midway through a spin, thumping to a most inelegant halt and putting her hand out to the glass to catch herself. She hadn't even been thinking of Erik—only of the steps, her movements—but she still felt as though she was breaking her promise to Marianne. She could imagine exactly what her friend would say if she knew Lia was choreographing a piece to one of his songs. She could imagine exactly what Scott would say, too. The dance, along with everything else, was best forgotten about.

Only, she couldn't forget about the dance. With Scott away, and no performances scheduled, Lia's natural instinct was to spend her quiet evenings at the studio practising for *Sleeping Beauty*, and while she was there alone, she couldn't resist occasionally running through her own little routine, gradually perfecting it. Perhaps it wasn't much, and perhaps she couldn't tell anybody about it, but it was her own creation, and she couldn't help but feel proud of it. There was something so cathartic about pushing her body through the strange, twisting, uncomfortable steps while

Erik's song blasted loud through the deserted building. It felt as though she was letting out something she hadn't even realised was within her: all the confused emotions she had never confessed to anybody, including herself.

It was during one of these solitary dance sessions that Tomas walked in on her. Lia didn't notice him until her routine came to an end, and she looked up from her position stretched out on the floor to see his tall, dark figure silhouetted in the doorway.

"Tomas!" She got to her feet, breathless, throwing a towel around her neck. "I didn't realise you were still here."

Tomas was Lia's regular dancing partner. They'd first worked together at American Ballet Theatre, before Lia had even met her husband, and their partnership had been so popular with fans that Tomas had chosen to follow her to London for the season rather than dance with anybody else. Lia was glad. Getting used to new partners was part of her job, and she would never have complained about it, but she and Tomas had the kind of solid, mutually supportive working relationship that made her transition to a new company so much less nerve-wracking.

"It is Sacred Ravens' music, yes?" Tomas gestured toward Lia's portable speakers. She stretched over and turned the song off.

"Yes."

"My boyfriend, he loves that band." Tomas had changed out of his practice gear into jeans and a fitted t-shirt, and he looked rakishly handsome as he leaned back against the barre. "He wanted me to ask you to introduce him, but I say no, no, no. Not gonna happen!" He laughed. "He was very disappointed."

Lia smiled. "Tell Charlie I'm sorry."

"Ah, is no good. He already hates you for bringing me here to dreary London. I tell him he should visit, see some sights, you know? But he thinks it rains too much here."

"It does rain too much. But tell Charlie we'll take him out if he comes over. You and him, me and Scott. A double date. It'll be fun."

Tomas shook his head, smiling his best Prince Charming smile, the one he used to dazzle the clutch of adoring fans who always waited for him at the stage door after performances. "I think he would like Scott better than he likes me, and then what?"

"Then you and I will just have to run away together."

"It will happen one day, my princess, it will happen." Tomas slipped an arm around her waist. "Now, you are going to show me?"

"Show you what?"

"What you were dancing."

"Oh, no!" Breaking away from him, Lia started to pull her hair from its tight bun, picking the pins out one at a time. "It's nothing. I was just messing about."

"I think not. What I saw was very good. Show me."

Lia ran her fingers through her loose hair, combing out the kinks. "Okay." She got to her feet and turned the music back on, heading once more for the centre of the studio. "But it's really not all that good."

She danced the piece again, hair flying, and when the song ended, Tomas treated her to a small round of applause as she pulled herself up off the floor.

"I think it is good," he said. "You will perform it, I think."

"Oh, God, no."

"Yes. I say yes. We can make it longer. Add more songs.

I will help you." He approached her and took her arm, twirling her around. "We add a *pas de deux*, a solo for me, a story … They will make a space in a triple bill for you."

Lia laughed. "No, they won't."

"For the great Lia Céline, they will. Her choreographic debut. What is the story?"

"I don't know. There isn't one."

"I think there is. Watching you, I felt you were angry. Trapped. Torn. A love triangle, maybe?"

Lia dropped his hand. "This isn't funny anymore." She turned away and collected up her things.

"We bring in another girl, maybe? Your friend Marianne? She is a soloist, she will like to have a role. I will allow you both to fight over me."

"We're not bringing in anybody, because we're not performing it. Anyway, Marianne would never do it."

"Another boy, then?" When Lia turned around, hoisting her bag onto her shoulder, she found Tomas eyeing her with a half-quizzical, half-amused look. "That would be better?"

She pushed past him. "We're not discussing this anymore."

"It is a ballet, my princess, nothing more. Do not stifle yourself. Talk to me when you change your mind."

7

Wren sat at the head of her sister's hospital bed as Detective Reeves called her mother. Delphi had gone to get drinks, and all was quiet apart from his low, serious voice. As he paced the room, Wren held Bethany's limp hand, wondering whether it would have been better if she told Harper the news herself. Reeves had given her the option, but she had let him do it because ... She didn't quite know why. A moment of weakness, she supposed. She hadn't been able to face the thought of explaining to her mother that Bethany was as good as dead because of her.

A million 'if onlys' ran through her mind. If only she hadn't shouted at her sister. If only she hadn't come to San Francisco. If only she had stayed at home, where she belonged, none of this would ever have happened. She squeezed Bethany's fingers, holding her breath, waiting, praying for some response, but there was none. Her sister's face was blank. Wherever Bethany was, she was not in her body any longer.

Reeves hung up the phone and took a seat on the opposite side of the bed. "Your mother is making preparations to come over to California."

"And Jared? Her husband, I mean."

"I don't think he'll be joining her." Reeves scrutinised Wren's face. "But you're not sorry about that."

"He's scared," Wren said. "He thinks if he comes over here, you'll arrest him."

"Nobody's given me any reason to. Yet."

Wren looked at the floor. After a few moments, she heard Reeves get up. "You'd best get home and get some rest," he suggested.

"Sure."

"I mean it. Get in touch if you need anything."

"I will." Wren watched him go, and then she was alone with Bethany in the silent ward. She stared at the lights blinking around Bethany's temples until they left bright imprints on her eyes. So now she was just supposed to give up? Just accept that Bethany was gone, doomed to wander in some virtual limbo forever more, until her body died and she was nothing but a digital ghost, a consciousness floating in the DreamScape? They could wait, Naveen had told her, and hope, but nobody who was lost had ever awoken before, and Wren knew that one day they would simply be expected to let her go.

"No," she whispered, squeezing Bethany's hand tightly. "No, that's not okay. That's not how it's going to be."

Wren and Delphi returned home late, to a quiet house. Jon and Ramona were both out for the evening, while Kazuo had holed up in his own room. Wren was relieved—she didn't feel like explaining what had happened. Delphi made her signature hot chocolates with marshmallows, cream, and a dash of whisky, and they shut themselves in her room to talk.

"You okay?" She passed a steaming mug over to Wren.

"Cold." Wren curled up on the end of her friend's bed and pulled a blanket over her legs. Delphi's room was a shrine to Sacred Ravens, holograms of Erik Dacre glowering from every angle. He was striking rather than handsome: gaunt and coldly beautiful with piercing green eyes. Wren found it hard to shake the feeling that he was watching her from the walls.

"Don't you ever get tired of having all these posters around?" she asked, more to keep the subject away from Bethany than because she cared about the answer.

Delphi laughed. "Of course not! Who could get tired of having Erik to look at? My future husband, I promise you." She sat in her desk chair and propped her heavy-booted feet up on the table.

"You really are one step away from getting a Draven tattoo."

"Soon as I've saved up the cash. You can help me choose the design of the wings."

"I'm honoured."

"There, you almost cracked a smile. Do it again."

Wren took a sip of her hot chocolate, but it only seared her tongue. "I don't feel much like smiling."

"She'll wake up, Wren. You have to believe that."

"And if she doesn't? You've been in the DreamScape, Delph. Do you think she's still conscious in there? What must it be like for her?"

"Hard to say," Delphi said, suddenly serious. "I didn't stay in there for very long, and it's a big place. As big as the Earth, or even bigger. There's every kind of place in there you can think of. Countries, historical eras, fantasy worlds. Some are wonderful. Some are … not so nice."

"Don't you think it must be scary for her? Trapped in there all on her own? I just can't help thinking …"

"Don't. Don't think about it. Hey," Delphi forced a smile, "she's probably sunning herself on some beautiful beach, having the time of her life. Perhaps she doesn't even want to come out." Wren could tell by her tone that she didn't really believe what she was saying.

"How do people get lost in there?" she asked.

Delphi frowned. "Not sure. It's like the doctor said—it's an unstable system. Nobody's really looking after it any-more. Sometimes things go wrong, I guess."

"I can't accept that's it," Wren said. "How can I sit around here and do nothing when she's trapped in there?"

"What else can you do?"

"I could go in. I could look for her."

"Wren, that's crazy. She could be anywhere by now. It would be like looking for a needle in a haystack."

"But I've got to do something! If I could find her, couldn't I bring her back somehow?"

"Maybe. I suppose it's possible. But still …"

"Help me. Get me in there, and I'll do the rest."

"How?" said Delphi. "I mean, I don't have a Corona, and I don't even know any dealers in this city. You can't just stroll up to someone and ask if they Scape."

"So, what *do* you do?" Wren sat up straight. "Come on, Delph. I thought this was the sort of thing you were into?"

"I am! I mean, I was. But my parents sent me here to get away from all that, and you gotta know somebody …"

"What about that girl I bumped into on the pier? Er … Andromeda? That was her name, I think. What if we could track her down somehow?"

Delphi frowned. "Sure, but how are you going to find

her?"

"I don't know." Wren got to her feet. "But I bet I know someone who does."

She darted out of Delphi's room and knocked on the door across the hall.

"Enter," came a solemn voice. Wren opened the door.

Kazuo's tiny bedroom was a coder's paradise, one sleek silver box on his desk projecting dozens of screens of information onto the walls and even the ceiling, while Kazuo lounged on his bed controlling them all with a series of intricate gestures, as though conducting a symphony. Above him, a movie was running, which he quickly silenced, and to all sides, notes, reams of code, and half-finished projects littered the walls. He swept each one away with a flick of his fingers, tidying them into virtual files at the corners of the room, and sat up, making space for Wren and Delphi to squeeze onto the bed. In a rush, Wren tried to explain what had happened to Bethany, while Kazuo nodded along, frowning.

"We're looking for someone who might be able to help," Wren finished. "A girl called Andromeda. Any idea if you could find her?"

"Andromeda?" Kazuo gave her a quizzical look. "Is that all you've got?"

"There can't be many Andromedas in San Francisco," Wren said, apologetically.

"Are you sure that's her real name?"

"I wouldn't know."

"Who is she?" Kazuo pulled up a search for the name and started scrolling through the results. "What else do you know about her?"

"Not much. She's about our age. Maybe a little older. I

met her on the pier at the Masquerade. She was with a bunch of Scapers."

"A Scaper? Sure, okay. Perhaps she only uses that name in the DreamScape. Most Scapers go to a lot of effort to hide their real identities, but there are ways of tracking them down." Information flew around the walls like a whirlwind. "Leave it with me for a bit," he said, already intent on his task. "I can do this."

8

Wren was dozing in the early hours of the following morning when she heard a soft knock on her door. She got out of bed and threw on some clothes before opening it to find Kazuo leaning against the frame. He looked exhausted, his unruly green hair sticking up at all angles.

"You look like you haven't slept a wink," she whispered, not wanting to wake the other housemates.

Kazuo grinned. "I like a challenge. I had to break a few laws, but I got what you wanted." He pulled up a social media profile on his phone, with a picture that was unmistakably Andromeda. "Anna Louise McKee. Unemployed. Majored in psych but dropped out of college two years ago. I didn't get an address, but I found a phone number. She ought to know that she's on an FBI watch-list," he added, yawning. "You can tell her that when you meet her later."

"Meet her?"

"I sent her a message. Said I was interested in buying some Slip—that's the drug they use to enhance the Scape experience. Part hallucinogen, part muscle-relaxant.

Anyway, she's expecting to meet me down near the old ferry terminal at eight this morning." He patted Wren on the arm. "You can go ahead and thank me now."

"Wow, Kaz, that's …"

"Amazing. I know."

"Kind, talented, and modest too. Thanks, Kaz, seriously. I'd better get ready to go." Wren went to close the door, but Kazuo stopped her.

"Look, are you absolutely sure you want to do this? This girl's into some serious shit. The FBI aren't watching her for nothing. You don't want to get mixed up in all that."

"I'll be careful," Wren promised. "I have to do this."

"All right. Good luck." Kazuo yawned again. "I'm gonna crash."

He stumbled back to his room. Wren glanced at her watch and realised she'd have to hurry if she wanted to make it to the meeting place in time. She ran a comb through her hair, grabbed a cereal bar from the kitchen, and headed out.

Down by the bay it was cold and windy, early morning mist still hanging low along the seafront. Wren headed to the pier and leaned on the rail, gazing into the choppy grey sea. Barely anyone was out so early, and apart from the occasional dedicated jogger or keen tourist, Wren was entirely alone. Eight o'clock came and went, and she scrutinised every person who came close to the pier, hugging herself and stamping her feet to fend off the cold. There was no sign of Andromeda. By eight-thirty Wren was sitting on the wooden slats, legs dangling over the water, unsure of whether to stay or go. By nine, she was frozen to her core and convinced Andromeda wasn't going to show. She got to her feet, shoved her numb hands in her pockets, and prepared for the long trudge home.

She was disappointed, but not surprised. Kazuo ought to have realised a girl who was being watched by the FBI wasn't likely to answer an anonymous summons by someone looking for drugs. The more she thought about it, the stupider it sounded. Andromeda had seemed pretty flaky, but clearly she was clever enough to avoid an obvious set-up. At least Wren had her number, she reminded herself, as she tramped up the steep hill towards her house. She would have to think of another way …

"Hey!"

A hand gripped her arm from behind. Startled, she pulled away and spun around, gasping. Andromeda stood there, breathless, her misty blue eyes wide.

"I know you. I met you the other night," she said, as though Wren's appearance was something mystical and fascinating. "You were waiting for me just now, and I don't think you really wanted to buy Slip. Why are you here?"

"I wanted to talk to you."

In the light of day, Andromeda looked older and prettier than Wren had remembered. She wore blue jeans and a loose white top, her pink hair tied back in a scruffy ponytail, a battered old brown leather satchel slung over her shoulder. Dozens of cheap, colourful bracelets hung on each of her wiry arms. Her round, angelic face was scrubbed clean of make-up apart from a slick of mascara on her lashes.

"If you knew I was there, why didn't you show yourself?" Wren asked. "Why follow me all the way home?"

"Can't be too careful." Andromeda's eyes wandered vaguely, as though she couldn't quite focus. "I wanted to know what you would do, where you would go. But you seem safe enough. Is this where you live?"

"Yes." Wren glanced up at the little grey house.

"So? What did you want to talk to me about? Have you changed your mind? Would you like to try Dreaming?"

"I guess. I need your help."

"My help?" Andromeda gazed at her through heavy-lidded eyes. With the sunlight behind her she looked ethereal, almost otherworldly, with her faraway stare and flawless ivory skin.

"My sister went into the DreamScape," Wren began, "and she ... she didn't come out."

"She got lost," Andromeda laid a gentle hand on Wren's arm, cocking her head to one side. "I'm so sorry."

"I thought if I went in there, perhaps I could get her back."

"Oh." The fingers slipped from Wren's wrist. Andromeda looked away. "I'm not sure it works how you imagine. The lost ... they don't come back."

Wren felt a chill. "But she's still in there, right? Her mind, her thoughts?"

"Yes, but ..."

"And if I went in there, if I found her, I could see her—talk to her?"

"Maybe. If you found her." Andromeda shook her head. "But I don't know how you would. If there was a way, believe me, I'd know."

"I can't just give up. I have to at least try."

"You can try, and you can try," Andromeda held Wren's gaze with a sad, sincere stare. "There's a thousand worlds in there. A galaxy of stars. You could hunt for years. Believe me, I've done it. Nobody knows where they go. The lost ones stay lost."

She sounded as though she spoke from experience.

"Did you lose somebody?"

"A long time ago." Andromeda smiled slightly. "I will help you, girl whose name I don't know, but you have to promise me something."

"Wren. My name is Wren. And of course, just tell me what you want. I can pay you for your time …"

"No, I don't need money. I only want you to promise, Wren … while you are searching, don't lose yourself, too."

Wren led Andromeda into the little grey house, to find Delphi, Kazuo, and Ramona still lounging in the sitting room in their pyjamas, eating frosted flakes and drinking tea while they watched an old episode of *Uptown Girls*.

"Man, Scott Lincoln. My wall used to be covered in posters of him," Ramona was saying. "Did you hear he got married? Such a shame …"

"To a woman?" Kazuo replied. "Funny, I always assumed he was gay. Maybe she's, like, his beard or something."

"No!" Ramona put her hands over her ears, shaking her head vigorously. "I don't even want to hear it. Don't burst my bubble, Kaz!"

The conversation died away as Wren and Andromeda entered. Kazuo, in his boxers and dressing gown, was the first to look up, his eyes brightening at the sight of Andromeda. Ramona followed his gaze and frowned. Delphi, too, regarded her cagily.

"That was quick," she said.

"That's a master at work," Kazuo replied. "You ever

need to hunt down a mystery girl—a *beautiful* mystery girl—you know where to come."

"It was you?" Andromeda gave him a surprised glance. "How did you find me out?"

"Everybody leaves a trail. You need to be more careful. I'll show you how, if you like."

"Later. Right now, I need a volunteer. Your friends are cool, right?" she added in an undertone, glancing at Wren. When Wren nodded, she went on, "Wren and I are going into the Dream. Somebody needs to be our Root."

"I'll do it," Delphi said, quickly.

"What's a Root?" Wren asked.

"The Root holds us down in the Mono—the real world, I mean. She watches over us as we sleep and monitors us to make sure we don't come to harm. When you met me the other night, I was acting Root to my friends. We take turns, so that everybody gets a chance to dream. I'll be your guide in the Dream. Your friend …"

"Delphi."

"Delphi will look after us here. I hope she knows what she's doing."

They went to Delphi's room, where there was enough space for both Wren and Andromeda to lie down, and settled themselves beneath the watchful gaze of Erik Dacre, still glaring out from his holographic posters. Wren sat on Delphi's bed, while Andromeda rummaged in her battered brown satchel, drawing out two Coronas and a small plastic package. Powered down, the Coronas were nothing more than slim, coloured metal bands, one pink and one blue, with a glass visor that covered the eyes, and two padded, round applicators on either side. Andromeda fitted the blue Corona around Wren's head, adjusting the applicators so that they pressed firmly against her temples. From her desk chair, Delphi eyed their new companion warily, and when Andromeda left the room briefly, she scooted closer to Wren.

"Did you see her eyes?" she hissed. "She's such a Slip-head."

"She said she'd help me, no questions asked." Wren toyed with the unfamiliar band around her head as she tried to get it to sit comfortably. "I don't care what she is."

"I'm just saying, that shit makes people go crazy after a while. That and the Scaping. I've seen it before—they lose their grip on reality, forget whether they're here or dreaming. You must've seen the news reports."

"Of course I have. Nutters who think they're still in the Scape and go on mad killing sprees or jump off buildings. But Andromeda seems pretty okay."

"Yeah, so do they all," Delphi frowned. "Until they're not. I told you, I ran with a few at school. One of them nearly pushed me onto a railroad track once. Thought he was dreaming. You just can't trust them. Any of them."

"I'm surprised at you," Wren said, glancing up at the poster of Erik Dacre. "Everybody says *he's* the biggest Scaper of them all."

Delphi looked sullen. "I like the guy's music. Never said he was perfect."

When Andromeda returned, she was carrying two glasses of water. She placed them on the desk and shook two pale pink pills out of the plastic packet, downing one with a gulp of water. The other, she held out on her palm. Wren plucked it gingerly from her hand.

"What's this?"

"The red pill." Andromeda grinned.

"Slip," said Delphi.

"Do I need it?"

"You don't *need* it," Andromeda said, "but these Coronas are old. Nobody makes them anymore—not officially, anyway. The tech's not what it was. The Slip will make it easier for your mind to accept the DreamScape, and it will stop you from moving around in your sleep. It's safer."

Wren glanced at Delphi, who nodded. "I don't want to have to restrain you. The Slip will relax your muscles and help you drift off. You're better off taking it, really. If you're gonna do a thing, you might as well do it right."

Wren took the red pill and swallowed it with a sip of water.

"Now," said Andromeda, "just lie down and relax. The Corona will scan your features and build an avatar for you while it puts you to sleep."

Wren lay on the bed and closed her eyes. She felt tense and nervous, watching the Corona's lights flicker from behind her eyelids, but after a few seconds a golden, glowing sensation built in her temples, gradually spreading through her scalp and down her neck. Soon, it flowed through her entire body, bathing every muscle in a delicious, molten warmth. There was nothing she could do but relax, melting away, drifting on a gently flowing sea. She was nothing, nobody, in pieces, disappearing. Gone.

9

On Friday afternoon, Lia left the studio early to catch the supersonic shuttle to Venice, where one of Scott's bodyguards waited on the station platform to usher her to a car. Lia had never quite got used to the way Scott's big, burly minders followed him everywhere, dressed in their civvies and Ray Bans like undercover CIA agents. They hinted at a level of fame that didn't feel real from within, where a man who wandered around in his boxers eating leftover pizza on a Sunday morning suddenly became a person who couldn't stand on an ordinary station platform without risk of harm.

It was all show. Erik had never bothered with minders, even when the record company had briefly tried to insist on them, and the sharp-nailed Dravens were more likely to cause harm than any of Scott's fans would ever be. Erik had treated it as a game, giving the bodyguards the slip repeatedly until the record company had given up bothering. Perhaps it was because they all secretly understood that the biggest risk to Erik was Erik himself, and what could a minder really do about that?

When Lia arrived at the restaurant, Scott was waiting at

a candlelit, canal-side table, while his minders ate pizza and drank soft drinks a few feet away. He stood as she approached, always the gentleman, and pulled out her chair for her.

"You look beautiful."

Lia put her arms around his neck and kissed him. "I missed you." As she took her seat, she added, "You were right about this place. It's lovely."

"I wish you could stay here all week with me."

"Ah, I'd love to." Lia picked up her menu. "But what would I do with myself?"

"Whatever you wanted. Shop. Sightsee. Sunbathe. You don't need to work, you know."

"I know."

A waiter approached the table. "Are the lady and gentleman ready to order?"

Lia looked down at her menu. "Oh, I haven't …"

"They do great seafood here," Scott suggested. "Why not try the crab?"

Lia folded the menu up and passed it to the waiter. "Crab sounds lovely. And a green salad."

"Steak for me, please. Well done. And a bottle of your best Champagne."

"Certainly, sir."

When the waiter was gone, Lia said, "Champagne? What's the occasion?"

"Do I need an occasion to treat my gorgeous wife?"

"But you've got something on your mind. I can tell."

"Hell," Scott grinned. "You know me too well. I've been thinking, Li. I don't like being away from you like this."

"I came to London to be nearer to you."

"Sure, and I appreciate that. But this isn't how imagined

marriage, you know? I thought perhaps, after your London season is over, you could join me. Permanently."

"You want me to quit my job?" Seeing the waiter approaching again, Lia lowered her voice abruptly, and they sat in silence as he poured their Champagne.

"We agreed it would happen sometime," Scott went on, once the waiter was out of earshot. He reached across the table to take her hand. "Lia, I'd love for us to have a kid."

"God, Scott, we've been married a month!"

"You need more time?"

"I don't know … I guess I just assumed we'd wait a year or so. Enjoy being married, you know?"

"How can we enjoy being married when you spend every waking moment dancing? Hell, you even got up every morning to practice on our honeymoon. Not that I want to start that argument again," he added, quickly. "It's your job, I understand that. But you said yourself that a dancer's career only lasts so long, and I want us to be together. Perhaps it's time to move on."

Lia fingered the stem of her Champagne glass. "I have to think about this."

"Sure. You do that." Scott looked out over the glittering water of the canal. Lia could tell by the set of his jaw that he was upset.

"What, Scott? What is it? Did you really expect me to agree immediately?"

"Gee, I don't know. I guess I just thought you'd be more enthusiastic."

"You know I love my job."

Scott pushed back his chair and folded his arms. "Is that really all it is?"

Lia sighed. "Tell me what's bothering you. Really."

"Erik Dacre." Scott spread his hands. "All right? That's what's bothering me."

"I thought we agreed to forget about that."

"And I thought you told me it was all in the past. Ancient history."

"It is!"

"Sure."

"You have to trust me, Scott."

"You know, I've been racking my brains all week and I just can't tell what the hell you ever saw in that guy, Lia. I mean, damn, you're the girl who likes a mug of cocoa and an early night. What were you doing with that hellraiser?"

Lia looked up at the sky. "Please, can't we just not talk about Erik?"

"No. I want to talk about Erik. I want to understand why my wife has history with a guy like that. Look, just look at this." Scott withdrew his phone from his pocket and scanned through it, turning it towards Lia to show her a photograph. It was an old paparazzi shot of her and Erik leaving a club in Los Angeles, Lia in a short dress with her hair loose and messy, Erik's leather jacket slung across her shoulders. She was laughing, but her face was puffy and pale, her eyes ringed with smudged mascara. She didn't remember exactly which night it had been, but it probably wasn't too much of a stretch to guess that she'd had a few too many cocktails and ended up crying at some point.

"So we went for a night out? So what? If what we're looking for is terrible old pap pictures, I'm sure I can find a few of you and Rachel Gibson."

"Everybody knows he takes all sorts of shit."

"I never took drugs, if that's what you're asking. I never Scaped. Erik did enough of that for the both of us, and I saw first-hand how it messed him up."

"But why, Lia? Why were you even there? When I look at this," he jabbed his finger at the photograph, "I feel like I don't even know you. Hell, you look wasted."

"People change."

"Not that much." He glared at her as though she'd crossed some sort of boundary in his mind. Lia got to her feet.

"I came here for a nice dinner. I'm not going to sit here and be treated like a criminal for having a past."

"Then don't."

Fuming, Lia snatched up her clutch bag and strode off. As she headed along the canal away from the restaurant, she was aware of one of the minders following from a respectful distance, but Scott himself did not come after her. She stopped on a bridge and got her phone out of her bag, looking out at the canal as she dialled a number.

"Hey, Tomas. I've been thinking about what you said. I think we should go ahead and choreograph that ballet."

10

Wren came to slowly, her consciousness gradually surfacing as though she was pushing her way up through deep water. First, she felt the ground beneath her feet, firm and springy, like grass. Next, the breeze, gently ruffling her hair. She reached up to touch it—short, choppy, just like her real hair. She ran her hands down her body, feeling her leather jacket, her cotton top, her denim jeans, all just as they had been when she lay down to sleep. And her skin: soft, warm, and alive, springing into goosebumps at her touch.

The mist cleared, and Wren found herself in a lush, green garden. There was grass beneath her feet; blue, cloudless sky above her head. From up ahead came the trickling of water: a calm, clear river with a red, Japanese-style bridge curved over it. A cherry blossom tree stood on one side of the river, while on the other a weeping willow dipped its leaves in the water. In the distance, the bright red roof of a pagoda emerged above a copse of trees.

Wren headed for the bridge and climbed its humped back, running her hand over the smooth painted wood, feeling the grain beneath her fingers. If this was a dream, it was unbelievably detailed, so realistic that it was impossible to distinguish it from real life.

"Welcome new ... Welcome new ...Welcome new ..."

The cracked, metallic voice came from nowhere, repeating like a broken record. On reaching the other side of the river, Wren turned towards the pagoda and stopped, frozen with horror. A huge gash sliced the sky, glittering blue pixels falling into a black void.

"Welcome new ... Welcome new ... Welcome new ..."

With an ear-splitting crack, another black gash ripped across the ground between Wren and the pagoda, cutting off her pathway like the slash of a knife through cloth. As she struggled to maintain her footing, the earth crumbled, pouring like a waterfall into the abyss. Wren turned to run, only to find her way blocked by a woman in a blue uniform and a pill-box hat who stood behind her. She was flickering, only semi-solid, one arm and half of her left leg missing completely. She stared at Wren glassily, repeating her welcome phrase over and over.

"Welcome new ... Welcome new ... Welcome new ..."

"Wren!"

Wren swerved the ghostly figure and ran back over the bridge to where the ground was more stable and Andromeda waited.

"What the hell was that?" Wren asked, trying to catch her breath.

"A rupture." Andromeda looked effortlessly ethereal in a draped white gown, her pink hair falling elegantly around her shoulders. She was taller and slimmer than her real self, with china-perfect skin and blue eyes as clear as a child's. "Don't go near them."

"I wasn't planning to."

"This is the orientation screen," Andromeda said. "The system dumps all new users here, but as you can see, it's seen better days."

"Clearly." Wren looked down at herself. "I look exactly like I do in real life."

"I took a moment to calibrate your avatar so it would project an image you were accustomed to. You can change it if you like, within reason. Basic human traits are free. Anything more out there will cost you Credits."

"I'm fine like this for now, thanks."

Andromeda nodded approvingly. "So you should be, little bird. Now, follow me, and tread carefully." She led the way along the riverside, giving the rupture a wide berth as she headed for the woodland alongside the pagoda. "There's only one proper way out of here, and that's to follow the orientation process, but we can't do that because of the ruptures, and we wouldn't want to, anyway. It's boring. I know a back door we can use."

"How did the ruptures get here?" Wren couldn't take her eyes off the void in the sky. It scared her more than she cared to admit.

"This network is vast, and since it was officially shut down a decade ago there's been no real infrastructure. Somebody somewhere is keeping it going—or lots of somebodies, more likely—but whoever they are, they don't have the processor power to hold it all together. It's crumbling faster than we can rebuild."

"What would happen to me if I fell into one of those holes?"

"That's how you get lost. Look behind you and you'll see a faint data trail."

Wren glanced back to see a slim golden thread running

from her feet towards the red bridge.

"The DreamScape creates a copy of your consciousness," Andromeda continued. "Thoughts, memories, self-image. In effect, it downloads you. The 'you' who is walking about and talking right now is just a set of binary ones and zeroes, and that data trail is the system tracking you, linking the information about you to your sleeping body. But if you were to fall into a rupture, the system would lose you, and the connection would be severed. You would still feel like you, in here, but because the system can't match 'you' up with your body, it won't allow you to wake. It happens to more and more dreamers every day."

Andromeda picked her way around the edge of the rupture and disappeared into the shade beneath the trees. Wren followed, glad to be out of view of the ruptures.

"That must be what happened to Bethany."

"Yes." Andromeda wove through the trees, her pace quickening. "And many others. But you should know that even if you did find her—and that itself is unlikely—I don't know if there's any way you could reunite her with her physical body."

"I'll cross that bridge when I come to it. Where do people go when they fall into a rupture?"

Andromeda stopped and faced her. "If I knew that," she said, softly, "I wouldn't be the person I am today."

"You said you lost somebody too?"

"Yes. My boyfriend, Reza. He fell into a rupture two years ago. I've been searching for him ever since."

"I'm so sorry."

Andromeda shook her head. "It's okay. We didn't know much about the Dream, or the ruptures, back then. We were just tourists, messing about. I've learnt a lot since then. I'm a native now—I come here every night while I'm sleeping. I might not be able to help you find your sister, but I can at least guide you. I want to make sure you don't get lost, too."

"You never know, perhaps together we can find out where they both went."

"Perhaps." Andromeda smiled sadly. "But it's too late for Reza. His body is dead. His parents let the hospital turn off the life support a couple of months ago. Still, I would like to find him, if he's here somewhere." The ground began to tremble beneath their feet, and Andromeda started walking again. "Come on, we're not safe here."

She led the way to a mossy glade, in the middle of which stood a tall birch tree.

"A back door," she explained. "Every environment has one. Originally, they were there so the coders could get in to do maintenance."

She took Wren's arm with one hand and touched a knot in the tree with the other. The woodland vanished in a burst of white light that seared across Wren's skull.

When the light cleared, they were standing on a clear promontory—ice, perhaps, or glass—which shot out through a vast starry sky, tapering to a point like a shard. Andromeda made her way towards the point of the shard, and Wren followed, unsteady and nervous on the transparent surface. When she looked back, she saw an icy cliff edge that ran for miles in either direction, shards jutting out into the sky at regular intervals. She even thought she could spot tiny figures standing on each one, just as she and Andromeda were.

"This is the StarScape," said Andromeda. "Our navigation system."

Wren gazed at the sky. A nebula of soft, twinkling

clouds floated like a living creature against the deep ocean of the sky.

"How does it work?"

"Every one of these stars is a location—an environment, we call them. You just reach for the one you want," Andromeda stretched out her hand, "and take it." She plucked an orange star from the sky and drew it towards them. It was small enough to fit in the palm of her hand, but Wren could feel its heat on her face.

"That's incredible."

"Isn't it?" Andromeda smiled lovingly at the star. "Can you believe they made this place illegal? It's a masterpiece. Gade Sorensen deserved a Nobel Prize for building it. Instead he was vilified." She took the star in both hands and tugged until it cracked open. Out shone a glaring white light just like the one that had transported them there. "All the information about this destination is contained in here. When I touch it, the Dream sends it all direct to my brain. Touch the light and you'll see."

The moment Wren's fingertips brushed against the light, information flooded her mind, a rush so powerful it almost knocked her off her feet.

"A city," she breathed, seeing it all at once in her mind's eye. Streets, buildings, and a name. "Reverie."

"That's right." Andromeda parted her hands and the white light expanded, growing wide enough for them to step through. "Welcome to Reverie."

11

Wren stepped out from the StarScape onto a sleek black surface. A rush of sudden noise assaulted her ears: people
talking and shouting, traffic hurtling past, music playing in
the distance. An elbow hit her in the stomach, and she span
around to find the culprit long gone, just one of many bodies
rushing along a busy sidewalk.

The city of Reverie bustled with creatures of every shape
and size: beautiful humans with long, lithe limbs and glowing tans; faeries with pastel-coloured skin and gauzy wings;
gnarled warlocks in full armour; cat-people with glowing
yellow eyes and twitching tails … The variety of avatars
was endless. On the corner closest to Wren, a blue-skinned
punk conducted a noisy argument with a woman in a neon-
pink sari, who was trying to convince him to buy upgrades
for his laser weaponry, while just a few feet away a girl with
leopard-print fur beckoned to a group of flying lizards.
Laughing, they flapped their wings in appreciation.

Wren looked past them at the city itself, and nearly lost
her balance.

Reverie was more chaotic and overwhelming than

anything she could have imagined. Every building and vendor's stall seemed to have been built piecemeal and designed to grab as much attention as possible. There was nothing that wasn't intended to advertise or sell something—game experiences, upgrades, sexual escapades—and the entrepreneurs had, it appeared, free licence to do whatever they wanted in order to entice potential customers. Whole skyscrapers had sprung up made entirely of neon, blinking and sparkling and twisting into ludicrous shapes in their effort to draw the eye.

Other architects had constructed traps for their prey: pavements that turned into slippery slopes to force people into bars and clubs; or sticky patches that froze them in place in front of a stall. Some buildings rearranged themselves as they sensed pedestrians approaching, erecting new walls or curling over the sidewalk in an attempt to funnel people towards their light-framed doorways.

No surface was left unexploited: not the pavements, or the walls, or the sides of the fast-moving pods that ferried passengers around. But the worst thing—the most unexpected, mind-numbing, dizzying thing about Reverie—was that all this did not end at the horizon. There was no sky in Reverie: the streets simply turned upwards and carried on: vertically, diagonally, even miles above their heads. The buildings on the ground jostled for space with those pointing in the other direction. Pedestrians finding themselves blocked by a building nonchalantly changed angle and walked up the walls. There was no up, no down, no sense of physics at all.

Wren, taking all this in for the first time, quickly became light-headed. Black spots invaded her vision. Stumbling, she reached for Andromeda, who held onto her as she bent over the ground—if it really was the ground—retching.

"Dream sickness." Andromeda rubbed Wren's back. "Everyone gets it the first time. But just think about it, little bird. How can you be sick when your body is safely back at home, lying on your bed? It's all in your mind. Sit down over here and take deep breaths."

Andromeda led her to a bench, and Wren sat with her head between her knees until the nausea subsided.

"What the hell is this place?" she asked, gasping for breath. The body she was in may have been virtual, but the nausea felt real enough, and so did the sweat trailing down her temples.

"Reverie was built as a central hub for all the activity in the DreamScape," Andromeda explained, with a patient smile. "Originally it was a much more pleasant place to be—well-kept and welcoming, or so I'm told. It was supposed to be the first port of call for new dreamers after orientation, where they could learn what entertainment was on offer. The providers could advertise—that was the whole point of the place—but it was kept within reason. Not like now. Since the system was made illegal this city has been a free-for-all. Anyone can build anywhere, anyhow."

"That explains why it's so ugly," Wren said.

"Yes." Andromeda sighed. "It's a shame. There's so much potential in this world, yet so many people only build ugly things. All they want is for their building to stand out more than the one next to it. But I suppose anyone can come here, and most people do, first of all. I prefer the environments that are harder to access."

"Do you think Bethany came here?"

"I expect so. It seems a good enough place to start." Andromeda got to her feet. "Where we go from here is another matter. Look at this place, little bird. Look how big it is. Where do you go? Who do you talk to? Which door do you enter? And this is only one environment among millions."

"Don't you have any ideas?"

Andromeda shrugged. "I said I'd get you here. I didn't say I had all the answers. If I did, I wouldn't be here. I would have Reza, and I wouldn't be wandering this place like a restless spirit."

Wren stood up. "Okay." She looked down each bustling street in turn, trying to gauge which direction her sister might have taken. Andromeda was right: finding one fifteen-year-old girl in amongst this multitude of people would be like looking for a needle in a haystack, but Wren didn't have time to despair. She could only spend a few hours at a time inside the DreamScape. She had to find some kind of lead while she had the chance. She had to trust she knew her sister well enough to guess where she might have gone …

"This way," she decided, striking off in the direction of a game advertisement that resembled the vampire novels Bethany loved to read. Andromeda followed, and they wove through the crowd of avatars until Andromeda grabbed Wren's arm.

"Watch out," she hissed, indicating a group of shadowy creatures moving down the vertical street above them. They were bland-faced and dark-suited, with a wispy quality about them, as though they might simply drift away if a breeze passed by them.

"What are they?" Wren asked.

"Gangsters. Dream mafia. This is a wonderful place but …" Andromeda drew Wren gently in the opposite direction. "There are plenty of people here you don't want to get involved with. Nasty people, in the Dream and out of it. They use the network for anything they want to keep away from the eyes of their governments. Drug dealing. Weapons smuggling. Money laundering." Andromeda wrinkled her nose. "Child pornography."

"I promise to give them a wide berth," Wren said.

"Hypnos is working on a way to get rid of them for good." Andromeda ducked down a side alley, away from the gangsters. "Then those of us who wish for peace and prosperity can live freely."

"Who exactly is this Hypnos?"

"They say the Architect chose him as his successor before he died."

"The Architect?"

"The creator of the DreamScape. Gade Sorensen. You will have heard of him."

"Of course I have," Wren said. "Would it kill you to call people by their names? I thought Sorensen disowned his creation when the network was made illegal."

"Publicly, he did," Andromeda replied. "Privately, he felt differently. The DreamScape was his life's work, and he did not wish to see it fall to waste and ruin. Hypnos strives to carry forth the Architect's vision."

"So, this Hypnos runs the place, then?"

"In a way. The Dream is free for all to do as they please. Hypnos is only here to guide us."

"But out there, in the real world," Wren pressed, "he's a person like the rest of us. So, who is he?"

Andromeda shrugged. "I don't know. I don't think it's important. We are all equal souls here. Our bodies, whoever we might be in the Mono—none of this matters. Come on. You had an idea, didn't you?"

"No. I mean, yes." Wren shook her head, remembering

the vampire game. "Follow me."

No sooner had she stepped back out of the alleyway, though, than she froze, staring at the sky between the layers of city.

"It's snowing," she said, bemused. Large white flakes drifted down onto the city from a black portal that had opened up in mid-air.

"That's not snow." Andromeda's voice was deadly serious. "This is a raid. We need to find an exit. Now."

Others were beginning to notice the portal and the snowflakes, and panic spread through the crowd. Some ran, some screamed, some simply stood and stared as the fist-sized icy shards fell on them. To Wren's horror, the moment the flakes touched an avatar they began to expand and spread, coating each recipient in a shimmering, liquid covering. A horned warlock howled as the ice flowed across his whole body, from his feet to his neck, and crept up his throat. It consumed his head, forced its way down his throat, choking off his screams. Frozen solid, his face contorted into wide-eyed desperation, he crashed to the ground and shattered into a million tiny fragments.

"Come on!" Andromeda yanked Wren's arm and they ran, dodging the snowflakes and their frozen victims as they raced back to the portal where they'd entered the city. "Whatever you do, don't let the snow touch you!"

"I wasn't planning to!" Wren yelled over the din. "What's happening?"

"It's an FBI raid," Andromeda shouted back, ducking a snowflake. "They use the ice to dump Dreamers out of the system and track their exits, so they can arrest them in the Mono. If either one of us gets iced, we're both finished."

Andromeda ground to a halt in front of the shimmering

white portal. There was a crowd at least thirty people thick, all trying to push their way through. She turned on her heel and pulled Wren off in a different direction.

"I know a better way." She forced her way across the road, towards a red neon building hung with Chinese lanterns, and dove through the door, ignoring the angry shouts of the bouncers. They ran through what looked like a strip-club, full of confused patrons and impossibly long-limbed, saucer-eyed dancers, until they reached a dressing room crammed with sequined costumes. Andromeda plunged right into the midst of the dresses and Wren, following, shoving feathers out of her face, was certain they were about to hit the wall, when she found herself in darkness, falling.

She woke up at home, back in Delphi's bed.

12

"A little longer in that hold, I think."

Lia picked herself up off the floor where she had ended her dance and crossed the rehearsal studio to Tomas. Through the panoramic windows that ran along one side of the room, the setting sun bathed the rooftops of London in an orange glow. Elsewhere in the Opera House, a performance was beginning, and there would be a bustle of people rushing around in the heart of the building beneath them, but here, upstairs in the studios, it was peaceful—almost deserted. A perfect opportunity for them to practice her ballet without interruptions. Tomas raised a hand, gesturing to the student they'd roped in to start the music again, and took hold of Lia's waist as the song began.

"We will run it through just from the second lift," he suggested, "and then perhaps a break."

He was worried about pushing her too hard. Lia could tell from the way he glanced at her from the corner of his eye as they walked through the first few steps. Not physically—Tomas knew perfectly well that she could handle everything that they were doing and then some, despite having to slot their practice sessions into an already heavy schedule. But emotionally, Lia found the work draining. Actually creating something, herself, was different to simply following the steps mapped out for her by another choreographer.

If anyone had ever criticised her as a dancer, it had been to comment on the lack of emotional connection in her dancing. Sure, she could act, and most of the time that sufficed, but every now and then a particularly perceptive critic would complain that Lia did not allow herself to really feel the experiences of, say, a Juliet or a Giselle. Bland, smiling, audience-pleasing princesses like the Sugar Plum Fairy were her forte, not roles that demanded she open herself up to the depths of love, despair, or longing. Tomas seemed determined to drag all that out of her, if all his harping on about getting to the raw heart of the piece was anything to go by. At times, the whole thing felt like a battle against her better judgement. Lia wasn't at all sure she wanted to say anything sincere about her feelings. Not to Erik's music. Not on stage.

Tomas helped her into the hold he'd wanted to practice, his hand supporting her bent back, one of her legs lifted, arms flung back in a posture of total abandon.

"Now wait, wait …"

Lia wobbled, lost her balance, dropped her foot to the ground. She shook her head, using Tomas's shoulder to pull herself upright.

"I'm sorry."

Tomas waved at the student again, and the music stopped. "No, it is late. You should eat. We will go to the canteen, no?"

"You go. I'm not hungry." Lia sat down by her bag and

unlaced her ballet shoes. "Let's call it a night. Scott will be wondering where I am."

"He is not in Italy tonight? You can go home," Tomas added to the student, who seemed glad to be released.

"No, he's not in Italy," Lia said, "and I said I'd be home for dinner."

Tomas sat down beside her. "You are not happy with me, Princess."

"I'm tired, that's all."

"And …"

"And … I think we should change the music."

"You want to use different songs?"

Lia pulled the pins from her hair, lining them up side by side on the linoleum floor. "I want to use a different band."

There was a moment's pause, during which Lia did not look up, and then Tomas said, "I don't think it would be the same, Princess."

"Good. I'm not going to dance this in front of an audience. Not how it is. I can't." She swallowed and shook her hair out, feeling like crying. "You're not looking at this from my point of view, Tomas. People talk about me—about me and Erik. It's been three years and they still do. And then there was that stuff at the wedding, and Scott's still really upset about it, and he doesn't say anything, but I know he can't let it go, and if I tell him about this ballet … and it's to Sacred Ravens music … and if I go out there and dance it in public …" She took a deep breath. "You know what it will be like."

"People will be fascinated. They will flock to see it."

"Yes, and pick over it and pick it apart and pick … and pick me apart." She was crying now. Wiping her eyes irritably, she went on: "And Scott will be furious, and

Marianne will be furious and my mum and Esmé too, because they'll see it and they'll know … they'll know …"

Lia trailed off, aware of Tomas looking at her intently. "You give people powers of perception that they do not have," he said. "They will see a story, that is all."

"So why do I feel I'll be letting everyone read my mind?" Lia whispered. "I never said a word, all those years. Not to the press, or anybody. I never told anybody anything about what went on, or how I felt. That never stopped people from making it all up. I don't want to give them any more fuel."

Tomas put his arm around her shoulders and hugged her close. "I want everyone to know how talented you are, that is all. You are a beautiful dancer. You have made a beautiful ballet. And yes, people will want to see it, and talk about it, and you will have to let it go and be a thing separate from you, and trust that nobody sees anything but a story. Go home and rest, and think about it." He kissed her on the forehead, before getting to his feet and picking up his bag, but just as he was about to leave, he turned back to look at her, still sitting where he had left her.

"You miss him," he said. "That is okay. It is allowed. It doesn't mean you don't love Scott."

He smiled at her, and left. Lia stared at the empty doorway where he had been. "You see," she said softly. "*You knew.*"

As Lia stepped out of the stage door into the cool September night, her phone rang. She glanced at it and saw a name that stopped her dead on the side of the road, in the ebbing light of the setting sun. The blood rushed from her body; her legs went weak. She took a deep breath, steeling herself for the worst, and answered.

"Kent." Her voice quivered. "I see your name and I know this can't be good."

"Hey Li. All right, don't panic," Kent said, in his Texas drawl. "We're all good here. All good."

Lia breathed again. Taxis rushed by, headlamps illuminating the twilight. "Then why are you calling?"

"Erik's gone AWOL, that's all."

Kent Austin was Erik's long-suffering, unwaveringly dedicated manager. The sight of his name on her phone's screen had sent Lia back to a time when a late-night call from Kent invariably meant a harrowing dash to the hospital, or a frantic hunt through L.A.'s nightclubs and Scape dens. That heart-in-the-mouth, is-he-really-dead-this-time? feeling was hard-wired into her, and it left her shaking and angry.

"I don't care, I don't want to know. It's nothing to do with me."

"I thought maybe as you'd been in touch recently …"

"I haven't seen Erik since the wedding."

"You called him the other day." Kent's tone was a touch accusatory. "He hasn't fucking shut up about it."

"I didn't even speak to him!" Realising that she was getting strange looks from passers-by, Lia started walking, heading for the tube. Scott preferred her to get a car, but she needed to be moving, for now, not trapped in a taxi.

"He's got this fucking idea in his head … about Scott … he's worried that …" Kent hesitated. "It's all bullshit. The Scaping makes his sense of reality a bit slippery, you know.”

“I know.” Lia wove through the busy street, past a gaggle of tourists watching a silver-painted human statue, and a crazed Sliphead on a soap box shouting about how everyone should abandon their mundane lives and join the Dream. She pressed the phone closer to her ear, the better to hear Kent over the ranting.

“… haven’t seen him for a couple days, and we’ve got a show tomorrow night. I thought he might be in London.”

“If he is, I don’t know a thing about it.”

“All right, Li. Hey, I’m sorry. I shouldn’t have bothered you. It’s … tough without you. He’s been pretty cut up since the wedding. I think he hoped …”

“Enough, Kent. Seriously. Enough.” Lia darted into Covent Garden station, squeezing through the milling crowds and up to the barrier. “I’m about to lose signal.”

“Hey, it’s cool. I’m gone. Good luck with everything, Li.”

Lia scanned her card on the barrier and headed for the lifts. A flock of girls in black joined the queue next to her. Lia spotted the tattoos on their backs and looked away.

“Kent …” she said, in a low voice.

“Yeah?”

“Let me know when you find him. Don’t tell him we spoke. Just … let me know, okay?”

“Sure thing, Li.”

Lia hung up just as the lift arrived. As she shuffled inside, she realised she’d let herself become surrounded by the Dravens. Stupid. She got out her phone and pretended to be absorbed in looking something up, letting her hair fall across her face. The girls were chatting excitedly about some club they were going to that night—a Scaper place, judging from their description—and then one of them muttered something to the others and they all went quiet.

"… could be. They do ballets near here …" The Draven spoke under her breath, but Lia caught a few words. The lift came to a halt and, relieved, she made to leave.

"Hey!"

Don't look. Don't look. The crowd moved slowly, creeping towards the elevator doors.

"Hey!" Black-painted talons gripped her arm. Lia shrugged free and managed to push her way out of the lift. Undeterred, the Draven shouted after her. "You should just go fucking kill yourself! Just go and die, gold-digging whore!"

Something snapped inside Lia. After the shock she'd just had, this was more than she could deal with. She spun around, surprising herself.

"Do you really think he likes you?" she spat. "You think he likes you people following him around like lovesick puppies? You're a bunch of dumb little girls who pay for the Coronas and the crack, that's all. Do yourselves a favour and go and get a real life. You have no idea." She took a shaky breath, looking properly for the first time at the stunned group of girls. They were all so young. "No idea," she repeated, in a softer voice, and walked away.

13

The first thing Wren did when she woke up from the Dream-Scape was to rush to the bathroom and throw up. Her head was spinning, her vision misty, and as she gripped the edge of the sink, she had a horrible, falling sensation, as if the whole room was sliding away beneath her. Nothing felt real. For a few confused moments, she couldn't remember whether she was awake or still dreaming. Then she caught sight of her own clammy, pale face in the mirror and came back to her senses. She splashed her face with cold water and returned to Delphi's room.

Andromeda sat on the bed, leaning against the wall looking as calm as ever. Delphi, her legs curled beneath her in her desk chair, watched Wren sit shakily beside Andromeda.

"You feeling okay?"

"Like crap."

"It's the Slip in your system," Andromeda said. "Your body's not used to it."

"Great." Wren lay on her back, her head near Andromeda's feet, legs dangling off the end of the bed. Erik Dacre scowled down at her from the ceiling. "How long were we out?"

"About four hours." Delphi gestured at her open sketchbook. "I got more work done today than in the whole of the rest of the term. Mr Branning will be pleased."

"Four hours? Seriously? It felt like less than half that time."

"That's why it's so easy to get lost in there." Andromeda sighed. "You lose track."

"Did you find out anything useful?" Delphi asked.

"I don't know. It's a huge place. We'll never track Bethany down without help. But this Hypnos of Andromeda's …"

"Ugh, don't tell me you believe that shit."

"… I think he could help us," Wren finished. "I want to talk to him."

"He's not even real!"

"He's my only hope, Delph. He may be a god inside the DreamScape, but out here he must be a person like anybody else. What if we could find him in the real world?" She looked at Andromeda, who shook her head.

"I'm sorry, little bird, but I can't help you. To dwell too long on Hypnos' mortal existence is a sin."

"Of course it bloody is." Wren sat up, but her vision clouded with grey dots, and she was forced to hunch forward, head between her knees, until they cleared.

"There must be something we can do." She hooked her fingers together at the back of her neck. "I refuse to believe that we've hit a wall so soon."

"Perhaps …" Andromeda began.

"Yes?" Wren looked up.

"Perhaps there is somebody we can talk to. But we

would need to go back in, and I don't think …"

"Let's do it." Wren picked up her Corona.

"Wren, don't. You need a break," Delphi warned.

"She's right." Andromeda put a hand on Wren's arm. "You're not used to it. Your mind needs rest."

"So, what? I'm supposed to just sit here while Bethany wanders around that … that nightmare alone? Forget it. If there's something I can do, I want to do it. Please, Andromeda."

Their eyes met, and Wren was sure she saw something like pity in Andromeda's eyes as she said, "All right, little bird. Here, take another pill."

"I guess I'm going to get a lot of work done today." Delphi sighed, turning back to her sketchbook as Wren swallowed the pill and fitted the Corona onto her head.

"I'm sure Kaz will switch with you if you need a break."

"No. I feel … I kinda feel responsible, you know?"

Wren lay down, the golden glow already creeping up her limbs. "All right. See you on the other side, Andromeda."

They met once more on a rocky outcrop in the StarScape. Entering the Dream the second time round felt far less overwhelming, more natural. Looking out at the millions of stars spilled across the night sky, Wren began to appreciate the sheer breadth of human experience collected there. So many worlds, each one created entirely out of somebody's imagination. It was a work of art, in a way.

"Where are we going?" she asked.

"Here." Andromeda plucked a star from the sky and

opened it, just as she'd done when they visited Reverie. Wren followed her into the light, and an icy chill hit her like a blast of winter wind.

They stood in a cavern carved from solid ice. It was as vast and empty as a cathedral, frozen pillars stretching upwards, before curving overhead like the stems of gigantic flowers. Light poured in—from where, Wren couldn't tell, but it was a light more pure and perfect than any she had ever seen in the real world. Refracted by the ice, it scattered a rainbow of colours across a frozen block that looked like an altar.

"It's a church," she said.

"One of many. Built to honour Hypnos." Andromeda walked down the aisle between the pillars. "I come here often."

"You really believe this person is a god, then?"

"Of course."

Wren found herself treading lightly across the ice, afraid to disturb the sense of deep peace settled over the cathedral. When she spoke, her voice was muffled by the vast space.

"Has this, er, Hypnos ever visited here?"

"No." Andromeda whispered. "Perhaps he doesn't wish to. Or perhaps he simply doesn't know we're here."

"How do you know for sure that he exists? If you don't mind me asking? Where does the legend come from?"

"Follow me. The priest will explain everything." She slipped through a doorway at the side of the chamber, leading Wren into a second, more compact room where rugs and cushions were scattered over the icy floor. About half-a-dozen men and women lounged there, curled up against the silken pillows, talking in low voices as they studied holographic displays of information. All of them were young, all beautiful, and most sported the same Grecian-inspired out-fits and pastel-hued hair as Andromeda.

"Andromeda." A young man got to his feet. He looked like an Adonis, with bronzed skin, aquamarine eyes, and golden hair cascading down his shoulders. "I'm so glad you could join us."

"This is Wren, your worship. She's come to learn more about the church. Wren, this is our priest, Apollo."

Apollo took Wren's hand and held it between his own. "We're always happy to welcome new recruits."

"Oh, I'm not a recruit." Wren withdrew her hand hur-riedly. "Just … curious."

Apollo's expression didn't flicker. "Of course. Please, sit down. Hestia, please fetch our guest some honey tea."

One of the women waved her hand in a dreamy curve. A china teacup full of steaming golden liquid appeared on her palm, and she passed it to Wren.

"You eat and drink here?" Wren asked.

"We like to retain some rituals from the Mono world." Apollo said. "It helps people to feel at home. Try it. You are tense, and it will relax you."

Wren took a tiny sip. It slid down her throat exactly like warm honey, and her body softened, her heart rate slowing.

"I feel more relaxed already," she admitted. "How does it do that?"

"The code taps into pleasure receptors in your brain," Andromeda explained. "Different substances are coded to have different effects."

"Like drugs?"

"Exactly. You need never be sad or anxious here. Have some more."

"No thanks." Wren put the cup down. "I'd rather have

my wits about me."

Andromeda only nodded. "Wren has lost somebody," she said, turning to Apollo. "She thinks …" Andromeda looked down guiltily, letting her hair fall in front of her face a little, "… she has an idea that perhaps Hypnos can help her find her sister."

"Still searching for lost ones, Andromeda?" Apollo's expression remained neutral, but Wren sensed a hint of judgement in his voice. "I'm surprised at you. You know what we are striving for. You know that the lost ones are among the blessed, and it is not for us to question where they have gone."

"I understand that." Andromeda looked sheepish. "But Wren … she's new here. It's hard for her, and there may still be a chance for her sister. Isn't there anything we can do?"

"Andromeda," Apollo took Andromeda's hand. "Do you doubt me? Do you doubt Hypnos? You've been with us for a long time now, and I know all about your loss. The way to retrieve your loved ones—both of you—is to help Hypnos in his mission. You know that."

Wren shook her head. "Sorry, but I've just about had my fill of crazy. Who exactly is this Hypnos, and what is his mission about?"

Apollo flashed her a white-toothed smile, but his eyes remained glassy and unemotional. Wren couldn't shake the suspicion that his real-life counterpart was older than his handsome avatar made him appear. "You have many questions, my friend."

"I just want my sister back. You say Andromeda's been part of your church for a long time, but she hasn't found her boyfriend yet, has she? Perhaps this Hypnos of yours isn't all he's cracked up to be."

"He requires faith. You should pray to Him."

Apollo let go of Andromeda's hand and took Wren's instead. His grip was gentle but firm, and he resisted a little as she pulled her fingers away for a second time.

"Sorry," she said, "but I'm looking for a more practical solution. I'm interested in the person, not the god. Who is he really? How did he become so powerful?"

"Very well." Apollo got to his feet, gesturing for them to follow him into the cathedral. They crossed the ice-hewn hall, Apollo walking barefoot with his white toga draped around his muscular form, and headed through a door on the opposite side, where an ice staircase descended in a tight spiral. As Apollo led the way down, he spoke again.

"You must understand that Hypnos' corporeal form is of little consequence to those of us who follow him. What matters is what He represents."

"And that is?"

"Creation. The dawning of a new age. Look around you, child. Can you not see the potential? The Architect didn't just design this network as a game. He designed it to be a whole new world for humanity—something infinite, unspoiled. A home for us all."

"No offence," Wren replied, thinking of Reverie, "but I wouldn't exactly want to live here. It looks pretty spoiled to me."

Apollo reached the bottom of the staircase and pushed open a small wooden door, leading Wren and Andromeda into a tranquil woodland glade.

"Not what you were expecting?" he said, smiling at Wren's surprise as he took a seat on the ground. "Please, sit."

Wren was reluctant to obey, but Apollo crossed his legs and folded his hands in his lap, watching her expectantly, and she realised he wasn't going to speak any further until she did. She settled herself on a comfortable-looking tuft of grass, and Andromeda did the same.

"I thought you would like a quiet place to talk, so I can answer your questions more honestly away from listening ears. The destruction you see in this place—the crime, the anarchy, and the ruptures …"

"Those tears, you mean?"

"The tears in the fabric of the system, yes. All of those things are Thanatos's doing."

"Thanatos?"

"Some call him the Dark God. He is a cancer, filled with bile and hatred, bent on destroying The Architect's creation from the inside. He tears Dreamers from their bodies and imprisons them for his own ends. Most likely he has your sister, Wren, and your boyfriend, Andromeda, but the two of you alone are no match for him. If you try to find him, you will only lose yourselves, too. That is why I implore you to put your faith in Hypnos. Only He has the strength to stand up to Thanatos. Only He can reverse the terrible plague that is ravaging this world."

"Andromeda said that Hypnos was chosen as a successor by Gade Sorensen," Wren said. "So, what about this, er, Dark God? Where did he come from?"

"He, too, was chosen. The two of them were supposed to counterbalance one another and ensure that the Dream-Scape was run harmoniously." Apollo shook his head, sadly. "Unfortunately, Thanatos has decided to use his power for his own selfish ends. You would do well to avoid, him, child. He would only poison you, as he has so many others."

Wren held the gaze of the beautiful avatar for a long moment, wondering what was behind that glassy stare.

"I'll take that under advisement," she said, eventually. "Come on, Andromeda. I think we've learned all we're likely to learn here."

14

"Wren? Wren! Wake up."

Wren sat up on Delphi's bed and pulled the Corona off her head. For a moment, she stayed very still, waiting for the sea-sick sensation gripping her stomach to subside. Delphi pressed a glass of water into her hand, and she took a hesitant sip.

"How the hell do you do this every day?" she asked Andromeda, who lounged on the floor.

Andromeda shrugged. "You get used to it."

"You build up a tolerance," Delphi said. "And then you get addicted. Nobody's really sure if it's the drug or the Dreaming that does it." She glanced sidelong at Andromeda. "Only that once you've started, it gets hard to stop."

"I can see how you'd end up losing your grip on reality." Wren passed her hand in front of her eyes a few times. Her vision was misty, casting a dream-like fog over everything. "All that shit about the gods … No offence, Andromeda, but I think you and your friends have lost all sense of perspective. Even if that stuff about Gade Sorensen choosing two successors is true …"

"It is," Andromeda said, gently but firmly.

"Even if it is true, they're just people like you and me. People who happen to have the cheat codes to a massive computer game, that's all."

Before Andromeda could reply, there was a knock at the bedroom door, and Ramona slipped inside.

"Wren," she whispered, "your mom's here."

Wren went downstairs. Only Delphi followed her. Harper stood stiffly in the middle of the sitting room, clutching a small pink travel bag that looked designer, but that Wren knew was fake from the market. Her dark hair was pulled back into a harsh ponytail, doing nothing to disguise the lines on her face from years of worry and cigarettes, and her long fingernails were freshly painted. When Wren entered the room, Harper greeted her with a hard slap across the face. Delphi yelped. Wren herself barely flinched.

"That's for leaving us," Harper spat.

"Glad we've got that out of the way," Wren replied, blinking back tears. Her cheek smarted, but she refused to show it. "You didn't bring Jared, then? He'd have done a much better job of that."

"He didn't want to come. I hope you're pleased with yourself. He's so angry with me." Her voice cracked a little. "Said he wouldn't let me back into the house if I left to come here. But I had to, didn't I? I had to see my poor little girl." Her fingers flexed and clenched around the handle of her bag.

"Could this be a first? You're putting Bethany before Jared? Why did it have to take her being in a coma for you to do that?"

"I just don't know what I done to deserve this." There were tears in her eyes. "My poor Bethany."

"You don't know what you've done? Are you serious?"

Harper looked Wren full in the face, searching her eyes as though trying to read her mind. "Why do you hate me so much?"

"Well, the fact that you just slapped me isn't high in your favour right now."

"This is your fault! If you hadn't left us … Bethany missed you so much." Harper sniffled and looked around, as though she might spot Bethany hiding in a corner of the room. "Where is she?"

"At the hospital. Come on," Wren grabbed her coat from a nearby chair. "Are we going or not?"

"Wren," Delphi interjected, quietly, "what do you want to do about … you know, Andromeda and everything?"

Wren sighed. "I don't know. I don't even know where to start. I think we all need a break tonight. Perhaps we can start again in the morning."

The hospital was dark and quiet by the time Wren and Harper arrived, after a tense taxi journey together. As they travelled, Wren had discovered, to her extreme annoyance, that Harper was expecting to stay at her house. Some irritable negotiations followed, and eventually Harper agreed to use her credit card to pay for a room at a motel.

"I hope you're happy that you're putting me into debt," she complained, as they got out of the cab and she swiped her card to pay for the journey. "Not like Jared would give me any money. Not when he wants rid of me. All the trouble you girls have caused him—he's had enough, he said. And then I had to leave Alfie with him, and who knows when I'll be able to see my little man again."

Sensing that she was about to start sniffling again, Wren said nothing to encourage her, instead leading the way silently into the hospital and down the quiet maze of corridors to the room where Bethany slept. The route had become second nature to her over the past few days. Official visiting hours were over, and the lights in the ward had been dimmed so that the glittering of Bethany's Corona cast an ethereal flicker of colour over her features. The room was silent but for her soft sound of her breathing and the occasional beep from the equipment monitoring her.

"Oh, my poor angel." Harper rushed to Bethany's side and took her hand. She looked down at her younger daughter and then up, appealingly, at her elder. "Why can't they just wake her up?"

"It's too dangerous." Wren explained what Doctor Nandra had told her.

"Oh, but surely they can do something? They can't just leave her like this." Harper's voice rose. "What kind of a hospital is this? She should be seen by another doctor. I want a second opinion. Look at her—she's absolutely fine, just sleeping."

"It's not that simple."

"When you think of all those Scapers who go in and out of the horrible bloody place all the time! Why did it have to be my Bethany who got stuck? What was she doing, going in there?" Harper dissolved into tears, clutching Bethany's fingers, and Wren felt a pang of sympathy for her.

"We'll get her back somehow, mum," she said, sitting on the opposite side of the bed. "I promise."

Harper sniffled. "I know I haven't always been the best

mum to you girls. But I do try. Honest, I do try."

"I know."

"It ain't the same without you, Wren. We all miss you. Poor little Alfie doesn't understand where you've gone."

Wren shook her head. "Can't you see why I did it though?"

"I know Jared can be hard to live with, but he does love you girls, in his way. It's just … he had a tough life, didn't he?"

"Don't make excuses for him."

Harper sighed. "Perhaps when you're a bit older and you meet a man you'll understand."

Wren glared at her. "I will never understand."

"You got a nice life here though, don't you?" Harper tried to smile. "Nice house to live in. Nice friends. I can get why you want to stay."

"Well, I'm glad we can see eye to eye on something."

"Any boys on the scene?"

Wren rolled her eyes. "No."

"Nobody at all?" Harper grinned. "Oh, come on, tell me some gossip. Take my mind off things. Must be someone you fancy, eh? I saw a cute boy in that house of yours. Said his name was Jon, didn't he? Well? Eh?"

Wren couldn't help but laugh a little. "You don't change, do you?"

Harper looked back down at Bethany, and her smile faded. "When're you gonna wake up, eh, Bethany? My poor little girl."

15

Somewhere in the DreamScape
No time at all...

Here, the wind ruffles Bethany's hair as she sits with her back against the hard bark of a willow tree. Here, the grass is fresh and green, the flowers pure white, the trickling stream as clear as the moonlight above her head. Here, the air is warm, and the nights are short and honeysuckle scented.

In this place, it never grows completely dark. Instead, the sky is washed with a deep purple glow, a perpetual wistful twilight, constantly on the edge of a sunrise. A short walk away is a village where people in old-fashioned clothes exchange cloth and apples for coins of gold. There is a smithy who makes weapons, and a tavern with a buxom wench. It's only a fantasy game, but it's the most peaceful place Bethany's found so far. Here, close to the safety of the village, she's learnt that the raiding hordes of orcs won't disturb her sleep, and so she lies beneath the trees on the soft ground, and drifts in and out of darkness.

The boy watches.

For a long time after she entered the DreamScape, Bethany didn't sleep. There was no need to rest or eat, nor even to pause for a moment. She wandered tirelessly, looking for a way out, but the portals only turned her upside down and spat her out elsewhere. Time here is impossible to measure. Hours, days, weeks … none of it means anything in the Dream. Her body could have kept going forever, but her mind was exhausted. When she fell into this environment, the familiar rhythms of night and day came as a relief. She decided to sleep, as best she could, and stay a while.

The boy watches, and Bethany watches the boy.

Although she understands in her bones that time moves more quickly here than in the real world, she has been here for five cycles of night and day, and she knows the village and its inhabitants well enough to realise that the boy does not belong. He is close to her age—perhaps a year or two older—and extremely handsome, with deep blue eyes, sandy hair, and suntanned skin. Bethany doesn't think he's part of the game. He's been watching her since sunset, from a branch in the willow tree, where he sits with his bare feet dangling in the air. He wears a simple pair of dark linen trousers and a white shirt which is only half-tucked.

"I think you're lost," he says, eventually. There is a tinge of amusement in his voice.

Bethany is in no mood to be mocked.

"Why don't you get lost?" she snaps. "Or do you want me to chuck a stone at you?"

"All right, all right." The boy jumps down from the tree, landing softly on the grass near Bethany's feet. "There's no need to be cranky."

Bethany scoops up a stone and brandishes it. "I'm

warning you."

"Hey, have it your way." The boy shrugs and saunters off. At first, Bethany has every intention of letting him leave, and good riddance to him, but then she remembers that this is the first actual person she's spoken to in days. Assuming he *is* an actual person, which is by no means guaranteed around here.

"Wait!" she says. "Who are you?"

The boy turns back, an insufferably smug look on his pretty face. "You can call me Boy."

"What sort of a name is that?"

"A perfectly good one, if you ask me."

"Are you a real person?"

"Does it matter?" Boy grins, showing a row of perfect white teeth. "Here, we can be whatever we want to be."

"Right." Bethany turns away, irritated. "Unless what you want to be is at home."

"The lost ones can never go home," says the Boy, suddenly serious. "You should come with me, girl."

"It's Bethany. And why should I come with you?"

For a long moment, Boy is silent. Then he walks right up to Bethany, leaning close and looking her right in the eye with a thoughtful expression. "Why," he says, softly, "shouldn't you?"

He has a point, Bethany is forced to admit. Here, there, anywhere. What difference does it make? Besides, Boy is the first person, avatar, whatever, to have taken any interest in her at all since she got here.

"All right." She gets to her feet. "Which way?"

"Follow me." Boy darts off through the glade, moving quickly, all lithe, long limbs.

"Do you look like that in real life?" Bethany calls, and

Boy turns, walking backwards with a grin.

"What is real life, after all? The life we're living, surely? So, yes, I suppose I do look like this in real life."

He turns back around and leads the way to a calm, moonlit lake. Before Bethany can say a word, he walks straight into the water, deeper and deeper, only stopping when he is immersed up to his shoulders.

"Come on," he says.

Bethany folds her arms. "I'm not going in there."

"You think this is real water? You think you'll get wet? You think you'll drown? Follow me. Or don't. Your choice." Boy plunges into the water, vanishing beneath the surface. Bethany waits a moment, but he doesn't reappear. After a few seconds hesitation, she wades into the lake. The warm water laps gently at her ankles. She walks deeper and deeper, until she is almost submerged, then takes a deep breath—remembering even as she does it that there is no air here, anyway—and dives into the heart of the lake.

Boy is waiting, his sandy hair wafting slightly with the flow of the water. The lake seems to go down forever—Bethany can see no bottom, only darkness. She follows Boy as he swims towards an opening in the rocks at the lake's edge, a tiny crack barely big enough to squeeze through.

"You first," he says, bubbles rising from his mouth. Bethany turns on her side, wiggling through the gap, trying not to think about drowning. Where she emerges, the water is colder and clearer—she can see the sun shining from above and she pushes up towards it, up, and up, and up, until she bursts, gasping, out of the lake. It is not the lake she has just left. Around her there is a thin film of ice, and as Boy surfaces he breaks through it, shards shattering around his head.

"This way," he says, not sounding in the least bit cold, although Bethany's teeth are chattering. She's soaking wet and shivering by the time she clambers onto the banks of the lake, but Boy is perfectly dry.

"Think yourself dry, and you will be dry," he says. Bethany tries to focus her mind on the thought of dryness, imagining her clothes and hair as dry and warm as if it were a hot summer's day. To her astonishment, it works.

They are in a large garden, one that looks as though it was once neatly maintained, although now it has become unruly and overgrown. A weed-strewn lawn sweeps upwards from the lake's edge towards a gravel path lined with tall trees. Creepers snake across the path, and ivy curls around the statues at either side of the stone steps that Bethany and Boy now make their way up.

Emerging at the top, they face a vast palace, like something out of a fairy tale. Like the garden, it's seen better days. The once magnificent stone frontage has been covered with grey moss, the carvings around the rotten oak doors are crumbling, and most of the castle's numerous windows are smashed or missing. Boy trips lightly up the steps and puts his shoulder against the door to force it open, and they tiptoe inside.

The castle's inside is just as scruffy as the outside. The marble floor is encrusted with dirt and rubble, while weeds creep through gaps near the walls. The mirrors are tarnished and black, and the grand staircase in the centre of the hall is missing a stair.

"It looks like Sleeping Beauty's palace," Bethany breathes, following Boy into a cavernous ballroom with a shattered crystal chandelier in the middle of the floor. The walls are lined with people, every one of them dressed in sumptuous rags. The men wear laddered breeches and torn frock coats in grubby velvet; the women moth-eaten silk gowns and elaborate, wilted headdresses filled with drooping feathers and dying flowers. They sit silent and motionless, watching Bethany and Boy with weary eyes. A stench of decay fills the air. Bethany shudders.

"What are all these people doing here?" she whispers.

"Waiting," is Boy's only reply.

"Waiting for what?" Bethany tiptoes around the ragged hems of the ladies' dresses, trying to avoid their staring eyes.

At the end of the ballroom, Boy pauses in front of a pair of huge, elaborate, firmly closed doors.

"Waiting," he repeats with a shrug, as though the answer doesn't interest him at all. Bethany looks back at the ragged horde, her throat tight with a horror she can't quite explain.

"Are they … dying?"

The Boy shakes his head. "Death is only the beginning," he says. Turning his back to Bethany, he flings the doors open. Seeing what's on the other side, Bethany starts to back away.

"No," she whispers. "No, I can't go in there."

Behind the doors is blackness—not emptiness, but a living, breathing blackness, like the dark inside of a gaping mouth, just like the horrible void she stumbled into days? … months? … years? ago. The darkness from which she could not escape, which has been clinging to her like slimy fingers the whole time she's been wandering in the Dream.

Boy, standing in front of the darkness, watches her with a cold stare.

"You can come," he says, "or you can wait. Make your choice."

Without another word, he steps into the rupture and vanishes. Bethany looks back at the ragged people, takes a deep breath, and follows him.

16

"Sometimes I'm afraid you're just a dream."

That was what Erik used to say to Lia, in that twilight between sleeping and waking.

"Sometimes I'm afraid you're just a dream."

Perhaps that was the most hurtful thing of all. That he couldn't even be sure she was real.

"You look a state." Scott was relaxing on the sofa when Lia finally made it home. He stood as she entered, coming over to take her kit bag just as she was about to drop it on the floor.

"Gee, it's nice to see you, too."

"I'm sorry." Scott placed the bag carefully on the shelf above the coat rack and gave her arm a squeeze. "I just mean you look exhausted. Why were you working so late?" He indicated two steaming bowls of noodles on the kitchen island. "Dinner's getting cold."

"Tomas and I are working on something new." Lia

shrugged off her coat and draped it over one of the kitchen stools. She picked up a bowl of noodles and took it over to the sofa. "Thanks for dinner."

"They work you too hard." Scott frowned, picking up his own bowl. "I thought you said as a guest artist you'd have a lighter schedule."

"It's not the company, just me and Tomas."

"So, you're taking on extra work voluntarily?" There was a hard edge to his voice as he sat beside her.

"Shouldn't I?"

"After what we talked about the other day? I thought we'd agreed you would take it easy."

Lia opened her mouth to argue, but before she could speak, Scott continued, "I'm worried about you. You seem so worn out. You haven't been yourself since … well, since the wedding."

Lia put down her bowl and sat back, nestling into the sofa cushions. He was right, she was worn out. She ached all over.

"I just need some sleep," she said.

Scott rubbed her shoulder. "Sometimes I feel like you're not really here, you know. Like your mind is elsewhere."

"I'm sorry. It's been a hard day."

"So why don't you tell me about it? Get it all off your chest?"

"It's nothing." Then, feeling as though she should give him something, at least, "I ran into some Dravens on the tube."

"Goddamn Lia, I told you to take a car."

"It's all right, they just shouted a bit. I guess it shook me up."

Scott's expression darkened, but he said nothing. They

had formed a kind of unspoken pact not to mention Erik, and yet here he was again, casting a shadow over their relationship. All he'd needed to do was to show his face, just once, and now he was haunting Lia's every waking moment. Scott's too, if the look on his face was anything to go by.

She thought of all the secrets she now found herself keeping. The ballet, the call from Kent. The thought that Erik might be in London, which had wormed its way into her mind like a parasite and was eating up her thoughts.

"I think I'll go to bed," she said. "An early night will do me good."

"All right."

He glanced at her still-full bowl of noodles, but didn't comment.

"We'll spend some time together tomorrow, I promise," she said

He nodded. "Sleep well."

Lia went to the bedroom and slipped off her clothes, changing into a pair of silk pyjamas and a robe. She opened the French windows that led onto the balcony and looked through the rain at the park opposite. White street-lamps cast their bright glow onto the trees, making the tips of the leaves look as though they'd been dipped in silver, but otherwise the park was black and still. Lia stared into the darkness until she started to imagine shapes moving in the shadows between the trees. The back of her neck prickled with the sensation that she was being watched.

Was that a figure she saw, or was she just being paranoid?

Paranoid ... or hopeful?

Heart racing, she turned away from the window. When

she switched on her phone, its screen so was bright it made her squint. Hastily, checking over her shoulder that Scott wasn't anywhere nearby, she typed a message.

Go home. I'm fine. Kent is looking for you.

She pressed send, and it was gone.

She waited a long while, but the park remained still and silent. Eventually, she closed the window and went to bed, but as she began to drift into a restless sleep, her phone pinged, and a reply appeared.

Just say the word and I'll come back. xxx

Lia deleted the message. When she woke in the morning, she couldn't be sure whether it had just been a dream.

17

When Wren arrived at college the next morning, she found Kazuo already in the classroom, sitting at his laptop surrounded by holographic projectors. He was working on his holo-sculpture, a pixelated Chinese dragon that twisted and refracted light like a prism. He looked up as he saw her approach.

"Hey, Wren. How'd it go with your mom?"

Wren shook her head. "Is it terrible that I don't like her being here? It just makes me feel so … on edge. Like Jared's going to turn up at any moment."

"From what you've said about him, I can't blame you for feeling that way. But it's good for Bethany that your mom's, here, right?"

"Yeah, you're right." Wren put her hand through the holo-sculpture and watched the pixels dance over her fingers as she turned it one way and then another.

"Andromeda hung around for a bit after you left last night," Kazuo said.

"Yeah? Did you manage to get it together with her?"

"We just talked, believe it or not."

"You? Just talking to a girl? I find that difficult to believe."

"Ah, ye of little faith," Kazuo said. "She told me about your visit to the church. All that stuff about the two gods …"

Wren made a face. "I'm not sure we're going to get much sense out of her, unfortunately. The people at that church creeped the hell out of me, and they've been brainwashing her for years."

"I dunno. I thought it was interesting."

"You mean batshit?"

"A bit. But there's something going on there that could give us some clues about what happened to Bethany."

"Really?" Wren had begun to despair of getting anywhere with the DreamScape—it seemed so vast and unnavigable—but Kazuo was good with computers, and the thought that he had an idea brightened her mood considerably. "Well, spit it out, Kaz!"

"This is going to take some explaining." Kazuo lowered his voice as the teacher arrived in the studio. "Bring your painting over here and I'll try and get you up to speed while we work."

Wren edged around the back of the room and dragged her easel over so she could stand beside Kazuo, brush in hand, pretending to add to the painting when, in reality, she was listening intently to what he had to say.

"It's just a theory, okay?" he began, when the teacher was out of earshot.

"Sure, sure. I'm not getting my hopes up, promise," Wren lied.

"Okay." Kazuo made a sweeping gesture in the air and his dragon span around, the better for him to examine some detail on the tail. "So, I was interested in what Andromeda had been saying about this Hippo …"

"Hypnos."

"Whatever they call him. Anyway, she kept talking about the good work he was doing for humanity, and I wanted to know what it was. And, you know, it's not completely insane."

Wren groaned. "Oh, she's got to you, hasn't she? One look at a pretty face and you'll come around to anything."

"It's true," Kazuo grinned. "But in this case, I really do think she's onto something. In a way. I'm not saying it's possible or anything, but it sounds like Hypnos is trying to create a utopia in the Scape. A place where people can live permanently, free of government, free of violence, free of wars and all that."

"Sounds lovely, but how does he plan to achieve that? From what I saw, the place is falling apart."

"Yeah, the amount of server power needed to even keep it running must be out of this world. To bring it anywhere close to what Hypnos wants would take an insane amount of cash, not to mention someplace safe to store all those servers. Andromeda reckons the current ones are secreted away down an abandoned mine shaft somewhere in Venezuela, or something like that. And then there's the problem of keeping people in there permanently … We're talking about people uploading their entire consciousnesses to the Scape. Just take a moment to think about how much information makes you you. Thoughts, feelings, memories. Patterns of speech, physical appearance … everything you ever were or will be. Now imagine trying to upload all of that to a computer network. The contents of just one person's brain would probably be enough to completely overload the system as it stands."

"But it's full of people right now," Wren said, puzzled.

"Sure, and they're all still connected to their bodies. The information is still stored in their brains, not in the network itself. Even, I'd guess, in the case of people like Bethany. And there I come to my point. She's still in there. Her consciousness is still in her body. It couldn't be otherwise. If all those lost people were complete consciousnesses wandering around in the DreamScape, the system couldn't cope with it."

"What about someone like Reza? His body's dead. They took him off life support."

Kazuo looked solemn. "Andromeda asked me that. I had to be vague. What could I say? I doubt there's anything left of him, or if there is, then it won't be much. An echo of an echo, if you know what I mean? A few corrupted files, maybe, left over from information the network obtained from him when he first logged in."

"So, if Bethany's still in her own brain, really, why can't we just get her back?"

Kazuo fell silent as the teacher passed by. Once she was gone, he continued:

"How can I put this? I've been researching how the DreamScape actually works. When you first enter the Scape it takes a kind of ... inventory of you. It connects with your brain through a neural link and copies a few basic traits such as appearance and mannerisms from which to create you an avatar. From there, as you move through the environment, it tracks your neural signature in order to feed your brain with the correct sights and sounds for whatever place you happen to be in."

"Andromeda told me about that," Wren said. "There's a

glowing breadcrumb trail that follows you around everywhere. She said when Bethany fell through one of the ruptures, the system must've lost that trail."

"Correct. The system can't connect Bethany's mind to her physical location anymore. That doesn't mean her mind's not in her body. It just means the files the Dream-Scape has created for her, to track her progress, no longer include information about her whereabouts in the real world. Normally, when you decide to leave the Scape, you choose to log out and in response, the system guides you back to your body, and gently wakes you up."

"Not sure it's all that gentle," Wren muttered. "But go on."

"The reason we can't just disconnect Bethany is because her mind really believes it is out there, wandering the DreamScape, and the system isn't able to guide her back. If we were to simply break the connection, we would sever the neural link without knowing what information was passing between her and the network at that moment. It could cause a complete mental break as she struggled to work out what was reality and what wasn't, or even worse, actual brain damage, if we cut the link at a moment when the network was interacting with her mind."

"Well, this is all unrelentingly shit," said Wren. "I thought you had an idea that might help us?"

"I'm getting to it." Kazuo waved his hand impatiently. "Listen, the DreamScape network is still tracing Bethany's movements, right? It's just not connecting them with her physical location. That means if we can get to the heart of the network itself—the hub where it does all the processing of avatars' movements—we might be able to follow a trail back to Bethany from there. Once we've got her, if we can find her, we can tell the system where her body is, allowing it to link her up again."

"So, we need to find …"

"The CPU. Central Processing Unit."

Wren frowned. "That doesn't sound like it's going to be easy."

"What in life is, Wren? What in life is? You're right, though. It's not like they advertise the location of the CPU for all to see, and even if we can work out where in the network it is, that's not going to help us get inside it. Gade Sorensen probably locked that thing down like Fort Knox. I'd guess that Andromeda's gods are the only people who can access it."

"So where do we start? The gods haven't been a lot of help so far."

"It's a computer program like any other, right? The DreamScape you see when you go in there is just the interface, put there to obscure all the cogs and wheels of the inner workings. We just have to figure out how to get behind all that, so that we can see where the information is flowing."

"Just?"

"Well …" Kazuo ran a hand through his green hair, grimacing slightly. "Not just. No good programmer wants randoms tinkering around with his nuts and bolts. But Andromeda told me she uses old portals set up to get engineers in and out of environments so they could make changes. That's our way into the scaffolding of the program, right there. I think we should be able to use those portals to get behind the scenes somehow. We agreed Andromeda would come over after college, and then she's going to take me in there, see if I can make sense of it at all."

"I'll come with you," Wren said, as the class finished,

and everyone began packing up their materials. "Meet you at the house this afternoon, all right?"

When Wren, Delphi, and Kazuo arrived back at the house that afternoon, they found Andromeda sitting on the steps waiting for them. She unfurled herself slowly and stood, casting a dreamy glance over the three of them.

"Are you ready to keep searching?" she asked. "Perhaps Apollo will have some new ideas about how to help us."

"Kaz said your Hypnos was working on some hare-brained plan to upload people into the DreamScape permanently," Wren replied, slipping past her into the house. "I'm not sure I can get on board with that."

"When the Dream is stable and complete, safe from the evil influence of Thanatos, it will be very different from the place you saw the other day. Surely you can see the potential? It's a whole universe where nobody need ever be hungry, cold, or afraid. Or will be, once the darkness is banished."

"From what Kaz said, that day is a long way off."

"You underestimate the power of Hypnos," Andromeda replied, as the four of them made their way upstairs.

"Well," Wren headed into Delphi's room, "how about we concentrate on the here and now? We need to go back into the Dream and investigate these portals of yours."

Andromeda nodded, settling on the same spot on Delphi's floor where she'd lain the day before, during Wren's first trip into the DreamScape. She curled her legs beneath her and looked at Kazuo, who stood behind Wren in the doorway.

"Kazuo had some interesting thoughts," she conceded. "Perhaps it will help to have fresh eyes to look at things from a different perspective. Are you coming in with us?"

Kazuo nodded. "I want to see how this place works from the inside."

"Guess I'm doing root duty again." Delphi brushed past them and sat down at her desk. She pulled off her boots and socks, put her feet up on the desk, and rifled through a drawer until she found a pot of black nail varnish. "Have a great time, guys. Don't do anything I wouldn't do."

Andromeda handed out Coronas to Wren and Kazuo, then fitted hers to her head and lay back on the floor. Wren and Kazuo did likewise, and moments later, all three of them were back in the Japanese garden orientation screen, with its pagoda in the distance and the horrific black gash splitting across the sky. Kazuo looked around and then down at his own body, examining his hands just as Wren had the first time she'd entered. He looked exactly the same as in real life, except his eyes had the slightly glassy look that Wren was becoming accustomed to in avatars.

"I can't believe I've never done this before," he said. "This place is … Wow. It's so much better than I imagined."

Andromeda smiled. "I told you. The portal is this way." She led the way through the forest to the glade with the birch tree in the centre, just as she had done with Wren, but before she could touch the knot that would transport them to the StarScape, Kazuo stopped her.

"How did you find out about this door?" he asked, peering at the knot. From what Wren could see, there was nothing to distinguish it from any other part of the tree.

"There are Dreamers who spend their lives hunting for

them. The portals are worth a great deal. Some try to sell the knowledge of their whereabouts, but luckily for the rest of us, there are others who believe that they should be free to use for all."

"Why are they so valuable?"

"To move around the system the way it was intended, you need Credits," Andromeda explained. "That's how Sorensen monetised his creation originally. Movement, avatar upgrades, entry to the most exclusive environments and games … all of it costs Credits. But those are hard to come by these days. A few users have managed to monopolise everything that was left over after the official shut-down, and they're not willing to share."

Kazuo frowned. "So, these back doors are the only way ordinary users can move around freely?"

"Not freely, exactly. They take you to where they were programmed to go—nowhere else. This one goes to the StarScape. I've never been able to get it to take me anywhere else."

"Like a hyperlink?" Wren said.

"Exactly."

"How do I get it to work?" Kazuo asked, but he was already reaching for the knot, and once his fingers rested on it, he vanished. Andromeda took Wren's hand and the two of them followed, finding Kazuo again on a rocky outcrop in the StarScape.

"Incredible," he breathed, staring at the sky awash with stars. "All these stars are separate environments?"

"Yes. But we can only travel to a few of them from here—the free to access ones, like Reverie," Andromeda said.

"Reverie?"

"Let's give Reverie a miss," Wren said, quickly. "Where else can we go, Andromeda?"

Silently, Andromeda selected a star.

18

When the blinding light subsided, they stood on a cliff edge in the middle of a thick fog. All they could see was the ground beneath their feet, and a rope bridge that stretched endlessly into the mist.

"Where are we?" Kazuo asked.

"I spent the last of my Credits to get us here," Andromeda said. "It's not a free environment. In fact, it's very expensive to enter. That's why I've only been here once before."

Wren looked around at the blanket of fog. "Why go to all that trouble to bring us here?"

"Kazuo is interested in the ways Dreamers move between environments. There is a portal here—one many Dreamers believe has great significance. I thought he should see it."

She put a foot on the first rung of the bridge, and it swayed alarmingly beneath her. Wren followed her across, her feet slipping on the damp wooden slats, trying not to think about the invisible drop beneath them.

"What happens if we fall?" she asked, her throat dry.

"We can't die here … can we?"

"No, little bird," Andromeda called back, her voice drifting on the wind. "But I would not recommend you try it. If you hit the ground, you will feel pain."

"I've got no intention of trying it," Wren muttered.

Behind her, Kazuo swore under his breath as the bridge rocked and swayed. Their progress through the mist was excruciatingly slow, all the more so because there was no end in sight. Wren lost track of how long they'd been inching forward for, and by the time they finally spotted solid ground, she couldn't have said whether they'd been crossing for minutes or hours.

"Thank Hypnos that's over," she said, relieved to take her first step onto a surface that did not slip and sway beneath her. Her relief was short lived. An obsidian-black cliff rose high and sheer directly ahead, and all they had to move along was a narrow stone ledge. Andromeda led the way, edging forward with her back to the cliff, palms pressed flat against the glass-like stone.

"I didn't like this the first time I did it," she admitted. "I don't like it any better now."

"And people pay a lot of money to come to this place?" Kazuo called.

"Not many do," Andromeda replied. "I think that's the point."

Eventually, they made it around the sheer cliff edge to face the gaping mouth of a cave. Andromeda pressed onward into the blackness, Wren and Kazuo in her wake. Inside, it was so dark they could barely see a thing, but they followed the flicker of Andromeda's white dress until she stopped, facing a featureless wall. She ran her hands over it methodically, covering every inch of the rock as though searching for something.

For a split second, Wren thought she saw a flicker of red light appear beneath Andromeda's fingers. Andromeda noticed it too, and moved back to the area of wall where it had appeared, working her hands across it until it glowed red again.

"There." She held a finger against the spot and stepped back so Wren and Kazuo could see it better. As Wren squinted at the red light in the darkness, the shape emerged more clearly, the edges becoming ever sharper. It resembled an ink blot, like something out of a Rorschach test.

"What's that?" Wren asked.

"They say it's the Mark of Thanatos. The Dark God." Andromeda shuddered. "It's never worked for me."

"What is it supposed to do?"

"It's a portal. People say a chosen few can touch it and be transported to the Dark God's lair. But I don't know the secret. I just thought you would like to see it," she looked at Kazuo, "since you're interested in the portals."

She let go of the Mark and it faded. Kazuo stepped up to the wall and ran his hands over it, making it glow red again.

"This Thanatos," he said, "he's another of your gods?"

"The other who was chosen by the Architect."

"A person with special access to the workings of the network." Kazuo frowned at the glowing shape. "He's piggybacked on the developer access points to create his own pathway."

"There are more of these, scattered around the Dream," Andromeda said. "But this is the only one I know how to reach." She cocked her head and examined the blot. "What do you think it's supposed to represent?"

"I don't know," Wren said. "Something winged? A bat?"

"Really? I always thought it was a person with his arms outstretched. An angel, maybe—or more likely a demon," Andromeda replied. Wren could just about see her pale face in the darkness, her eyes sad. "The last time I came here was with Reza. He wanted so badly to make the Mark work for him. He wanted to find the Dark God."

"Why? I thought Thanatos was supposed to be bad?"

"Reza didn't think so. He thought there was something more going on. Something that we didn't understand. He became obsessed with the idea of the Dark God. He stopped believing in the teachings of Hypnos and went to look for him, and then one night in the Mono I found him sleeping, just like your sister, and he wouldn't wake. It was the Dark God who took him from me, I'm sure of it. Besides," she added, "it's hopeless. Nobody but Thanatos's inner circle can get close to him, and I can't find anybody who can even tell me who they are."

"I can work out how this functions." Kazuo examined the blot. "I can find a way to access the code and get us in there, and once I've done that, I can figure out how to re-route the hijack to take us straight to the CPU. Just give me time."

Wren and Andromeda left Kazuo to study the Mark of Thanatos, and logged out of the DreamScape for a break. When Wren woke, she was staring up at the Sacred Ravens poster once more. Erik Dacre glowered down at her through sharp, green eyes. He was dressed all in black, of course, and the poster's designer had added a pair of dramatic, holographic wings behind him, black feathers spreading out from his shoulder-blades, making him look like some kind of demon.

A thought bobbed dozily through Wren's mind, looking for a place to settle. She pushed herself up onto her elbows, feeling woozy. Andromeda was already awake, watching her. Kazuo lay stretched out on the floor, and Delphi was nodding off in her desk chair, her work abandoned. It was dark, and when Wren checked her watch, she found it was late in the evening.

"Do you think he'll get anywhere with the Mark?" she whispered, nodding at Kazuo.

"Many have tried," Andromeda said, doubtfully.

"Kaz is good with computers, though." Wren's gaze strayed once more to the Sacred Ravens poster. "I'll bet *he* knows something about all this," she mused.

"Who is that?"

"Erik Dacre," Wren replied. Delphi stirred and opened her eyes. "He's the most famous Sliphead there is, right Delph? Everybody says he spends half his life in the place. Surely he must know something about these gods, or how people are getting lost in there?"

"Well, okay …" Delphi yawned. "Perhaps. But how does that help us? It's not like we can just rock up to his house one afternoon and ask him."

"No, but …" Wren indicated the list of tour dates on the poster, "we do know where he's going to be on certain specific days and times. And then there was that competition you entered, to get backstage passes …"

"Yeah, me and every other girl between the ages of fifteen and twenty-five. I don't think we can rely on my winning it. I mean, like, I'd love to, but I've never been that lucky, you know?"

"When are they announcing the winner?" Wren asked, getting to her feet.

"Wednesday."

"Then we've got time."

"Time for what?"

Wren looked down at Kazuo. "Can we wake him, Andromeda?"

"Now? I can go back in and ask him to come out, if that's what you want."

"Please do." Wren gazed at the poster. "I've got an idea."

"So let me get this straight," Kazuo said, once he had fully woken and managed to get up to speed. "You want me to hack into the magazine's internal network and rig the competition so that you two can go see Sacred Ravens and maybe meet Erik Dacre?" He was sitting on Delphi's bed, leaning against the wall, looking ashen and sipping from a glass of water as he tried to shake off the dream-sickness.

"That's about right, yes." Wren was sitting on the floor with Andromeda, while Delphi perched on the end of the bed, handing out beers she'd just fetched from the kitchen. Wren accepted hers gratefully and cracked it open. "I'm not sure if you're saying it's going to be hard, or easy."

"Oh, I can do it, all right." Kazuo grinned. "You should know better by now than to doubt me."

"Great!" Delphi clapped her hands gleefully. "Can you, then, Kaz? Please, please, please?! I'll do all your chores for a month."

"I'll do it. For Wren, right?"

"For Wren, sure! That's totally what I meant." Delphi nodded vigorously.

Kazuo looked at Wren. "You think this Mark of Thanatos thing is something to do with him?"

"That ink blot … we thought it might be a winged person, or a bat, but it's not, is it? It's a raven. Just like the one in the poster. I knew it the moment I woke up—it just took me a while to realise."

"You think that man in the poster is Thanatos himself?" Andromeda looked doubtful. "Are you sure, little bird?"

"Sorry, Wren, I hate to say anything that might jeopardise our trip," Delphi said, "but I think you're clutching at straws."

Wren shrugged. "Well, at least you two seem to agree for once. But what else do I have to go on right now? It might be him, or he might know something. Honestly, I don't know where else to turn."

"Just be cautious, little bird," Andromeda said, softly. "If you turn to Thanatos, you may not come back."

19

The first thing Bethany becomes aware of are the vibrations beneath her feet. She is moving. Then the sound: a steady *clunk, clunk, clunk*, in time with the vibrations. A train? But the image fading into existence around her looks more like a restaurant. Rows of tables set for dinner with white table-cloths, and napkins folded into fans, and way more cutlery than any normal person could possibly need. Gentle piano music plays quietly in the background, as dark countryside speeds past outside the windows. One of those posh steam trains, then, like out of an old movie.

Bethany looks around for Boy, but he is nowhere to be seen. She's alone in the carriage, but not for long—a door opens at the other end and the dinner guests start to arrive, making their way to their tables. The men are dressed smartly, in jackets and bow ties; the women wear beautiful evening dresses and jewellery that reflects the candlelight, bouncing it all around the room. Bethany wonders how much those necklaces cost. More money than she will ever see in her lifetime, no doubt. As the carriage fills up, the guests take their seats and consult the menus, while dapper waiters buzz around pouring drinks and taking orders. Nobody pays any attention to Bethany.

The food, when it arrives, looks fancy and strange, but Bethany is nonetheless seized by the desire to eat. She hasn't eaten a thing since she came to the DreamScape, and although she isn't hungry, she misses the sensation of food. It's been days, at least. Weeks, perhaps. Maybe if she sits down, somebody will let her have some chips. If they even serve chips in a place this posh. She looks around for an empty seat.

In fact, there is only one space available, at a table for two opposite a pretty, blonde woman in an emerald-green dress. She is young and kind-looking, so Bethany sits down shyly, wondering whether she's a real person or part of the game. The woman notices her through clear blue eyes and smiles, and Bethany feels immediately at ease.

A waiter stops at their table. The kind-looking woman orders something called *soo-flay* and Bethany asks for some chips with ketchup. He returns moments later with their food, and Bethany tucks in gratefully.

"You must have been hungry," says the woman. She has an English accent, which is comforting to Bethany's ears.

"Not really," Bethany replies, between mouthfuls, "but I like chips."

"What is your name?"

"Bethany. And you?"

The woman just smiles. "I'm not important here. You are. Bethany who?"

"Silver. Bethany Silver." Should she be giving her real name away, Bethany wonders? Does it matter? Nobody here knows her anyway.

"Where are you travelling to, Bethany Silver?"

Bethany frowns out the window at the moonlit fields. "I don't know. A boy brought me here, but he's gone, and I want to go home."

"Perhaps I can help you. Where is home?"

Bethany hesitates. Home is Lancaster, but that's a place she doesn't really want to go back to.

"San Francisco," she says, at last. "Where my sister lives. That's where I was when I ended up in here. Can you help me get back?"

"I know someone who can help you." The woman smiles. "Don't worry, we're almost there."

20

"Ohmygod ohmygod ohmygod!"

Wren was sitting at the kitchen table with Kazuo, eating cornflakes, when Delphi came clattering down the stairs and burst into the room, still in her dressing gown, brandishing her phone.

"Oh my God, he did it!" she shrieked, waving the phone in Wren's face, too quickly for Wren to actually see anything. "He seriously did it. Two tickets to see Sacred Ravens tomorrow night, and backstage passes! Kaz, I could kiss you."

"Be my guest." Kazuo proffered his cheek, and Delphi gave him a quick peck. Wren couldn't help but smile.

"Thanks, Kaz," she said.

"Anything for you, beautiful." Kazuo winked. "You can thank me properly later."

"Seriously, I owe you one. But how are we going to get there?" Wren said. "I don't have any money for shuttle tickets."

"Don't worry about that," Delphi said, quickly. "I've got the cash. My parents gave me some money to tide me over while my bursary comes in."

"I can't ask you to use that for me."

Delphi shrugged. "You can pay me back in instalments or something, if it makes you feel better. Or just consider it a thank you for getting me the chance to *meet Erik Dacre*!" Her voice rose to a squeal, and she clapped her hands, bouncing on her toes. "Oh my God." A look of horror crossed her face. "What am I going to wear? Wren! You have to help me! Come on." She pulled Wren out of her seat. "This is urgent!"

Twenty-four hours later, Wren was sitting on a supersonic shuttle, speeding towards New York City. Beside her, Delphi was in the highest of high spirits, bobbing away silently to—undoubtedly—a Sacred Ravens song on her headphones. She'd spent most of the morning agonising over her outfit and bemoaning the fact that Wren had managed to talk her out of getting a Draven tattoo.

"I'm sure if he's going to fall in love with you on sight, the presence or lack of a tattoo won't make any difference," Wren had told her, as they got ready in Delphi's room. Delphi paused in applying her thick black eyeliner to glare at Wren.

"You're making fun of me. That's rich, coming from the girl who now thinks Erik Dacre is some kind of Dream-Scape deity."

"Hey, I don't think he's omnipotent or anything—that's Andromeda's theory—but you have to admit it all makes perfect sense. It's got to be someone with resources;

someone who uses the DreamScape all the time, and has done for years …"

"… And then there's the raven symbol. Yeah, yeah, yeah, you said." Delphi finished applying her eyeliner and pouted at her reflection, sweeping her hair to one side to show off her skull earring. "I just hope you're not going to embarrass yourself when we finally get to talk to him."

"No, no, I'll leave that to you, Delph," Wren replied, earning herself another filthy look. "I just want to find out if he knows anything that might help us find Bethany."

Delphi's enthusiasm was infectious, though, and Wren had to admit she was starting to feel quite excited at the prospect of not only seeing New York for the first time, but meeting a famous rock star to boot. She could only imagine how envious Bethany would be if she knew. She gazed out the window at the inside of the shuttle tunnel and tried to plan what she would say to Erik Dacre. She only had a short time to explain Bethany's situation and persuade him to help her—if he even could—and she had no idea how she was going to do it. Andromeda had been desperate to come too, but they didn't have a ticket for her and besides, Wren secretly felt that having somebody along who actually believed in the Dark God might be more of a hindrance than a help. She was rather hoping that Dacre would turn out to be a perfectly rational person who just happened to be good at manipulating the DreamScape, and not the kind of megalomaniacal nutcase who would deliberately start a religion around himself. But then, if the Dravens were anything to go by, perhaps rational was a bit too much to hope for.

They pulled into Grand Central Station late in the afternoon. Wren did her best not to gape like an obvious tourist as they passed through the vast, arch-ceilinged hall, dodging floods of smart-suited businesspeople on their way home from work. The commuters were purposeful and polished, a world away from the chilled-out Californians Wren had gotten used to.

Wren and Delphi grabbed hot dogs from a stand just outside of the station and ate them as they walked towards Central Park, where the concert was taking place.

"This way." Delphi took charge, weaving through the crowd with her phone in front of her, consulting her map as Wren hurried to keep up. "I think we need to head down this … no, that road."

Wren looked up … and up, and up, searching for the tops of the skyscrapers that stretched seemingly without end, their tips separated by only the thinnest sliver of grey-blue sky. It was as though the human race had used up all the available space on the planet, and had decided to start their quest for the stars at ground-level, building as they went. They walked under miles of scaffolding, passing everything from upmarket jewellery shops to cheap laundrettes, while a sea of yellow cabs crept past in a permanent snarl of traffic, their drivers honking and shouting at one another.

By the time they made it to Central Park, Wren's feet hurt, and her head was pounding from the bustle and lights. Thankfully, they were soon able to join the crowd queueing to get onto the great lawn. In the distance was the stage, a towering jumble of metal, video screens, and lighting rigs on a scale Wren couldn't have imagined. She'd never even been to a rock concert before, let alone something of this size, and she couldn't help but stare in awe. There must have been tens of thousands of people pouring into the park—guys with long hair and band t-shirts, Cyborgs, blue-veined Wraiths, and, of course, an abundance of Dravens.

The steward at the gate took a look at their passes and directed them into the VIP area close to the stage. Delphi was about ready to spontaneously combust from happiness. Wren got her a beer to try and cool her down a bit, and they staked their claim to a prime position right up against the barrier, as near to the front as they could possibly get.

They waited a long while as the park filled up, listening to tinny music from the speakers near the stage, watching adverts flit across the giant video screens. And then, everything fell silent. The screens went black. A whisper of anticipation rustled through the crowd.

A heavy beat started up, thudding through their feet as if it came from the heart of the earth, so loud Wren was afraid her teeth would vibrate out of her head. Then the backing guitar, a glittering baseline just above the beat, building upwards and upwards until, with a great splash of light and sound a figure appeared, high above the stage on a pedestal. He spread his arms wide, soaking up the applause, then bent over his guitar, and a riff like a buzzsaw slashed through the night.

Delphi thrust her arms in the air and screamed along with the rest of the crowd as he descended the stairs, coloured lights flickering this way and that over his sharp-boned visage, lighting up his dark, skull-like eye sockets. He stepped up to the microphone and began to sing in a deep, guttural purr, his voice gently menacing in a way that gave Wren the shivers. She let herself get washed away in the moment, soaking up the music, the heat, the enthusiasm of the crowd. There was something primal about it, all these people gathered together to sway and dance, the beat creating a simple, transcendent connection between them all.

Whatever he might have been in reality, Wren thought,

and whatever he might have been in the DreamScape, here, in this place, in this moment, Erik Dacre was more than just a man. He became a vessel for the emotions, desires, pain of every person in the crowd. A creation of their collective imaginations. A kind of god.

When the final encore ended, and the stage went black for the last time, Wren and Delphi shuffled their way—hot, sweaty and exhilarated—out of the VIP area along with the rest of the crowd.

"That was so amazing," Delphi kept repeating, breathlessly. "So amazing."

They showed their passes to the steward, and he guided them into a tent-covered area just behind the stage, where roadies in jeans and checked shirts milled around, already packing away the drum kit and clearing up the plastic cups littering the floor.

"Wait here please," the steward said, before heading out through a gap in the tent covering.

Wren looked at Delphi. She had gone pale.

"I feel a bit sick, Wren," she whispered. "I think I need to go outside …"

"Hold it together, Delph." Wren squeezed her shoulder. "You're fine."

A man in a shiny, blue three-piece suit and heavy-rimmed square glasses ducked into the tent and approached them. He had a white-toothed smile, sandy hair, and something of the air of a used car salesman.

"Ladies." He held out his hand to each of them in turn.

"Kent Austin. Sacred Ravens' manager. Pleasure to be able to show you around. You want a beer?" He plunged his hand into a nearby ice-box and pulled out two bottles of Bud.

"Thanks." Wren took them both, because Delphi seemed to have lost the power to move.

"Now." Kent spread his hands apologetically. "I know you're here to meet Erik, and you're looking forward to it, right? I just wanna warn you girls, though, he's not the best at this sort of thing. You gotta cut him a bit of slack, all right?" He led them out the back of the tent and across the grass to a vast black tour bus. "I like Erik to meet the fans every now and again," he added, taking the steps into the bus two at a time. "Helps keep him focused." He made a clicking motion with his fingers, as if to indicate bringing someone out of a stupor. "The other guys will look after you, though. They're okay."

Kent ducked through the black velvet curtain behind the driver's cab, holding it back for Wren and Delphi to follow into the interior of the bus. As her eyes adjusted to the dim light, Wren made out about half a dozen people crashed out on black leather sofas. The air was full of the smell of cigarettes and Chinese takeaway, and in the centre of a small coffee table sat a half-empty bottle of vodka and a collection of used shot glasses. A couple of Dravens were cosied up with some of the band members on one sofa, occasionally casting wistful glances at a dark figure who lay stretched across the other, his feet up on one armrest and his head thrown back against the other. One arm hung down close to the floor, a cigarette slowly burning itself out between his fingers. He wasn't moving, or doing anything at all, but Wren could sense the focus of the whole room gravitating toward him, as if he were a black hole, sucking them all in.

"You got fifteen minutes or so and then we gotta split," Kent said. "It's a long way to DC in this goddamn whale of a thing. Erik!"

The cigarette made its way up to Erik's mouth. He took a slow drag, blowing the smoke out into the air above his head.

"Erik, you got fans here. You remember? The competition winners?"

"Fuck." Erik lifted his head slowly, looked at them fuzzily, and then pulled himself the rest of the way up to sitting.

"Great start," Kent muttered.

Erik rubbed his forehead with the knuckles of the hand holding his cigarette, smoke spiralling into the air around him. His gaze was piercing, his eyes almost unnaturally green, but there was a cloudiness about them that reminded Wren of Andromeda. He was shirtless, wearing the same tight leather trousers and biker boots he'd been wearing on stage. His arms and torso were black with tattoos, the most striking a huge ink-blot raven splashed right across the centre of his chest.

"Fu-uck," he repeated, in his lazy drawl. "I'da stayed a bit more sober if I'd remembered. Sorry." He squinted at them as if unsure whether they were really there. Wren was forced to conclude that he was pretty much wasted. She wondered how he'd managed to hold it together so well on stage.

"You girls got names?" One of the other band members cut through the awkward silence, gesturing to a third, empty sofa. "Take a seat."

"Wren," Wren said, and when Delphi didn't seem to be able to speak, she added, "and this is Delphi."

"Doesn't say much, does she?" Erik observed.

Wren glanced at Delphi, who stared back in abject panic. "She's just really excited to meet you."

"Likewise." Erik treated Delphi to a grin that lit up the room like a camera flash, and she sat down, quite heavily, on the sofa opposite him.

"Um …" she said.

Erik reached for the vodka bottle, poured himself a shot and downed it. Wren could sense his attention waning again. Glancing around to see that Kent was occupied, she dodged the attempts of the other band members to make polite conversation, sat down and leaned forward to Erik.

"Listen, I don't have long and there's something I want to ask you."

"Shoot," he replied, without looking at her.

"What do you know about the people who get lost in the DreamScape?"

That got his attention back. He eyed her suspiciously. "People ask me a lot of shit, but that's new."

"My sister—her name's Bethany—she got lost and she's lying in a hospital right now, in a coma. I want to get her back and I thought maybe you could help me. Please?"

He took a drag of his cigarette, curious but unmoved. "Why me?"

"You … you seemed like someone who would know."

Erik leaned forward so his head was close enough to Wren's that she could smell the scent of stale sweat and cigarette smoke coming off him. He reached across her to the ashtray on the table. As he stubbed his cigarette out, he looked her right in the eyes, unblinking.

"Whatever you think you know about me, you're wrong. I can't help you. But if you want my advice? Let her go. Stay out of the DreamScape. There's shit going down there that you don't want to be a part of. Trust me."

With that, he got to his feet, pushing his dark hair back from his face, nodded at Delphi, and stalked off into the back of the bus. Seeing this, Kent soon came hurrying over to usher them out, apologising profusely for the briefness of their visit without appearing to care at all.

"Hey! Hey, wait a minute!" Wren tried to call back to Erik, but Kent kept walking forward, forcing her to back away down the steps of the bus. Once she stood on solid ground again, she turned to him. "Please, just let me talk to Erik for a minute longer."

"I'm sorry, girls. Visit's over. Tell you what, here's some signed posters, all right? Have a great evening."

"Stay out of the DreamScape," Wren muttered darkly, as the coach door slid closed. "Doesn't look much like he takes his own advice, does he?"

"He was even more gorgeous in real life, though," Delphi sighed.

Wren looked at her sharply.

"He's a junkie bastard," she spat. "He knew exactly what I was talking about, and he gave me nothing. What a fucking waste of time. What am I going to do now?"

Delphi patted her on the back. "Hey, don't be upset. We'll think of something, won't we? Come on, we'd better go and catch the shuttle."

21

"You're very quiet."

In one of the Royal Opera House dressing rooms, Lia and Marianne were preparing for the dress rehearsal of *Sleeping Beauty*. Marianne, dressed as the Lilac Fairy, helped to fasten Lia into the pink tutu she would wear for her first entrance.

"You can't be nervous, surely?" Marianne continued, pulling the laces of the bodice tight.

"I wanted to ask you something, actually." Lia glanced over her shoulder at Marianne. "Tomas and I have been working on something." She had been wavering for some time about discussing her ballet with Marianne, but she and Tomas were reaching the limit of what they were able to do alone. As a duet, the work lacked tension and depth. A third dancer would change the dynamic entirely.

"Ah ha! I knew it." Finished with the tutu, Marianne stepped back. "I've seen you guys whispering in corners and sneaking off to the studio after class. I knew you were up to something. Well, spill!"

"It's just a short abstract piece we're choreographing."

Lia leaned towards the mirror to check her make-up, trying to sound casual. "Something to make part of a mixed bill, maybe, if anybody wants it. But we need a third person, and I wanted to ask you first."

"Are you kidding? I would love to. Count me in!"

"It's just …" Lia hesitated. "I was afraid you wouldn't approve."

"Why the hell not? It sounds like a great idea."

"Because the music we chose … well, it's Sacred Ravens."

Lia had been bracing herself for a reaction—anger, perhaps, or at least exasperation—but Marianne just cocked her head on one side and peered at her.

"Why?" she asked, curiously. "I mean … was that your idea or Tomas's?"

"Mine, I guess. But Tomas was the one who persuaded me to work on it."

"Yeah, like hell he did." Marianne's eyes narrowed. "That sounds like just the kind of attention-seeking stunt he'd pull."

"It's not like that," Lia protested. "He's just trying to encourage me to be creative."

"You know your problem, Lia?" Marianne jabbed a lipstick at her. "You're too goddamned nice, and you think everybody else is the same. You know how much Tomas loves the limelight. That's why he dances with you. He's trying to encourage you to show yourself up so he can get some column inches."

"Excuse me? You think I'm showing myself up?"

"I think you know as well as I do that if you choreograph a ballet to Erik's music, the press will be all over it. You always say you don't like the attention, Li, but sometimes, honestly, I do wonder."

"It's true! Do you think I like being attacked by crazy fans on my way home from work? Do you think I like having my personal life splashed across the news feeds?"

Marianne spread her hands. "What do you want me to say? Because it sure does look like you do." She sighed. "Look, I'm sorry. I know you hate it, so why do this? I'm sure we can keep the choreography and change the music. If you want me to talk to Tomas …"

"No," Lia snapped. "No, I don't. Look, if you don't want to be involved, I totally understand. But I'm doing this because I want to, not because Tomas talked me into it. Do you think I don't know my own mind? Because sometimes it really does feel that way, Marianne. You, my family, Scott … all of you treat me like a child."

"Don't be ridiculous, Li …"

Lia held up a hand. "No, I've had enough. You know what Scott said the other day? He said he looks at old photos of me with Erik and sees a person he doesn't know. Well, he does know her, because that's who I am. He might not like it—you might not like it—but you can't just erase the parts of me that you don't like. Those years of my life happened, Marianne. Maybe this ballet is my way of dealing with that."

"I did know that person," Marianne said. "Or perhaps you forgot? I was there the whole time, and you know what? She was fucking miserable." She frowned. "What's gotten into you lately? No, wait, don't answer that. I know exactly who to blame for the way you're acting."

"They're calling Act Two," Lia said, relieved to have the excuse to escape as a disembodied voice crackled from the speaker above the dressing room door. "I've got to go."

Lia and Marianne ran through the rest of the dress rehearsal with barely a word to each other beyond what was necessary. Lia noticed Marianne gave Tomas the cold shoulder as well. She knew she was being unfair. Marianne was only looking out for her, just as she always had. She'd been a good and loyal friend for so many years, and every concern she had raised had occurred to Lia herself plenty of times before. She *should* give up the ballet if she wanted a quiet life. She *was* acting like someone who craved the attention. And yet she just couldn't bear to drop it now.

It was like a compulsion. The choreography was all she thought of, day and night. She frequently woke at three in the morning, her mind buzzing with ideas, leaving her too wired to drop off again. Changing the music was unthinkable, she decided, as she headed home that evening in the car Scott had insisted she take everywhere since the incident with the Dravens. It was the life-blood of the piece. Nothing else would do. In fact, even what they had wouldn't quite do. If they really wanted the work to be seamless, original, and professional, they would really need to …

No. Lia shook the thought out of her head as she strode across the marble foyer of her apartment building, headed for the lift. No, that was not an option.

But once the thought was embedded, it wouldn't leave her. It stuck in her mind like a splinter. Scott was away filming again, and the flat felt so empty and quiet. Lia wandered over to the window and stared into the blackness of the park opposite. Nothing moved this time. Nothing made a sound.

She was thoroughly alone, and she felt it, a cold ache in the pit of her stomach.

She glanced at her watch. Almost eleven p.m. It would be around mid-afternoon in the states, but it might as well have been another century, it felt so far away. Lia switched on the TV screen and, taking a deep breath, dialled a video call.

It rang for a long time, and Lia was close to hanging up when a blur of dark hair appeared on the screen. The picture wobbled—a flash of bland hotel furniture in the background—and then Erik looked out at her, green eyes wide in astonishment.

"Li, is everything okay?" He sounded out of breath, as though he'd rushed back from somewhere to take the call. Lia was already convinced this had been a terrible idea, but it was too late now.

"I'm fine. Everything's fine. Where are you?"

Erik let out a breath, looking a touch more relaxed.

"DC," he said. "Touring."

He lowered his head, and for a moment the view was obscured by black hair again, then he lifted a cigarette, fumbling with his lighter. Lia recognised it—a silver antique that had once belonged to Chris Cornell. She'd managed—with some difficulty—to procure it for Erik as a thirtieth birthday present.

"How's it going? Well?" She tried to smile, feeling false.

"Not bad." He watched her intently. He obviously wanted to know why she was calling, but didn't like to ask. "You're in London?"

"Yes."

"Look, I'm sorry. About the wedding thing." He took a drag of his cigarette. "I crossed a line. No excuses."

"Yes, you did." Lia looked away, not wanting to say it was okay, but not wanting to admit how badly he'd ruined things between her and Scott. "And the coming to London to keep an eye on me?"

"That, I'm not sorry for. I'm worried about you. I don't trust your husband. I think there's something going on with him that you don't see."

Lia sighed and put a hand to her forehead. "Yes, Kent said you were having delusions again. Honestly, Erik, you look awful. Do you ever sleep? I mean, really sleep, not hooked up to that … thing."

"Does it matter? It's you I'm concerned about."

"That's a no, then. For heaven's sake, you need proper sleep, or you'll go out of your mind. And considering the amount of Slip that's probably running through your system, I wonder how you can be sure you're not hallucinating half the time." Lia bit her lip and took a deep breath, blinking tears out of her eyes. "I didn't call you to have this conversation. Frankly I'm not sure I should have called you at all."

"Well, you did, so how about you tell me why? It must be late over there, huh? Where is Scott?"

"Italy."

"Are you sure you're okay?" He leaned towards the screen and peered at her, as if trying to read her thoughts. "Somehow I don't think you'd be talking to me if everything was dandy."

"It's business, all right." Lia folded her arms. "I'm working on a project—a new short ballet. With Tomas. We're using your music, so I was wondering how you'd feel about putting together a new mix of the songs, you know, so they flow well for the piece?"

She'd tried to make it sound matter of fact, and not like the huge deal she'd somehow built it up to be in her mind, but the slow, almost triumphant smile that spread across Erik's face told her that he was willing to read into it everything she'd feared and more.

"You're not kidding?" he ventured.

"No."

"Can I come and watch a rehearsal?" he asked, far too eagerly. "You know, to get an idea of what you need?"

"I don't think that would be a good idea."

"But I can come and see the finished piece, right? Actually, those are my terms. I'll do whatever you want, free of charge, no royalties, as long as you let me come and watch the opening night." Lia didn't like how pleased he looked with himself. "Do we have a deal?"

"This isn't an opportunity for you to worm your way back in, you know."

"Hey," he spread his hands in mock-innocence that irritated Lia, "I'm asking to come watch the ballet, not take you out for dinner. You don't even need to speak to me. Just let me come along. God knows I need something to look forward to."

"Oh, for goodness sake. All right, it's a deal. Just, please promise me you won't cause any trouble, and you'll stay well out of Scott's way."

"I can probably fight the urge to punch him in his pretty face. Probably."

"Not funny."

"All right, I promise. You'll never even know I was there. So, let me know what you need, and I'll get started. Unless you want to hang out a bit longer ...?"

"I've got to get to bed. Thank you, Erik. Good night."

"Sleep well."

"You too. I mean it," Lia added, sternly. "Get some proper sleep. And eat something, okay?"

"Perhaps you should come over here and look after me?" He grinned—a strange, strained smile that did not reach his eyes.

"*Good night*, Erik." Before he could protest again, Lia hung up, and the screen faded to black. She leaned her head back and stared at the ceiling, biting her lip.

"What is it about you?" she muttered. "You crazy, useless, waste of bloody space. Why the hell can't I just give you up?"

22

"Wren. Wren?"

Wren blinked, shaking her head to clear away the warped shapes and colours that danced across her vision as she dozed by Bethany's bedside. From the fading kaleidoscope, her mother and Doctor Nandra's faces emerged. They stood on the other side of the bed, as though they had been there some time. Doctor Nandra cocked her head on one side and looked at Wren with that kindly-yet-detached concern that seemed characteristic of doctors.

"How are you feeling, Wren?" She made her way around the bed to pull up a chair beside her. "All this must be very hard on you."

Wren wondered whether her eyes were starting to show signs of that misty, soft-focus look that Andromeda always had. After Erik Dacre had turned out worse than useless, Wren and Andromeda had spent several nights in a row in the DreamScape, researching the Mark of Thanatos in the hopes of either finding another one, or figuring out a way of earning enough Credits to get back to the one in the cave.

She looked away. "I'm fine."

"We have people you can talk to, you know, if you need a bit of help coming to terms with the situation."

"Like I said, I'm fine." Wren forced herself to focus and stared back at the doctor with the steadiest gaze she could muster.

"All right. Well, if you change your mind, I'm always here. But I have some news that might give you both some hope." She smiled across at Harper. "A specialist from New York has approached us. Samuel Gendry. He researches the DreamScape and its effects on the human brain. Somehow, he heard about Bethany's case, and he's taken a shuttle over hoping to examine her. I must admit," Naveen added, "I hadn't heard of him myself, but I've been looking at his publications, and from what I can tell he comes very highly recommended."

"You think he'll be able to help her?" Harper asked.

"I can't promise anything. He's a research neuroscientist, not a medical doctor, but he could provide us with an alternative view of what's going on inside Bethany's head. At this point, anything we can do to increase our understanding of Bethany's situation is valuable." She looked at Harper. "He seems very keen to see your daughter. Did you contact him yourself?"

Harper shook her head dumbly.

"We haven't contacted anyone." Wren said.

"Will you give permission for him to come in?" Naveen asked.

"Yes, yes, of course," Harper said, quickly. "Anything that will help my little girl."

Naveen left the room, returning moments later accompanied by a tall, gangly Black man who looked young enough to be fresh out of university. He approached them nervously, watching Bethany's silent face as he shook Harper's hand.

"Samuel Gendry," he muttered, his gaze flitting restlessly around the room. "I hope we can do something for your daughter."

"I hope so too," Harper replied. "What is it you're going to do?"

"We'll be studying Bethany's brainwaves in response to external stimuli," Gendry said. "We may also attempt to make some changes to the configuration of her Corona. The Corona reads the electronic signals her brain sends out, and responds with stimulation to the visual and auditory sections of the brain. We would like to understand what happens if we intercept those signals."

"Do you think you'll be able to wake her, eventually?" Wren asked. Gendry turned in her direction, without quite looking at her face.

"We'll have to see what happens," he said. "We have many subjects that we are currently studying, and none of them have yet been woken successfully. It is my hope that Bethany will be different. But we will have to see."

"Mum ..." Wren began, "would you like to get us a coffee? I'm gasping. I'll bet Professor Gendry would like something, too."

Harper gave her a puzzled look, but complied, and left the room. Once she was gone, Wren turned to Gendry.

"You've got no intention of waking her, have you?" she asked, quietly. Standing on the other side of the bed, Naveen shot her a worried glance.

"There's a lot we need to understand before we can even begin to contemplate ..." Gendry began.

"She's just a research project to you, isn't she?

Something to gather data from."

"Wren …" Naveen began.

"Where is it you're from, anyway? Who's sponsoring all this research?"

"Wren, I think maybe you should go home, get some rest. *Proper* rest," Naveen said.

"Fine." Wren pushed her chair back and got to her feet. "Fine, I'll go. But you should remember—both of you— that Bethany's not a test subject. She's a person. My sister. And I want her back, all right? Please, just try. Try and get her back."

When she got home, she found Andromeda and Kazuo sitting together in the kitchen, eating noodles. They seemed to be getting along famously—so much so that Andromeda appeared to have moved in to Kazuo's room pretty much permanently. She wondered what Ramona thought about that.

"How are things, little bird?" Andromeda asked, as Wren sat down to join them. Wren was coming to find her dreamy way of speaking rather comforting.

"I need to find out more about somebody called Professor Samuel Gendry," Wren said.

"Who's that?" Kazuo asked.

"He came down from New York today to see Bethany. To study her, I mean. He's supposed to be some kind of expert, but I don't like him. I want to know who he is, and what he's really up to."

"Let's take a look, then," Kazuo said. "Everybody leaves

a trail somewhere."

The two of them spent that evening hunting through the internet for information about Gendry. What they found made Wren uneasy. Gendry was employed by the privately funded Foundation for Cognitive Research, a small but well-funded unit based out of a lab in Boston, and nothing Wren was able to dig up could tell her exactly who was bankrolling it. The benefactors clearly preferred to remain anonymous. All very well, but their main—nay, their only—line of research seemed to be on those who had either become addicted to, or been lost in, the DreamScape.

Gendry and his fellow scientists had published a number of papers that went into mind-numbing detail about the exact effects of Slip on the neurology of the brain, and the brainwave activity of DreamScape users, both normally functioning, and comatose, like Bethany. At no stage that Wren could see had they had ever tried to revive any of the comatose patients. A number of them had eventually passed away or been taken off their life-support systems.

One paper even investigated the possibility that a patient who had died might still be able to be located within the DreamScape. The researchers discussed their attempts to pinpoint the patient's consciousness in the DreamScape, in the hope of maintaining contact even as their physical body died. So far, they had been unsuccessful, but even so, Wren was certain that these people were not trying to save the lost patients. They were only interested in experimenting on them.

As night fell, Wren put on her Corona and lay on her bed. She'd long since given up on Andromeda's rule of having somebody nearby to act as Root. Nobody, not even Andromeda herself, knew that Wren was making solo, late-night trips into the DreamScape. She knew it was risky—very risky—but it just didn't seem to matter. Saving Bethany; finding the Dark God—that was all she could think of.

She materialised on a beach. This environment was more damaged than any other she had seen so far—vast black ruptures cut across the sky and the land. The moment she arrived, one of them widened even more, the dark, choppy sea vanishing into the emptiness like a waterfall from the edge of a cliff.

A wave surged up the beach, lapping at her ankles, bringing with it a few random objects: a handful of pages from a book, a torn photograph, a rusted Samurai sword, and even a broken keyboard from an old Spectrum ZX computer. The sea deposited them all on the sand, adding to a tide line of strange items that ran all the way down the beach. In the distance, shadowy figures sifted through the flotsam, some alone, some in small groups, picking out whatever treasures caught their eye.

Wren walked down the beach, wrapping her arms around herself against the cold drizzle, watching her footprints sink into the damp sand. She had come here on the strength of a whisper—a half-story she'd heard over and over as she and Andromeda travelled the DreamScape. Rumour had it there was a beach somewhere where the remnants of disused items tended to wash up—a kind of DreamScape recycle bin—and that somewhere amongst the detritus another Mark could be found. Nobody had been able to tell them exactly how to find it, though, and so once they'd located the beach itself, Wren had decided to keep searching until she figured it out. Hypnos' priest, Apollo, had told her Thanatos had caused the destruction that blighted the Scape, and here it was worse than anywhere. Something in Wren's gut told her that the Dark God was close by.

The sky darkened as Wren combed the beach, turning over decaying musical instruments, fragments of medieval costumes, a cracked wizard's staff. This really was the trash-heap of the DreamScape, she thought, shifting aside a mound of gems that looked as though they'd come from one of the more retro platform games. Yet again, there was nothing beneath them but sand. She straightened up, gazing out across the restless water, and a sudden realisation dawned on her. She'd scoured this beach, top to bottom, twice over, and found nothing. But the beach was only part of this environment. She had not thought to search the sea.

Tentatively, she took a few steps into the freezing water, waves pooling around her ankles, trying to remember that the cold was all in her mind. Rain whipped across her face as she waded on, the water resisting her at every step.

The light was fading, and an eerie stillness settled over the sea. Wren could sense a storm brewing; could almost taste the electricity in the air. She pushed herself off her feet and swam for a few meters, then took a deep breath and plunged beneath the water.

It took her eyes a moment to adjust to the murk. Reflexively, she'd held her breath, and she let it out in a sigh of bubbles, remembering she didn't need to breathe here. Through the cloudy water she could make out a sandy seabed just beneath her, cluttered with yet more discarded objects. Not for the first time, she wondered at the existence of this environment. Somebody had gone to the trouble of coding this place and all its broken, washed-up flotsam; its stormy skies and freezing rain. It was like a wasteland, but it had been put here on purpose. Was it part of a game? Was it supposed to convey something, like a work of art?

She swam on, peering through the depths until she spotted a huge, steel behemoth of a sunken warship. A jagged tear was ripped across its hull, and through it, Wren could just about see the interior of the ship. Something told her that was the place to look, so she swam inside, wriggling through the hole, trying to ignore the burning in her lungs. *All in the mind.*

The ship was still and silent. Heavy metal doors punctuated the corridor she swam down, hanging off their hinges, their round, porthole windows smashed to pieces. A shoal of fish brushed against her ankles. In the distant murk, a single electric eel hung in the water, twisting and writhing, flaring with bright, white light. Wren swam towards it, and it moved away from her, whipping its tail as it disappeared around the corner. She followed … and stopped. There, directly ahead, an ink-blot raven was splashed across the far wall of what looked like a mess room. The Mark of Thanatos. She swam up to it and ran her hands over its surface. Its red glow rippled out from beneath her fingers.

"I can get you in there," a voice rang out from behind her, "but it'll cost you."

Wren turned to face the eel. It contorted and expanded, growing into a humanoid shape. As it's light faded, it left behind a boy, a little younger than Wren, with sandy hair and a rakish smile.

"You can call me Boy," he said.

Wren stared at him, wondering if he was part of the game, or something else entirely. A beat of silence went by, and then she decided that, after all, it didn't really matter.

"Can you really get me in there?" she asked, surprised to find that her voice worked perfectly well beneath the water.

"Like I said," said Boy, "I can. But it will cost you."

"Cost me what?"

"Your soul. If I help you cross into the realm of the Dark God, you must pledge your soul to the DreamScape, and stay for eternity. Oh, it's not all bad. Think about it. Immortal life!" His laugh was cold, almost mechanical. "Don't you want to live forever, Wren Silver?"

"Not really," Wren said. "How do you know my name? Who are you?"

"Oh, I know a great many things." Boy's lips twitched. Wren looked at him dubiously.

"Well, thanks and all," she said, "but I think I'll try and make my own way."

"Sure, sure." Boy turned away and then, a second later, turned back as though he had just thought of something. "Only, I assumed you'd be interested in knowing where to find your sister … Never mind. I can see when I'm not wanted."

"Wait!" Bubbles foamed out of her mouth with the words. "What do you know about my sister?"

But it was too late. Boy's limbs shimmered and curled up as his body shrank away, collapsing back into the shape of the electric eel. It flicked its bright white tail and swam away, leaving Wren in the darkness with nothing to do but stare at the glowing red raven.

"Immortal life," she said to herself, a horrible, creeping feeling crawling up her spine as she thought of what she had read about Professor Gendry's research. He'd been trying to locate the consciousnesses of people like Bethany in the DreamScape, but not so that they could be woken—so that he could see if they would continue to exist, even if their bodies died. Wren continued to stare at the raven for a long moment, as the red glow slowly faded away to black. "Immortal life. That's what he wants."

23

The train slows. Bethany looks up from her chips to find herself alone. The kind woman and all her fellow passengers have vanished. Outside, the English countryside has disappeared, and bright sun beats down on a dusty red desert. Strange, gnarled, tree-like plants dot the landscape, but otherwise there is nothing to see except rocks and tumbleweed.

When the train finally draws to a halt, Bethany goes to the door, pulls on the heavy brass handle, and looks outside. There is no station, no people, nothing to see at all apart from a tower on the horizon. Bethany wonders again what happened to Boy. Not that she misses him, particularly, but at least he seemed to know what was going on. The train doesn't seem as though it's going anywhere soon, so Bethany starts a slow trudge through the baking heat towards the tower. Remembering that none of this is real, she tries to think herself cool and comfortable, but even this not-real sun is too much for her, and she soon finds herself sweating and thirsty.

The kind woman talked about someone who could help her. Somehow, Bethany imagines if she could only reach the tower, she might find that person. She feels a bit like Dorothy, off to see the wizard. Although, from what she remembers of that story, the wizard wasn't a real wizard at all, was he? Just some average Joe who was good at special effects. That would be just her luck.

A slight breeze starts up as Bethany reaches the tower. It isn't really all that big up close. Maybe three or four stories high, max, and all crumbling. It is made of red stone, just like the desert, and beyond it … Beyond it the whole world just drops off a cliff. There is nothing but empty space for miles in every direction, including downwards, but somewhere far below, Bethany can see a tiny river running through the red stone. *The Grand Canyon*, she thinks, impressed she has managed to remember something from school. She stands on the edge of the canyon for a while as the sun goes down, watching the colours of the rock change from red to purple to blue and then, realising it's getting cold, she decides to go inside.

In the tower, a campfire blazes, and the walls dance with lively paintings: child-like daubings of animals and figures that seem to bounce and spin in the flickering firelight. They are everywhere, and the effect is dizzying. Amidst the chaos, she spots a man on the other side of the fire, leaning against the wall with a cowboy hat tipped low over his face.

"Can you help me?" Bethany asks.

The cowboy looks up. He looks both young and old, with a face like carved wood, cut deep with lines and burnished by the sun. "Are you Bethany Silver?" When Bethany nods, he indicates a space beside the fire. "Come and sit with me."

Bethany sits on the dirt floor, hugging her knees. "Who are you?"

"Some people call me Hypnos," the cowboy says.

Bethany gives him a sceptical look.

"That's a dumb name. And what do you call yourself? The Wizard of Oz?"

The cowboy chuckles. "You're imagining there's nothing behind this whole façade? You might be right, Bethany. You might just be right."

"Can you send me home?"

"There's something you need to understand, Bethany. Can you picture yourself, right now, in the real world? You will look as though you are sleeping. Imagine it. You are right where you are supposed to be. You have not moved. All this travelling you have done, moving from place to place—all that is an illusion. You are right where you began. Do you understand?"

Bethany shakes her head. "Are you saying ..." she laughs, "are you saying I just have to click my heels or something?"

"I wish it were that simple. I have been searching for you through the DreamScape, pinpointing your true location. Think of your consciousness as a computer file, saved in a folder. Only, when you fell through that rupture, the system forgot where it had saved you. As you travelled, I was keeping track of you, hunting for your file. Now, I have found it."

"So, can you, like, tell the system where it is? Re-join my brain with my body, kind of thing?"

"I suspect I could." The cowboy frowns as though he's considering the possibility for the first time. "It would be a very simple process. Yes, I'm sure I could do that. But how would that help me? No, Bethany. You have a much more important purpose to fulfil. You'll be staying with me."

The cowboy gets up and turns to the wall, to a painting

Bethany hadn't noticed before: a hand-print encircled in red. The cowboy fits his palm into it, and the tower vanishes in an explosion of white light.

24

"You don't understand! He's not helping her; he's experimenting on her!"

Wren twisted her arm, trying to break free from her mother's grip. They were on the other side of the glass from Bethany's hospital room, where Professor Gendry had gathered an array of beeping medical equipment and white-coated assistants around the sad, sleeping form on the bed. As soon as she'd woken that morning, Wren had raced down to the hospital, frantic with the understanding that had dawned on her after her conversation with Boy. Bursting into Bethany's room, she'd demanded Professor Gendry leave, which only resulted in him calling hospital security, who, in turn, called Harper and Doctor Nandra.

"You need to calm down." Harper dragged her away from the door. "Just calm down, or you'll get a slap, all right?"

"He's going to kill her!" Wren turned desperately to Doctor Nandra, who had that infuriating expression of professional concern on her face once again. "You've read his research, right? You know what he's done to the lost patients he's worked with before. He's been taking them off life support and trying to track them through the Dream-Scape. They all died. Did you know that? They *all died*!"

"Wren," Naveen said, gently, trying to guide her to a couch, "please sit down."

Wren resisted for a moment, then sat, and Naveen continued, "I know Professor Gendry's research must look scary to you at first glance, but I can assure you he hasn't been killing his patients. Life support was turned off in some cases, that's true, but that was a decision made by the patients' families, not Professor Gendry. Other patients died naturally, but that, sadly, is a risk inherent in this condition. What we're doing here, Wren—what Professor Gendry is doing here—is simply trying to find out more about what is happening to Bethany. It's true, he's not a medical doctor, and he may not be able to directly help her, but at this point all information is helpful to us. Do you understand?"

Wren glared at her. "I thought you had Bethany's best interests at heart," she said, bitterly.

"I promise, I do."

"Well, *he* doesn't. Do you even know who he works for? Does anyone?"

"Wren." Harper passed a hand across her brow. "We can't get rid of the Professor now. I'm sorry, but we can't."

"What are you talking about?"

Doctor Nandra sighed. "Professor Gendry and the Foundation for Cognitive Research are paying Bethany's medical bills," she said. "In full. Unfortunately, as an illegal immigrant without a visa or medical insurance ..." she trailed off, glancing at Harper.

"I can't pay for all this," Harper said, flatly. "I ain't got any money. Even taking her home would cost thousands.

The Professor's offered to take Bethany to his own facility and pay for all her care from now on."

"This is about money?"

"What would you like me to do? I don't have a choice, do I?"

"This is my sister's life we're talking about! You can't put a price on that!"

"Wren." Doctor Nandra put a reassuring hand over hers. "I'm afraid you're not well. I can see you've taken what's happened to your sister very much to heart, and it's understandable that you're finding it difficult to deal with. Tell me, have you been going into the DreamScape? Perhaps you thought you might be able to find her?"

"No," Wren shook her head sharply. "No, no, no …"

"You do understand that excessive DreamScape use can cause delusions?" Naveen went on, in the same lullaby tone. "Especially if you're taking Slip. It can affect your reasoning, your sense of reality."

"No, you're not doing this. No. No. I'm not delusional. I know what I'm talking about. I *know*."

"Wren, maybe you need to get away for a bit," Harper suggested. "Take a break from all this."

Wren stood. "You're not sending me away. I want to talk to Professor Gendry." She spun around, heading for Bethany's room, but stepped straight into a large, shadowy form. She looked up.

The bottom dropped out of her stomach.

"No," she whispered. "No, not you …"

Jared.

He was there, large as life, standing in her city, her world, like he owned the place. Wren backed away, loathing flooding her veins at the sight of his black-button eyes. In his heavily tattooed arms, he held her little brother, Alfie, who squirmed and squealed at the sight of his mother.

"Alfie!" Harper ran over and scooped him out of Jared's grip. "I've missed you so much, baby."

Jared grinned, pulling them both into one big bear hug. "I've come to bring my family home," he announced, mostly for Doctor Nandra's benefit. None of the rest of them needed to ask why he was there.

"You don't know how glad I am to see you," Harper murmured from within his powerful grasp. "Both of you. Are you not angry with me?"

"Of course not, lass. Don't be daft."

"What about Bethany?" Wren snapped. "You can't just leave, mum."

"It looks like she's in good hands," Jared said. Harper threw Wren an apologetic glance—a look Wren had seen far too many times before.

"Alfie needs me too," she said, "don't you baby?" She looked through the glass at Bethany, still surrounded by doctors. "I feel useless here. What can I do for Bethany?"

"You can be there for her," Wren replied, "if she wakes up."

"It sounds to me like you're causing bother, Wren," Jared said, warningly. "Disrupting the doctor's work, are you? Perhaps you'd better come back with us, get away from all this."

"No! No way. Stay away from me. I'm not going any-where with you!" Wren bolted for the door, but she wasn't quick enough. Jared caught her by the arm.

"I heard what the lady said," he said, nodding to Doctor Nandra. "You've been having delusions, Wren. You need to come home and rest, eh?"

"I do think that sounds like a good idea, Wren," Doctor Nandra said. "We can look after your sister here, and you can take a bit of a break, come back when you're feeling more yourself."

"That's settled, then." Jared nodded.

Wren could only glare back at Naveen as Jared dragged her away, Harper following with Alfie in her arms.

Only a few hours later they were travelling back to the UK on the supersonic shuttle, speeding through a tunnel deep beneath the Atlantic Ocean. Harper was animated and happy, delighted to be reunited with Alfie, who ran up and down the aisle in a frenzy of excitement. Even Jared, working his way through a six pack of beers, seemed cheerful, despite his mutterings about how much hard work it had been looking after Alfie on his own. He actually seemed genuinely happy to have them back, but Wren knew it could not last. At some stage his mood would darken, and the recriminations would begin. He would lay on the guilt trip, Harper would try to defend herself, Jared would get angry, and, eventually, he'd lose his temper. It was always the same.

Wren stared out the shuttle windows into the blackness of the tunnel, feeling numb. She'd hoped she would never make this journey again. There was nothing in England she wanted to go back to. Nothing at all. And now she was leaving Bethany behind for a second time. Any little chance she had of getting her sister back slipped further and further away with every kilometre she travelled.

They arrived in London late in the evening, disembarking into the vast silver ribcage of St Pancras station. The passengers still milling around were tired and quiet, wrapped up in their coats and scarves against the autumn chill. The shops were shutting up, pulling down metal shutters, switching off lights. Wren shuffled along with Jared, who was keeping a close watch on her while Harper pushed a sleeping Alfie in his buggy. They descended into the guts of the building, heading for the Underground train that would take them the short distance to Euston, from which they could catch the last train to Lancaster. Their footsteps echoed on the concrete floor as they headed for the ticket barriers.

Jared swiped his credit card on the reader and the gate failed to open. He tried again, red faced, a vein in his forehead throbbing—a warning that Wren had learned to take very seriously indeed. Still, it failed to open. Irritated, he called a guard over, who tried to explain that his card had been rejected. Jared, worse for wear after all his drinking, seemed convinced that this was some sort of conspiracy designed to humiliate him. Voice rising, he barraged the guard with accusations that eventually levelled-up to threats. The guard reached for his radio to call for back-up, and Wren seized her chance.

She hopped the barrier and ran. Ran as fast as her legs could carry her. Ran without looking back, pelting down escalators, skidding through corridors, with no idea whether anyone was pursuing her and no desire to find out. She flung herself around a corner and found, to her intense relief, a train there just about to leave. She raced for the doors just as they were closing, wedged her foot in, and squeezed through the gap, forcing her way into the packed carriage.

Panting, Wren turned to look out of the window as the train pulled away, just in time to see Jared round the corner with the guard hot on his heels. She ducked behind another passenger and hoped neither of them had seen her.

She stayed on the train for a couple of stops, waiting for a moment when plenty of people were disembarking before pulling up her hood and slipping off along with them. When she surfaced, she found herself in Covent Garden, still packed and bustling even at this late hour. As she wandered down the street towards the market, she passed a silver-painted living statue with a Grecian dress on, and a fire eater with a large crowd of tourists around him. The flames lit up the night in bright bursts, and Wren, feeling on edge, slunk away to somewhere a bit darker.

She bought an overpriced hot dog from a market vendor and sat on the steps to eat it. A few feet away, a group of Chinese tourists chattered excitedly over a holographic map, arguing about which route to take, while behind them, a wave of well-dressed people left the Royal Opera House, clutching red programmes. As Wren ate, she caught sight of a life-sized poster hanging outside of the Opera House entrance. In it, a blonde-haired ballerina wore a white dress with fiddly little wings sticking out of her back. She looked vaguely familiar, but Wren couldn't quite place her.

The crowd of theatre-goers drifted away, and the market started to pack up and empty. Wren stayed where she was, unsure of where to go or what to do. She had a small amount of cash on her, but not enough to cover a cheap room for the night, let alone the shuttle fare back to San Francisco, and it was getting colder. At least she was out of Jared's clutches. He wouldn't want to waste good money staying in London to look for her. With any luck, he was on the train to

Lancaster by now, or banged up in a cell somewhere for causing trouble at the tube station. Wren felt she could deal with anything, even being cold and alone on the streets of London, as long as she was away from Jared. Nevertheless, she needed a place to stay for the night, and she didn't know a single person in the city. Out of desperation—or perhaps just for a friendly voice to talk to—she placed a video call to San Francisco.

"Wren!" Delphi answered, breathless. "Oh my God, are you okay? I went to the hospital looking for you, and Doctor Nandra told me you'd gone home with your mum and Jared. I've been trying to phone you all day."

"I'm okay. I got away from Jared. I'm in London now."

"God, what time is it over there? It looks dark."

"Late. I can't get back, Delph. I haven't got any money."

"We'll have a whip-round," Delphi said. "I'm sure we could scrape together enough for a shuttle fare if I asked everybody. Maybe the college would even help."

"Thank you." Wren hated to accept charity, but if she was going to get back to San Francisco she didn't have much choice. "I really appreciate it."

"Listen …" Delphi hesitated.

"What is it?"

"I don't know if I should bother you with this right now, but … well, I guess you'd want to know."

"Know what?" Wren demanded.

"When I went to the hospital I went up to Bethany's room, and … She's not there. She's gone. I asked Doctor Nandra where they'd taken her, and she wouldn't tell me anything."

"She's with Professor Gendry," Wren said. "He was going to take her to his own facility. But I have no idea where that is or what he's planning to do with her. Jesus! That's my little sister. Everyone's given up on her, even mum, and now I don't even know where she is!"

"Wren, hey … oh, God, don't cry. I seriously don't know what I'd do if you started crying. You're supposed to be the tough one, right?"

Wren smiled weakly. "I don't feel very tough right now. Actually, I'm bloody freezing."

"You can't sit out there all night. Is there anyone you can stay with?"

"I don't know anyone in London. But I wondered …" Wren wiped her eyes and tried to focus her mind. "Is Andromeda there? Can I speak to her?"

Delphi raised her eyebrows. "Sure, if you want. I mean, I'll get her." She disappeared, leaving the phone on her desk, a Sacred Ravens poster in view on the opposite wall. Wren glared through the screen at Erik Dacre for a while, silently blaming him for everything, until Andromeda's pale face appeared on the screen.

"Hello, little bird," she said. Then, peering at the view behind Wren's head, she added, "Is that London? I've never been. Well, not in the Mono anyway."

"Yes, that's London. Listen, Andromeda, I'm stuck here, and I need your help."

"Anything."

"Can you go into the Scape and talk to your friends and find out if any of them are based in London? I need a place to go tonight and, if they're willing, I need to borrow a Corona. As long as I'm stuck here, I might as well keep trying to help Bethany."

"I'll see what I can do."

25

Wren slunk down a dark alleyway, trying to surreptitiously check the map on her phone without letting the light from the screen shine too obviously. She had no idea what kind of people might be lurking here so late at night. She found the door Andromeda had directed her to—a peeling, red-painted entrance to a boarded-up tobacconist's—and knocked. Nobody answered. Wren knocked a second time. Eventually, the door slid open a crack, and an eye blinked out from behind it.

"Who are you?"

"Wren. Andromeda's friend. She told you about me?"

The girl—for it was just a girl, younger than Bethany—opened the door a little further so Wren could step through. She had powder-blue hair, numerous piercings, and a hunted air, like a deer in headlights. Her eyes were unnaturally large, the rest of her paper thin.

"My name is Calliope," she said, locking the door behind them. The little shop was packed with sleeping bodies, on couches or mattresses or just blankets on the floor, Corona lights glittering around their temples. In the darkness, Wren could just see that the walls were plastered with colourful graffiti—a frenzy of hallucinogenic visions.

"You're the Root," she said to Calliope.

"Yes. Tonight." The girl rubbed her bare arms, shivering. "Here, you can borrow my Corona. As you're Andromeda's friend."

Wren slipped off her leather jacket. "And you can borrow this, if you want."

"Thanks." Calliope put the jacket on and went to perch on a stool behind the shop's counter. Wren found an unoccupied piece of floor and squeezed in between a pair of silent figures. Lying on her back, she slipped the Corona onto her head, and slipped out of the world.

She arrived on the beach, where she'd arranged to meet Andromeda and Kazuo. The sky was alive with a raging storm, and several new gaping black tears had perforated the beach itself. The sand slipped away beneath Wren's feet as she picked her way nervously to where her friends stood. To her surprise, Delphi was there too, looking just like her usual self, and she greeted Wren with an enthusiastic hug.

"I'm so glad you made it! Are you all right? Are you somewhere safe?"

"I hope so." Wren smiled weakly. "What are you doing here? I thought you hated the Scape."

"I do, but I wanted to see you." Delphi cast a dubious glance around. "This place is bleak. Can't we go somewhere nicer?"

"Not yet," Wren said. "I've got something to show you."

"I've found something too." Kazuo folded his arms and looked out across the foggy, grey sea. "This place kinda gets into your head, doesn't it?" he said.

"You're telling me."

"I've been hunting through the raw code ever since we found the Mark of Thanatos. It was like … a compulsion. I just couldn't stop. I was looking for patterns that might help us hijack one of the portals. I keep telling myself it's just a computer program, you know? All this," he spread his hands, "is just surface. You have to look deeper, figure out how it works at a basic level."

"What did you find?"

Kazuo took a few steps towards the lapping waves. "I was staring at the code, late last night. Just staring and star-ing, and then I saw it. In between all the usual, functional stuff, there were patterns. It looked totally meaningless at first. Just redundant, I don't know, kind of computer babble. No actual coder would have written it. But there was some-thing almost organic in the way it repeated itself, over and over. Like cells dividing."

Wren frowned, puzzled. "What do you think it could be?"

"It seems to cluster in certain parts of the program—older parts, like this beach environment." Kazuo glanced back at her. "Did you know that this is one of the oldest environments in the Scape? According to the date-stamp on the code, it's one of the first places Sorensen ever built. A test environment. What did you find here?"

"Another Mark. Down there." Wren pointed into the sea. As she spoke, lightning slashed across the sky, burning a bright pathway into her vision. The thunder followed a frac-tion of a second later.

Andromeda shivered as a fine rain began to fall. "The storm's getting closer. Whatever we're doing here, we should be quick about it."

"This redundant code," Kazuo said, "the patterns—they cluster here more than they do anywhere else. They're all over the beach's original code, eating into it, displacing what's supposed to be there."

"The ruptures," said Andromeda.

"Right."

"Something is drawing the redundant code to cluster here and we ..." Kazuo took a deep breath. "We should probably be pretty worried about this ..."

"What?" Wren pressed.

"That code is growing, dividing, repeating itself. It's totally unregulated, unconstrained by any of the rules or protections that would usually be built into a program like this. It just spreads, like a cancer." Kazuo took a few steps into the water, waves lapping around his ankles. "You know, when we connect to the DreamScape, we make our own brains part of the program."

Realisation dropped on Wren like a heavy weight. "Shit. Are you saying this," she indicated the gaping black tears, "could be happening to our actual brains?"

"Exactly." Kazuo was knee-deep in the sea by now. He looked back at the three of them, still gathered on the beach. "Come on."

Wren waded out into the water. "Where are we going?"

"To the centre of the black hole. The place where the code clusters the most." Kazuo was in up to his waist now, and still walking. "You said you found a Mark of Thanatos down there. I'll bet I know exactly where it was."

He dove beneath the waves and the rest of them

followed—even Delphi, after some coaxing from Wren. As they swam, Wren explained what had happened the last time she'd been down there: finding the Mark in the shipwreck, the appearance of Boy, Boy's attempt to make a deal with her.

"He knew something about Bethany. Perhaps he knows where to find her, maybe even how to get her out," Wren said, as the ship loomed out of the darkness ahead of them. "The answers are in here somewhere. I'm sure of it. If making a deal with Boy is the only way to find out, then perhaps that's just what I need to do."

"No," Kazuo said. "No, you don't have to do that. The repeating code is everywhere here. Show me where that Mark was."

Wren led the way through the shipwreck's silent corridors. This time there was no glowing eel, no sign of Boy. But the Mark remained exactly where she'd found it. Kazuo swam up to it and ran his hands over the wall until the Mark glowed beneath his touch.

"There's something strange about this place," he said. "The source of the code clusters is right behind this wall. The Mark must be a way through to whatever's back there."

"So now what?" Wren asked.

"Perhaps I can find a way to hack in there. But it's going to take a while. You guys might as well log out and get some rest."

Wren logged out of the DreamScape and did her best to sleep for real, tossing and turning on the floor between the eerily still bodies of her fellow Dreamers. It was no good. Her mind was buzzing, and she couldn't switch off. When she closed her eyes, colours and shapes danced across her vision, lurching and whirling and occasionally collecting themselves into twisted representations of people or places she knew.

Bethany lay in the hospital, but as Wren approached, her sister's skin blistered and oozed, turning a lurid green before melting away. Wren flinched from the sight of Bethany dissolving into a puddle, and found Jared sitting atop a speeding shuttle, zooming towards her with his hands outstretched, ready to grab her. She whirled round again to see her mother shrink into the shape of a spider and scuttle away into a dark corner. Wren swelled up like a balloon, floating towards the ceiling, only to hit the ground with a jolt when she bolted awake. Her fingertips tingled with sparks.

She stared at the ceiling, her heart racing. What was happening must've been the effects of the Slip in her system, but knowing that didn't make any of it any less nightmarish. Wren sat up. The lights of the other Dreamers' Coronas sparkled like fallen stars in the darkness. Nearby, Calliope snored with her head down on the shop counter. And—*there*—in the blackest corner of the room, something moved. Insects. Creeping, crawling, inching out into the light with their blinking eyes.

Wren held her breath as they came closer. Tiny, scuttling things like deformed spiders, advancing on her in a wave. She tried to back away as they reached her, but she couldn't move. A dead weight pressed on her chest. The tiny feet tingled on her toes as the things raced up her legs. She screamed, but no sound came out.

And then she woke up.

Sitting up hastily, Wren put her hands to her head, gasping. She couldn't stay here like this. She reached for her Corona and fixed it back onto her head. If she had to hallucinate, she would at least make it a hallucination she could control.

"I'm almost done," Kazuo said, as she approached him from behind, back at the site of the Mark of Thanatos. He turned. "Wren. I knew it would be you. Can't sleep?"

"I feel like I'm going crazy," Wren admitted. "I can't deal with … out there."

"Andromeda told me that the Slip does that to you after a while. And you've been spending a lot of time here, haven't you?"

"More than I care to admit." Wren made a face. "Doctor Nandra knew it. She was worried I was getting delusional."

Kazuo shook his head. "Hang on in there, kid. I'm pretty sure there's something very strange going on in this place, and that at least part of the answer is behind this portal." He ran his hands over the Mark. "There. I think I've cracked it. Just let me send a message out to Delphi and Andromeda, and we can all head inside."

Wren swam up and down the corridor as they waited for the others, looking out of the corner of her eye at the Mark the whole time. It remained stolidly black and impenetrable looking. Where would it take them? Kazuo only wanted to find a way to the CPU, but she was becoming convinced that Thanatos himself held the answers she was looking for.

If only she'd found a way to make some better use of her

few minutes with Erik Dacre, she could have at least gotten a clear idea of whether he was involved or not. Whether it was the Slip or the effect of Kazuo's repeating code making its way into her brain, she felt as though somehow Thanatos—or Erik, if it was really he—was taking over her rational thought. Was this what had happened to Reza, when he had gone off in search of the Dark God and never returned?

"Wow, so we're really going in there?"

Delphi's voice shook Wren out of her reverie as she and Andromeda swam up to her. Andromeda, in particular, looked apprehensive.

"Let's go for it, Kaz." Wren didn't want to give them the chance to change their minds. Kazuo pressed his palm to the Mark. Wren held her breath, expecting to see it glow red, but instead, a bright white light exploded out of the ink-blot raven, engulfing all four of them.

They began in darkness. Then, holding onto one another's hands for stability, they took a few trepidatious steps forward. A pale orange light picked out sharp, narrow spikes like dragon's teeth, forming a gaping mouth.

Glancing at her friends, Wren crept into the light, realising she was following a path through a cave. Stalactites and stalagmites merged into lumpen forms of rock that looked almost organic. In the bulbous remains of lava flows, hints of features appeared—eyes here, mouths there—giving her the creeping sensation that their progress was being followed.

"Ugh, I don't like this place at all," Delphi whispered, as they made their way down a narrow pathway through the rocks. Here and there, the orange light was joined by an eerie glow of green or blue, casting strange shadows across the ground. The air was cool and damp, and Wren could just about hear the steady drip of water somewhere nearby.

The pathway turned into stone stairs, leading deep into the heart of the cave. The darkness grew ever thicker, while the few patches of light became stronger and more sharp-edged. The staircase grew narrower, and the four of them had to move in single file, Wren at the head of the line.

The walls pressed in around her, but just as she feared they would be able to go no further, she stepped out into a vast space with a ceiling that arched high over their heads. They stood at the top of a set of stone seats, arranged around a blue-lit underground lake. Above it, the shape of a huge black raven had been burnt into the sandstone wall.

Wren made her way down the aisle and took a seat.

"What are you doing?" Kazuo asked.

"Looks like we're here for some kind of performance," Wren said. "I thought I'd see what happens."

Kazuo joined her, shortly followed by Delphi and Andromeda. The light in the cavern dimmed, and ghostly music started up from nowhere.

Then, causing a slight ripple across the mirror-like surface of the lake, a pale figure appeared at the edge of the 'stage'. Wearing a white tutu, she danced across the water without ever seeming to notice that she had an audience. At the end of her performance, she disappeared into the blackness, only to begin the solo over again, like a looping film.

"That's Lia Céline," said Delphi.

"Who?"

"She used to date Erik Dacre. They were together for, I dunno, five years or so? And then she just walked out on him. Broke his heart. Such a bitch."

"I'm sure you'd treat him much better, Delph."

"I would. I don't know what he ever saw in her. Most of his songs are about her," she added, with more than a hint of envy. "Everybody says he never got over her."

Wren watched the ghostly dancer, imagining the cave through the eyes of the person who had designed it. A place of silence, reverence even, where he could contemplate what he had lost, over and over. A kind of mental torture dressed up as religion.

"I knew he knew more than he was letting on," she mused.

"You think it's really him?" Andromeda asked. "You think Erik Dacre is the Dark God, for sure?"

"For sure." Wren didn't take her eyes off the dancer.

"Then he must know how to find Bethany. And Reza. But how do we get him to talk to us?"

"We could wait here until he shows up," Delphi suggested. "He's sure to be back sometime, don't you reckon?"

"He didn't want anything to do with us at the concert. If he comes back and finds us sitting here in his inner sanctum, do you really think that's going to put him in the mood to chat?" Wren replied.

"She's got a point," Kazuo said. "So, what do you suggest, Wren?"

"Her." Wren said. "We know his weakness now. We need to get to him through her. And as it happens, I know exactly where she is right now."

26

Lia woke on the morning of her first performance of *Sleeping Beauty* with a sick ache deep in the pit of her stomach. She'd slept badly, unable to stop ruminating over her conversation with Erik the night before. From bitter experience, she knew the state of mind he must be in, with the stresses of touring exacerbating his chronic insomnia and causing him to reach more and more often for his Corona and Slip. He saw it as the only way he could get any rest; the only way he could turn off his ever-whirring thoughts and escape reality for a time.

There was no true rest involved, though. Being in the DreamScape was as much work for his brain as being awake and so, during these periods of Corona overuse, Lia had always been able to see the symptoms of lack of sleep taking hold long before Erik himself became aware of it. Wild extremes of mood, erratic behaviour, forgetfulness … and then there were the hallucinations. She'd learned to identify the misty look in his eyes that meant he would soon be seeing creatures crawling out of the walls and the floor melting beneath his feet.

At times, she'd been able to head off the worst of it by intervening at just the right moment. She'd always seemed to have a calming effect on him, becoming his bridge back to reality and sanity. Sometimes he would even manage to dwell there for a decent amount of time: long enough to make a new album, or—in one phase she found it particularly difficult to think about now—to begin planning a wedding with her. There would always come a point, though, when the pressure started to get to him again, and the whole artifice began to crumble. He was at that point right now. She'd seen it clear as day when she spoke to him, and there was nothing, short of jumping on a shuttle to the States, that she could do to stop it.

That, of course, was unthinkable. She could not go to America. She had *Sleeping Beauty* tonight, and Scott was on his way back from Italy—was probably on the shuttle right now—coming to see it. If she were to drop everything at this moment to go and see Erik … well, it would be the end of her marriage. That was a fact, and it disturbed her that the temptation nagged away at her, nonetheless. She couldn't shake the fear that nobody else could help him; that she could even have made things worse by encouraging him to pin his hopes on her again.

Lia took a car to the Royal Opera House, where she changed into her favourite practice gear in time for early morning class. When she entered the studio, she found several dancers already warming up, including Marianne, who only gave her a fleeting glance as she passed by. They hadn't spoken since their argument before the dress rehearsal, and Lia was tempted to let the stony silence continue, knowing Marianne would never be the first to apologise. After a moment's deliberation, though, she dropped her bag on the floor and went over.

"You were right," she said, quietly, drawing Marianne away from her friends.

"I was?" Marianne raised an eyebrow. Lia looked at the floor.

"I spoke to Erik," she admitted, in a low voice. "It was a terrible idea."

"Oh, God, Li, why would you do that?"

"I only wanted to ask him to do the music for my ballet." Lia turned to the barre, trying to hide the tears that sprang to her eyes. "It was a terrible idea."

"Lia …" Marianne put an arm around her shoulders and drew her into a hug. "Girl, you need to look after yourself, all right? Not him."

"What makes you think I want to look after him?" Lia sniffled.

"Because you always did. Right from the very beginning. Hey, don't cry." Marianne held her out at arm's length so she could look Lia in the eye. "It's a sweet thing about you. You like to feel needed, right? I guess Erik was pretty good for that. Scott, on the other hand … he's got his shit together. Maybe that leaves you feeling a bit purposeless."

"Maybe." Lia wiped her eyes. "I just … I worry …"

"Sure you do. That's okay. Just don't mistake anxiety for love. What you have with Scott is so real. I don't want to see you throw that away."

Lia bit her lip. "You're right. Of course. You were always right. You never liked Erik, even from the start."

"I can't deny that." Marianne looked up as the ballet master entered the room. "Come on, pull yourself together, Li." She gave Lia a gentle shake. "You've got a big night tonight."

Lia took a deep breath, forced a smile, and turned to the barre.

By the end of class, Lia had decided to text Erik once to tell him that the deal was off, then block his number and do her best to forget about him, the ballet, and everything connected with him. She'd even almost talked herself into Scott's idea of settling down and having babies. After all, if Marianne was right, and her problem was wanting to feel needed, perhaps a baby was the perfect way to fulfil that without running back to Erik. A baby would be far less disastrous, that was for sure. She had to consider the kind of life she wanted, and that was a life with a future, a family, a safe and loving home.

Lia headed out into Covent Garden market, where she stopped to get out her phone. She made several attempts at composing a message to Erik, but it felt like an impossible task. She'd opened Pandora's Box and she had no idea how to close it again without risking Erik doing something stupid, like rushing over to London to confront Scott directly. She tried several ways of wording the message in an attempt to persuade him that the decision to call off their agreement was hers, and hers alone, but everything she wrote came across as insincere, as though she was trying to convince herself as well as him.

"Excuse me!"

Lia looked up from her phone to see a young woman hurrying towards her. She was petite and tomboyish in her scruffy jeans and hoodie, with matted brown hair and freckles splashed across her pale cheeks. Lia noticed the misty look in her eyes and started to turn away, muttering something vague about not giving money to Scapers.

"I'm no Scaper!" The girl came to a halt in front of Lia. "Well, not usually. Are you Lia Céline?"

A Draven, then. There were many unfortunate conse-quences of Erik's addiction, but perhaps the worst of them was the way it spread to his fans, who would often start us-ing the DreamScape either to emulate him, or in hopes of meeting him in there. Lia had encountered a good few Slip-addled Dravens in her time, and the confrontations never went well.

"I'm sorry," she said. "I'm waiting for my husband, and I can't talk to you." She started to move away, but the girl followed.

"You don't understand," she said, breathlessly. "This is important! I need your help. I need to find a way to reach Erik Dacre."

"I'm sorry," Lia said. "I can't help you."

27

In real life, Lia Céline was a mere scrap of a person, tiny and startlingly slim, with a drawn look about her face and blue eyes that seemed to speak her every thought. She regarded Wren with a look of anxious pity.

"I'm not in contact with Erik," she said, nervously glancing over Wren's shoulder.

"But you know how to get in touch with him," Wren pressed.

"I can't help you. I'm sorry."

"You think I'm some sort of crazy fan, don't you?" Wren sighed. "Look, I'm not a Draven, all right? My sister, Bethany, is trapped in the DreamScape. I believe that Erik might know where she is, or what's happened to her. I need to speak to him. It's a matter of life or death."

Lia still looked doubtful. "Even assuming you're telling the truth," she said, "Erik can't do anything for you."

"You don't know that."

"He is not a well man. Do you understand? Whether you're a fan, or you're really looking for help, you truly would be better off turning your attention elsewhere. I say that not to get rid of you, but because it's the truth. Erik is very sick—he has been for some time." Lia glanced away. "He's not a person to pin your hopes on. Take it from somebody who knows."

"My sister," Wren said, as steadily as she could, "is in the hands of somebody who wants to kill her. Erik may be that person, or if not, he may know who that person is. All I need you to do is to persuade him to speak to me. Please. He'll listen to you. I know he will."

For a moment, Lia hesitated, but then a bulky figure in a bomber jacket and a baseball cap crept up behind her and grabbed her around the waist.

"Hey, gorgeous," he drawled, and Wren immediately recognised the man beneath the low-key disguise. She'd seen that face every week on *Uptown Girls* when she was younger. Scott Lincoln paused in nuzzling his wife's neck to look up at Wren. At first glance he seemed the same charming, open, almost goofy character she recognised from the show, but there was something cold about his eyes that Wren didn't like at all.

"Friend of yours?" he asked.

"A ballet fan." Lia shot Wren a significant look, clearly keen for her to leave.

"Really." Scott narrowed his eyes at Wren, and she had the feeling he knew his wife was lying. "Well, it sure is nice to meet fans. But right now, we have somewhere to be, don't we, Li?"

"We do." Lia turned to smile at him. "Thanks for stopping to chat," she added to Wren, as Scott drew her away. "I hope you enjoy the performance later. Why don't you pop by the stage door afterwards and say hi?"

Pop by the stage door? Was that an invitation to talk

further? Too surprised by Lia's apparent change of heart to say anything, Wren watched her and Scott walk away. Then Wren's phone buzzed with a message from Kazuo:

Meet me in the cave. Think I've found a way into the CPU.

It was very early morning back in San Francisco—Kazuo must have been up all night. Hopeful that they might finally be getting somewhere, Wren hurried back to Calliope's Scaper hideout.

The little tobacconist's was still packed with sleeping Dreamers, even in the middle of the day. Wren found a space on the floor and hooked up to her Corona. On reaching the cave, it took her a long time to find Kazuo. Eventually, she spotted him at the edge of the lake, waiting by a small rowing boat.

"What've you found?" she asked.

"I was wandering around this cave," he said. "Looking for some inspiration, I guess. The place is full of portals to various points in the DreamScape, but at first, I couldn't find any way of getting into the CPU. I figured, though, that if Thanatos really was one of Gade Sorensen's chosen replacements, he would have a way of getting in there. And then I noticed this."

"You think this boat goes to the CPU?"

"I took a look at the code from outside." Kazuo untied the knot holding the boat in place. "It definitely goes somewhere. But unlike all the other portals, I couldn't see what was at the other end. It was all locked down under a firewall. So, I figured—sounds like something Wren would like to see. What do you say? Shall we see where it goes?"

Wren didn't need to be asked twice. She hopped into the boat. "Let's go for it."

Kazuo sat in the boat, but rather than rowing it, he lifted his hands and started making strange movements: a sweep of the palm here; a twiddling of the fingers there. Wren watched him, puzzled, and when she could stand it no longer, she asked, "All right, what are you doing?"

"Looking at the code," Kazuo replied, staring at a point in the air between the two of them as he worked. "I guess you can't see it. Must look pretty strange."

"How do you do that?"

Kazuo shrugged. "There are developer back doors all over the system, if you know how to find them. Did you find Lia Céline?"

"Yes. She wasn't very forthcoming, but I think she was starting to change her mind when her husband showed up. If I can get back there tonight, I might be able to meet her after her performance."

"If we can get to the CPU, we may not need her. Okay, I think I've got it."

Serenely, they floated out onto the lake, passing the ballerina just as she executed an elegant pirouette. Soon, the cavern narrowed. They passed beneath a ceiling of stalactites so low they had to duck, and into a cramped rock corridor, lit by a dim orange glow. A fluttering sound caught Wren's attention, and she looked back to see black wings beating in the darkness. The raven hovered for a moment, watching them, then let out a loud caw and wheeled around, flying back out into the cavern.

"I think we've been found out," Wren said, quietly.

"You think that was Thanatos?"

"It figures he'd realise we were sneaking around here eventually." Wren shuddered. "I suppose the question is— what will he do about it?"

"I don't think he'll have time to do anything," Kazuo replied, looking dead ahead with an alarmed expression. Wren followed his gaze.

Ahead of them was a sheer drop, water tumbling over the edge. Where it went was anybody's guess, and they were headed straight for it.

They plunged over the edge of the waterfall and tumbled through the empty void, losing the boat, losing all sense of direction and time. Wren expected to hit water at the bottom, but they never did. The cave and everything around them simply ceased to be, and they floated in emptiness, listening to a female voice repeating the same words over and over.

"Please enter master credentials. Please enter master credentials. Please enter ... "

"Kaz?" Wren's voice echoed despite the fog that blanketed her vision.

"Here."

As the mist cleared, she found herself standing on a solid surface. Kazuo stood nearby, looking more intrigued than worried.

"Are you okay?" Wren asked. "Where are we?"

"Please enter master credentials. "

"It's a password entry screen," Kazuo said. "Of a sort."

"So, what's the password?"

Kazuo made a few swift hand movements, muttering to himself, and the world shifted like puzzle pieces clicking into place. A thousand screens flickered into life, above, below, and all around them, enclosing them in a dizzying sphere of images. And in the centre of it all, a black leather recliner materialised—the captain's chair. Kazuo threw himself into it, letting out a whoop.

"Oh, hell yeah!" He pushed off with his feet, sending the chair spinning. "This is it! This is the heart of the beast!"

"Where are we?" Wren peered at one of the screens, on which a plucky elf battled a dragon. "What did you do?"

"I entered the master credentials," Kazuo said, laughing.

"How?"

He spun to look at Wren, his laugh fading. "Call it an educated guess," he said, suddenly serious. "I convinced the system that I was Gade Sorensen. It wasn't that hard, really."

"Why not? What is this, his control room? Surely it was pretty damn well protected."

"Oh, sure, it was. But the password is everywhere, if you know where to look."

Wren frowned. "Care to elaborate?"

"The virus. The repeating code that's spreading all through the Scape. The login credentials are within it, repeated over and over. Looking at the code is kind of like … reading its thoughts. Except it's not an *it*," Kazuo added, "it's a *he*."

"This is the CPU, isn't it?" Wren said. "This is where Sorensen built everything from."

Kazuo nodded. "The oldest part of the DreamScape. The centre of operations."

"And the virus. You said it's …"

"A he. Right." Wren could tell he was enjoying being the one with all the answers. "If you remember, Gade Sorensen died last November. Everyone knew he'd been ill for a while, but he holed himself up in his mansion for a year. Barely anybody saw him in all that time. Nobody knew what he was up to. Well, I looked at the date-stamp on the code belonging to this virus."

"Let me guess? It was the day he died."

"Bingo. You're pretty quick, you know. For a girl." Wren glared at him, and Kazuo backed away in his chair, laughing. "I'm joking, I'm joking! But yeah. It was you who figured it all out, really. You started talking about immortality and that's what made me realise—if you were dying, and you had this place under your control, wouldn't you look for a way to live forever?"

"That's what Professor Gendry is doing," Wren said. "I'm sure of it."

"And I wouldn't be surprised if Sorensen had been bankrolling it. But I guess he ran out of time. I think he had to rush things. He tried to upload his consciousness into the Scape before Gendry's research was complete, and the virus is the result."

"You think those ruptures in the Scape are Sorensen's consciousness?"

"What's left of it. I mean, who knows what kind of a mess he's in. I don't know how much real, actual thought that thing is capable of, but the one thing it seems interested in is getting in here, into Sorensen's control room. Perhaps the login credentials are just an echo of his last thought, repeating itself endlessly."

"All right." Wren looked at the screens, hoping to find some kind of interface or control panel. "What can we do from here? Can we search for people? Can I search for Bethany?"

"We should be able to access anything from here,"

Kazuo said. A few gestures conjured up a shimmering key-board in mid-air. "Try it."

Wren stepped up to the keyboard and started to type Bethany's name. But as the letters appeared on the screen nearest her, she had the strangest sensation that they were fading, that the screen itself was fading, and the room around her. Her fingers faltered. She could no longer see what she was typing. Alarmed, she tried to look at Kazuo, and found that she could not move her head.

Something tugged at the back of her skull, and an excru-ciating pain shot through her, as though somebody was trying to turn her brain inside out. Wren screamed, but no sound came out.

And then she was awake.

Gasping, she opened her eyes. Someone stood over her; a shadowy figure clutching her still-blinking Corona. As the throbbing in her head subsided, she became aware of the many bodies who had been lying beside her in the tiny to-bacconist's. Some of them were still asleep, others were sitting up, rubbing their heads. Around them stood men in black uniforms. Police. A low thrum of panic vibrated through the room as the Dreamers realised what was going on.

"Get off me! Let me go!" Near the door, Calliope strug-gled to escape the grip of an armoured officer who held her arms pinned behind her back. Wren, still dozy, found her-self yanked to her feet and similarly restrained. There were only four police officers and at least a dozen Dreamers, but everyone was too muddled with sleep to put up much of a fight. Wren tried to struggle as the officer cuffed her, but her movements felt slow and useless, and soon she was shuffling, zombie-like, out of the shop with the others.

They were loaded into a police van, sitting in rows facing one another, and it was only as they moved away that the full desperation of her situation hit Wren like a punch in the stomach. Moments ago, she'd been in Gade Sorensen's control room, so close to finding Bethany. Now she was under arrest, being taken back to a police station where they would, undoubtedly, call her mother—and Jared—the moment they figured out who she was.

She looked around at the other Dreamers, their heads bobbing as the van bumped along. None of them were speaking to one another. They looked pale and dazed. Wren felt the same herself. Andromeda had once told her how dangerous it was to disconnect someone forcibly from the DreamScape. The police had risked causing them brain damage, not that they seemed to care.

She thought about Gade Sorensen, living a kind of half-life in bits in there. Certainly, he *had* achieved immortality, of a sort. He had infected the Scape and every Dreamer in there, and would continue to do so to everyone who entered the DreamScape, right up until the whole thing collapsed. But Sorensen wasn't the one who had Bethany. He couldn't be. Even if he had set up Professor Gendry's Foundation for Cognitive Research, he wasn't pulling its strings now. Not if Kazuo was right about him being little more than a repeating meme. There was somebody else controlling Gendry now. Somebody else looking to become immortal, somebody who was trying to avoid making the mistakes Sorensen had made.

Erik Dacre.

Wren made a decision as the police van drew to a halt. She was going to get out of this fix, somehow, and when she did, she was going to find the one person she knew could help her pin Dacre down. The one person she knew he would listen to. She was going back to Covent Garden, and she was going to get Lia Céline to help her, if it was the last thing she did.

28

Time passes. How long, Bethany can't tell. She is drifting through a white void, bodiless, shapeless, just a thought with no vessel. She could have been here for hours, or it could have been years. She feels so far away from what she used to be: a solid, actual girl with hands and feet and a life and friends and a home. Now she is nothing but a whisper. There is nothing to keep her *her*, no sense of being, no Bethany Silver. She feels she must concentrate hard on something, or whatever is left of her will simply break into pieces and blow away like dust on the wind.

She tries to think of home. Her mother. Wren. None of them really wanted her, did they? She was an inconvenience to Wren, a source of trouble to her mother. They're probably pleased she's gone.

Gone. Gone where? Is this even the DreamScape anymore, or just the inside of her own head? Is she dead? Is she just code in a computer somewhere?

Time passes.

Is there anybody there?

Her thoughts echo into the void and come back to her.

…body there? Body there? Body there?

Who is she, without a body? Is she still Bethany? She's not sure she can remember what it felt like to be Bethany.

Time passes.

She notices a sensation. A soft, feather like sensation, like a breeze blowing over her skin. If she had any skin. There is still nothing there, nothing to see, yet she senses she is gaining some kind of shape. There is a cool pressure beneath what, for lack of a better word, she will call her feet. A prickling, like damp grass between bare toes. She flexes her fingers, and the air moves around them.

Looking down, she can see the faint outline of a body. Pale arms and legs protrude from a white dress that falls to just above her knees. She moves her hands to her stomach and the linen crinkles against her skin. Blue sky spreads out around her like paint bleeding across one of her sister's canvasses. Clouds drift by. The warmth of the sun spills across her face as a gentle wind ruffles her hair.

She takes a step. The ground is solid, with the slight spring of a freshly mown lawn. Ahead of her is a small wooden house with gabled windows and a picket fence. It looks exactly like the dolls' house Bethany once played with. A house her real father—not Jared—built for her and that still sits, dusty and ignored, on a shelf in her bedroom. She remembers how, as a child, she used to dream that her father would return from wherever he had gone and take her away to this house, out on a hill somewhere with a stream running nearby and a swing hanging from a tree …

Bethany turns. *That tree*. That exact tree, filled with blossom, and yes, there is a wooden swing hanging from it, moving slightly with the breeze.

She rushes to it, jumps onto the swing, and moves herself

forward and back, pushing her way higher and higher into the air. She takes great gulps of air, almost crying with relief and delight at having a body again.

"Do you like it?"

Startled, Bethany stops swinging. As the swing slowly rocks to a halt, Boy walks into view from behind her. Like Bethany, he is barefoot.

"Do you like it?" he asks again. "The house? I made it for you."

"I thought you'd left me," Bethany admits, strangely relieved.

"Hardly. I've been with you all along."

"Who lives in that house?"

"You. If you want to."

"Who else? Does my dad live there too?"

"I'm sure he'll be here any day now," Boy says. "Will you stay and wait for him?"

Bethany slips off the swing. "I suppose so." She takes a few steps, enjoying the feel of the grass beneath her feet. "I don't have anywhere else to go."

"You can stay here as long as you like." Boy smiles and takes her hand. "You don't know how special you are, Bethany. You're the first of a new kind. A whole new species, in a way."

"I am?"

"Come on." Boy draws her forward, pulling her up the hill to the house. "Let's look inside. You can change anything you want."

29

"Are you going to the party after the show?"

"I wouldn't miss it." The dancer lowered her voice, but not enough that Lia didn't catch what she was saying. "I'm hoping to sneak a picture with Scott Lincoln. I hear he's even more gorgeous in real life."

"Shhh!" Her friend, a soloist dressed in a peasant costume, glanced back at Lia, giggling. Lia busied herself rubbing the toes of her point shoes in resin and pretended not to notice. It was the opening night of *Sleeping Beauty*, and everyone waiting in the darkened wings was a bit giddy with nerves and anticipation.

Lia was no exception. After her lunch with Scott, she'd returned to the Opera House and spent most of the afternoon going over her solo, but all she could think about was the girl who'd accosted her in the market. What had she meant, that her sister was trapped in the DreamScape? Of course, Lia had heard the stories of people who became lost in the network and couldn't be woken—she had always feared it would happen to Erik one day—but why did the girl think that he might have something to do with it?

Truth be told, Lia had never given much thought to what Erik actually did in there. It had never seemed to matter much. What did matter was that it was unhealthy, it disturbed the balance of his mind, and it took him away from her. It was a way to find oblivion for a few hours. What waited on the other side was, she'd always assumed, as unimportant to him as it was to her. Suddenly, that assumption seemed naive. Blinkered, even.

As Lia stretched, Tomas arrived looking dashing in his princely costume. He glanced at her, but moved on to talk to one of the peasant girls, seeming subdued. Nerves? That was unusual. Tomas never suffered from nerves.

"Did Marianne say something to you?" she asked, when he finally joined her.

"About what, Princess?" Tomas placed his hands around her waist, as if he were about to lift her, and Lia twisted around to look up at him.

"About our ballet. About Erik ...? She did, didn't she?" she added, seeing Tomas begin to look shifty.

"It is not the time to talk about it," Tomas replied in a hushed voice, as the first strains of the orchestra started up for act one. "We will discuss at the party later."

The performance began, and once Lia started dancing, all her worries fell away. She was nothing but her body and the music, and at the end of the show she received a rapturous round of applause and several bouquets. One of them, a dozen red roses, was signed only "E". She pulled the card off and threw it in the trash before taking the roses back to her dressing room with the rest of the flowers. He had sent roses to her every opening night since they'd met. It was just habit by now. Still, she couldn't help but pluck one from the bunch, holding it to her lips for a fraction of a second, feeling its velvety caress. Catching sight of herself in the mirror, she thrust the flower quickly back into the vase.

Lia took her time to shower and change for the party, massaging her tired legs and patching up her sore toes with plasters. She slipped on the green, bias cut gown Scott had bought her, and poured herself a quick glass of wine, taking a few sips for courage before trying to squeeze her swollen feet into her gold stiletto sandals. Once she'd finished her wine, she added a pair of earrings, checked her hair once more in the mirror, and headed out of the stage door.

There were a few fans there, and Lia signed a few autographs, but there was no sign of the girl she'd met earlier in the day. Eventually, she went back inside to knock on Marianne's dressing room door.

Marianne answered, dressed in blue, her curly hair piled on top of her head in the kind of effortless up-do that Lia could never manage.

"Are you ready?" Lia asked.

"Sure. Congratulations on a great performance," Marianne said, without meeting Lia's eyes.

"Thanks," Lia replied, but she sensed that something was up. "And you."

They went upstairs in a strained silence, heading through the heart of the opera house before emerging into the breathtaking Floral Hall, where a circular Champagne bar stood beneath a vaulted glass ceiling. The hall was already filled with people who, rather embarrassingly, broke into applause on Lia's appearance. Blushing, she dropped an awkward curtsy and made a beeline for Scott, who stood by the bar with two glasses of Champagne.

"You look beautiful." He kissed her on the cheek and handed her a glass. "And the performance was perfect."

Marianne and Tomas soon joined them, and the three dancers spent what was—to Lia at least—a painful half-hour receiving complements and talking through the performance with patrons. Meanwhile, Scott took selfies with the dancers, until eventually everyone's curiosity was sated, and they were finally able to relax and enjoy the party.

At least, Lia had been expecting to enjoy the party. As soon as they could extract themselves from the crowd, Scott led Lia, Tomas, and Marianne to a quiet table where he poured them each another glass of Champagne. Suddenly, the atmosphere felt strangely formal. Marianne and Tomas looked at Scott as if they were waiting for something, and when Lia tried to catch their attention, they both became very absorbed in people-watching or sipping their drinks.

Scott took a seat next to Lia and leaned in close to her. "Aren't you drinking?" he asked, nodding to her untouched glass.

"I think I've had enough already." Lia glanced at Marianne and Tomas. All three of them were staring at her now, and her skin was beginning to crawl. "Is something the matter?"

"I wanted a word with you, Li." Scott rubbed her back comfortingly. "Don't look so worried. Marianne called me earlier."

Marianne looked at the table.

Lia opened her mouth to speak, but Scott went on, cutting her off, "She's only concerned about you. You and I both know you haven't been acting like yourself since the wedding, and then Marianne told me about this little project of yours ..."

"Marianne!"

"Don't blame her," Scott said. "She's only trying to help.

She was worried that Erik Dacre's appearance at the wedding had …" he paused, searching for the right words, "spun you off course a little, let's say."

He fixed Lia with an intense stare that made her shrink. Now she was beginning to understand what he was getting at, she could see the anger simmering beneath his charming surface, tightly bound in a way that was more frightening than if he had simply let rip.

"You see, the trouble is, Li," he went on, "if I let you go ahead with this ballet, how is that going to make me look? Did you really think I'd be okay with it? With the idea of everyone talking about you and him, yet again?"

"It's just music …" Lia looked to Tomas for support. He, at least, had the grace to look ashamed of himself for staying silent. Marianne sat with her arms folded in a kind of defiant righteousness.

"It's not though, is it?" Scott clenched his fist, a little anger bubbling to the surface, before he forced it back down and smiled at her. "I checked your call records, Li. That was a pretty long call to the US you made the other night."

The sound of the party—the tinkle of glasses and laughter—receded into a muffled haze.

"You checked my call records?"

"And I think I was justified, given what I found."

"We were only discussing the ballet. I wanted his help with the music, nothing more."

"If you felt you were doing nothing wrong, why didn't you tell me about it?" Scott put a hand on top of hers, intertwining their fingers. "We care about you, Li. *I* care about you. I want you to drop this project, for your own sake. I'm willing to believe what Marianne tells me, that you were manipulated down this path for the gain of others," here he shot a sharp glance at Tomas, who winced. "I know you're the type of person who wants to make everyone happy, but you need to think of yourself now. Marianne told me what your life was like before. How unhappy he made you. The idea of you getting sucked back into all that ..."

"I'm not going to! I love you. I married *you*." Lia blinked back tears. "You're right, the ballet was a stupid idea. I never meant to cause so much upset. I only wanted to do something for myself for once."

"The best thing you can do for yourself, Lia, is stay away from Erik," Marianne cut in.

Scott reached over and slipped Lia's phone out of her purse. "I tell you what, I'll send a message to Erik for you, just let him know the whole thing's off. Then you don't even have to do anything. There."

Message completed and sent, Scott dropped the phone into his jacket pocket. Lia could only stare at him, astonished.

After a moment of uncomfortable silence, Marianne made her excuses and went to talk to some friends on the other side of the room. Tomas was quick to follow her example, leaving Lia and Scott alone. Not wanting to meet Scott's eye, Lia sipped her wine and let her gaze rove around the room, restlessly.

Which was when she saw him.

In true Erik fashion he had his feet up on the table and a cigarette in his hand—because naturally the no-smoking rule couldn't possibly apply to him—and he was scanning the faces in the crowd from beneath a curtain of dark hair. Any moment now, he would spot her, and Lia was not going to risk that happening in public. She got to her feet, whispering to Scott that she needed to go to the ladies, and wove her way through the tables to head downstairs, still holding her half-empty glass of wine.

Seconds after she stepped into the foyer, she felt a hand on her shoulder. She knew the touch like it was her own, rough fingers on her bare skin that made all the hairs on her body stand on end. She turned.

In the three years since she'd left him, his boyish good looks had sharpened into something colder and more unforgiving. He was still beautiful, there was no denying it, but his face had grown more gaunt, his bones more prominent, the look in his eyes more haunted.

"What are you doing here?" she asked.

"I was invited." Erik was all affronted innocence. Lia almost laughed.

"Invited? By who?"

"Your partner." Erik gave an exaggerated shrug. "Guy with a foreign accent. He seemed to think I ought to be here."

"Tomas?! That absolute …" Lia cut herself off before she could say any more. "Scott gave him a browbeating about the ballet, so he thought he'd get you involved, didn't he?"

"He seemed concerned." Erik took a step closer. Lia took a step back, holding her glass in front of her body with both hands.

"You can't be here," she said. "You have got to move on. This following me around … It's just not normal."

He was silent, but it was a forceful silence, breaking her down piece by piece. She felt very small, very delicate. She turned away, walked a few paces towards the big glass doors that looked out onto the night.

"We could just go," he said.

"Stop it, all right? Just stop." Lia put a hand to her forehead. "I cannot do this anymore. Get out of my life. Get out of my head. Leave me alone."

"Lia …" he took her arm, turned her around to face him. "Look me in the eye and tell me you never want to see me again, and I promise you won't."

He meant it, she could tell. It was the one thing she had never done. She'd left while he was away on tour, packed up and gone to stay with her sister in New York and refused to answer his calls, but the one thing she had never done was to look him in the eye and tell him it was over. That was why he'd never really let go. Why he'd always sort of been there, still, in the background, the one person she knew would come running if she called. It had been so selfish of her, she realised, and now was her chance to put it all to rest. Let him walk out that door and get on with his life while she got on with hers.

"I …"

She had opened her mouth without knowing what she was going to say, and she never got the chance to find out.

"Get your hands off my wife!"

Scott stormed through the foyer, a ball of furious energy, and grabbed Erik by the lapels of his jacket, slamming him back against the wall.

"I have had it with you, you fucking piece of shit. You're everywhere. Every time I turn around. You're like a fucking cancer."

"Scott!" Lia grabbed his arm, but he shrugged her off easily.

"She married *me*. She belongs to *me*. How about you get that through your fucking skull and leave her alone?"

Erik seemed infuriatingly unconcerned by the whole

thing. Scott was a couple of inches shorter than him, but stockier and probably stronger thanks to all the training he did to look good in his film roles. Erik didn't even try to fight back. He shot a glance at Lia over Scott's shoulder that seemed to say, "do you hear this guy?" and Lia understood he was giving Scott enough rope with which to hang himself. Unfortunately, she feared Scott was likely to do some serious damage to Erik in the process.

"Scott, let him go. Please."

"Not until he promises never to come near you again." Scott leaned in close to Erik, getting up into his face, and something in Erik's expression changed. He frowned slightly, looking into Scott's eyes with a calm, puzzled curiosity.

"It's you, isn't it?" he said.

"What the fuck are you talking about?" Scott spat, but Lia could see he'd loosened his grip a little.

To Lia's amazement, Erik began to laugh. "Jesus fucking Christ, it's you!"

Scott let him drop, backing away as Erik went on laughing: "I'd know you anywhere, old friend. You can't hide from me."

"The guy's crazy." Scott took Lia's arm. "He's high or something. Come on, Li. We've wasted enough time on him."

Lia looked back at Erik as Scott drew her away. He was laughing so hard he could hardly breathe, but it was a mirthless, bitter kind of laughter, as if some terrible irony had just crashed down upon him. He saw Lia looking but couldn't even collect himself long enough to say anything to her. Scott was right. He did look crazy.

"What did he mean, 'It's you'?"

Scott had ushered Lia straight out of the Royal Opera House and into his waiting car. Now, as they drove through London, he glared out the window with a stormy expression, and Lia had to repeat her question before he heard her.

"He's delusional," he snapped. "The guy's obviously lost it."

"He called you 'old friend'." Lia pressed. "Have you met before?"

"I've never met him before in my life." Scott's voice was a low growl. "I wouldn't give the time of day to that washed-out waste of space. And you …" For a moment Lia thought he was about to shout at her, but then, unexpectedly, his expression softened. "He doesn't deserve to breathe the same air as you. You know, that's what I don't get, Li. You're so much better than him. Can't you see it?" He sighed. "You know I'd forgive you anything. I just want to understand. Do you still love him?"

"Scott …"

"Do you, Lia? Hell, did you ever really love me, or was I just there at the right moment?"

"For God's sake, I'm not having this conversation." Lia looked out of the window, wishing she could somehow escape this invisible cage she'd found herself in.

"You can't answer me, can you? Can you?" She could feel him watching her, the air between them stretching taut, the silence growing heavier and heavier. And then, something broke. Scott leaned forward, knocked hard on the partition separating them from the driver. It slid open.

"Take us to the shuttle station," he said.

The driver glanced back at Lia. "Are you sure?"

Scott scowled at him. "You heard me. We need to leave."

30

Something jabbed into Wren's back. Half-asleep, she rolled away from the offending object and woke with a start as she almost fell off the concrete bench she'd been dozing on. She sat up and shook the cobwebby remains of her Slip-induced dreams out of her head, the events of the previous night slowly coming back to her as she looked around the tiny holding cell she and the other Scapers had been crammed into. Behind her, her bench-mate, Calliope, had stretched out, snoring, with one hand behind her head—it had been her elbow that had woken Wren. Most of the other Scapers were sleeping too, or sitting silently on the floor, watching the bolted metal door. An anaemic sliver of morning light edged through the one tiny, reinforced window near the top of the concrete wall. Wren pushed her hair back with both hands, feeling sick.

"Fuck," she muttered.

She vaguely remembered being brought into the police station, fingerprinted and photographed, and asked for her name and place of residence. She had given her address in San Francisco, figuring that as much as she didn't want the police calling college, she wanted them to call her mother and Jared even less. She wondered if they'd called anyone at all yet, and how long she was likely to be stuck here.

She got up and began to pace what little floor space there was, buzzing with frustration, exhaustion, and hunger. Every moment she was caged in here was a moment in which Bethany slipped away even further. She needed to be doing something. Her phone had been taken off her, so she didn't even have any way of knowing what time it was.

Gradually the other Scapers began to rouse, watching her in their dreamy, disconnected way. One of them, a woman with purple hair and a nose-ring, stretched her arms above her head and yawned.

"Would you fucking relax?" she said. "You're making me twitchy. They'll let us out soon enough."

Wren stopped to look at her. "Will they?"

"Wow, you must be a noob." The woman rolled her eyes. "You think they've got space in prison for every Scaper they scrape up off the street? They just want to scare us a bit. For Hypnos's sake, cool your boots."

Wren lent against the cold wall and tried to relax, but every minute seemed to stretch into an hour. She picked at the skin around her fingernails, feeling like she might just tear it all off if she didn't get out of here soon. At last, the metal door clanked open, and a police officer stepped into the room.

"All right, one at a time," he shouted. "When I call your name, come forward."

One by one, they shuffled down a bleak corridor to a desk, where they were handed back their paltry possessions and informed they would be given a formal warning or, in the case of those who'd been arrested for Scaping before, a fine. Wren breathed a sigh of relief as she stepped out of the station, blinking in the daylight. She looked at her phone. It was full of missed calls from Delphi, but it was 11.30am. It would be the middle of the night in San Francisco, so Wren couldn't call back just yet. Instead, she headed down the street and spent some of her remaining money on a coffee and croissant from a corner café. As she sat at the table, watching the first wave of smartly dressed workers arrive for an early lunch, she consulted the map on her phone and found that she was somewhere in Soho. Not far from Covent Garden, then.

After she'd finished her breakfast, Wren strode back outside, following her map until she reached the Royal Opera House. She headed inside and up to the ticket desk, acutely aware of the fact that she had not washed or changed clothes for several days now.

"Er ..." she began, addressing the lone clerk. "Do you know if Lia Céline is here right now? I need to speak to her. It's urgent."

The clerk looked down at Wren through a pair of black-rimmed glasses. "Are you a friend of hers?"

"I'm ..." Oh, what the hell. Wren took a shot in the dark. "I'm her sister."

The clerk looked dubious, but she picked up the phone, nonetheless. There was a long pause as she spoke in a low voice to somebody on the other end, and then she put the old-fashioned handset back in its cradle.

"She's not here," she said, frowning. "She should be, but she didn't show up this morning, and nobody's been able to get in touch with her."

"Oh," said Wren. "I mean, yes, exactly. That's why I'm here. I tried to call her, and she didn't pick up. You're saying she hasn't answered anybody else's calls, either?"

The clerk shook her head. "But if you know another way to get in touch with her … she's got a matinee in an hour and the director's frantic."

"Perhaps I can go round to hers," Wren suggested, "see if she's ill or something? Could you maybe call me a cab?"

She crossed her fingers behind her back as the clerk picked up the phone once more. "All right," she said, after a moment's conversation. "The taxi will pick you up out the front in ten minutes. Here," she handed Wren a card with the Royal Opera House phone number on. "If you find Ms Céline, please can you call us?"

"Of course! Look … er … sorry, but do you have my sister's address there? Could you maybe just pop it on the card for me? I never wrote it down and I just can't remember what number …"

"Okay, okay." The clerk narrowed her eyes, but scribbled something on the card and passed it back to Wren. "You will let us know if you find her, won't you? Or even if you don't."

"Yes, yes I will, thank you very much."

Wren darted out the building before the clerk had a chance to change her mind. Clutching her card, she hopped from foot to foot as she waited for the taxi, expecting every moment for someone to come storming out of the Opera House demanding to know why she was impersonating Lia's sister. But a minute later, a black cab pulled up at the side of the road and Wren flung herself inside, glancing at her card.

"Er … Kensington Square please," she said.

The cabbie glanced at her through the mirror. "Right you are, miss."

The journey seemed agonisingly slow in the busy week-end traffic, creeping inch by inch toward Kensington Square, but eventually they arrived, and Wren got out of the cab, thanked the driver, and paid him the very last of her credits. As he drove off, Wren made her way up the steps to the front door of a tall Georgian terrace and pressed the top button for the penthouse flat. Nobody answered. She pressed it again. Still no answer.

Sighing, she headed back down the steps. Yet again, she had hit a brick wall. If Lia was not at the Opera House, and not at home, Wren had no idea where else to look for her. Strange, though, not to show up for one of her own performances. Wren found a bench in the park opposite the house and called the Opera House to ask whether she'd arrived for work yet.

"Not yet," was the reply from the girl on the desk. "But hold on a moment. I mentioned to Marianne that you'd called, and she wants to speak to you."

Wren heard the click of a call being transferred, and then a breathless American voice on the other end of the line.

"All right, mystery woman. I've got two minutes before I'm due on stage, so let's make this quick. Who the hell are you and what's happened to Lia? Did Erik send you looking for her? Don't try to pretend you're her sister," she added. "I've spoken to Esmé and she doesn't have a clue about any of this."

Wren hung up in a hurry. She sat back against the cold park bench and looked at the sky. She was out of money, out of ideas, and rapidly running out of hope. Then a thought jolted her back to action. She picked up her phone and dialled the Opera House again.

"I'm so sorry," she said to the clerk, "I was speaking to

Marianne and I got cut off. Can you put me back through?”

"She's performing now," the girl said, apologetically, "you'll have to call back in a few hours.”

Wren hung up again, got to her feet and started walking. There was no way she was waiting for a few hours. This woman, Marianne, had mentioned Erik as if she knew him. She might know where he was, or if not, then she might be able to tell Wren something that would help her track him down. There was obviously something strange going on with Lia Céline, and Wren couldn't shake the feeling that whatever had happened to her was somehow connected with Erik and, consequently, with Bethany. It was a slim hope, but it was the only one she had, so it was back to the Opera House for Wren, on foot this time.

As she hurried along the boundary of Hyde Park, keeping one eye on her map, her phone buzzed. It was Delphi. Wren put it through as a voice call only.

"Oh, thank God," Delphi said, on hearing Wren's voice. "I thought you were dead or lost, or God knows what.”

"Just arrested," Wren replied. "There was a raid on the hideout. Thankfully they let me go with a warning.”

"So they just dragged you out of the Scape? They could have caused you brain damage!”

"Perhaps they have," Wren laughed dryly. "Not sure I'd be able to tell the difference at this stage.”

"What are you doing?”

"Walking. Looking for Lia Céline. Or one of her friends, at least. Seems she's gone missing lately.”

"What's that got to do with you?"

"Not much. But it's bound to have something to do with Erik Dacre, don't you think? He is obsessed with her, after all."

There was a long pause on Delphi's end of the line. "Wren," she said, gently, "I think you should just come back to San Francisco. The college have agreed to pay your shuttle fare. I can ask them to send you the ticket."

"You want me to abandon Bethany?"

"No! Of course not! That's not what I'm saying at all. I just think you should come home. What good is it doing you being stuck in London? You don't even know where Bethany is."

"Delphi, this is my only chance to get close to Erik Dacre," Wren snapped. "I know it sounds crazy, but if I can just figure out what's happened to Lia Céline …"

"Lia Céline is not your problem, Wren."

"Sorry, Delph, I've got to go. I'll call you back later, okay?"

"Wren! Just wait …"

Wren hung up the phone and broke into a jog. If she could get to the Opera House before the matinée ended, she would have a chance to pin down Marianne. It wasn't much, but at least she was doing something, and that was surely better than being stuck on a shuttle for the next few hours.

When she reached the Opera House, exhausted and out of breath after an hour's walk, the foyer was quiet, the clerk nowhere to be seen. A strange hush lay over the building—the silence of hundreds of people tucked away in the heart of the theatre, watching the performance. With nobody around to stop her, Wren darted upstairs and into a vast atrium with a glass ceiling. Her boots squeaked on the brushed wooden floor. Her only company were a couple of bartenders at the Champagne bar in the centre of the room, who watched her pass without curiosity.

Seeing a pile of cast lists on a nearby table, Wren picked one up and scanned through it, looking for Marianne's name. Sure enough, an addendum slip inserted between the leaves announced that due to 'unforeseen circumstances' Lia Céline's part of Aurora would be danced by Marianne Morrison. Wren slipped the cast list into her back pocket and headed onward, feeling as though she was making her way through the ribcage of some great beast, looking for its heart.

She took one of the escalators at the edge of the atrium, then followed a corridor plastered with old photographs of dancers and opera singers until she came to a pair of double doors labelled *Auditorium*. Gingerly, Wren pushed one open.

She was at the very top of the theatre. The stage was a pinpoint of light far away in the darkness, where a tiny creature in pink danced with one prince after another. The music filled the air like a physical force, layers upon layers of sound controlling the dancer like a puppet. Wren crept down the steps to the front of the balcony, ignoring irritated glances from the audience, and stood leaning against the rail, content for a moment to simply watch.

As the performance ended, Wren slipped out of the auditorium along with the rest of the audience, and retraced her steps out of the building, where she followed a pair of excited teenage girls around the corner and up to the innocuous stage door. She pulled her hoodie around her against the cold, and waited.

31

She waited around half an hour before the dancers began to trickle out of the theatre, one or two at a time. The teenage girls Wren had followed were keen to get as many autographs as they could on their cast sheets, but Wren overheard them bemoaning how disappointed they were to have missed out on seeing Lia Céline herself. That didn't stop them from flocking around Marianne Morrison when she appeared with a tall, handsome man who Wren assumed had played the prince.

Wren hung back as the girls took selfies with the dancers, waiting for her moment, but before she could make her move, Marianne paused midway through signing a programme, her attention suddenly arrested by something on the other side of the road. She thrust the programme and pen back at the startled girl and stormed past her, shouting:

"You! I'm sick of the sight of you! You're like a bad smell, always hanging around."

Wren turned to see the dark figure on the other side of the road, and her eyes widened in astonishment. All this time she'd been standing there, her attention completely focused on Marianne, and Erik Dacre had been meters away. She crossed the road, trying not to draw attention, while straining to hear Erik's low drawl over the hubbub of the small crowd who collected around him.

"Where's Lia?"

"I was about to ask you the same question." Marianne's voice carried much better. The handsome prince followed in her wake, looking curiously at Erik, who lounged against the wall in his leather jacket.

"You don't know where she is?" The prince raised his eyebrows. Wren took up a position a few feet away from the three of them and proceeded to lurk as inconspicuously as she could.

"Are you telling me she's not here? She didn't perform just now?" Erik sounded genuinely puzzled. Surprised, Wren crept a little closer.

"No, she fucking didn't," Marianne snapped. "Nobody's been able to get hold of her all day. And then there was that girl you sent looking for her, pretending to be Esmé ..."

"What girl?" Wren shrunk a bit as Erik went on, "I didn't send any girl. Has anybody tried calling Scott?"

"Of course," the prince said. "But he is not answering."

"The last I saw, he was dragging her out of the Opera House." Erik's edgy energy was palpable. "If she's vanished with him, she's in danger."

He was already making to leave when Marianne stopped him. "In danger? What are you talking about?"

Erik glared at her. "You always were stupid."

"Excuse me?"

"You were so busy hating me that you never took a real good look at him, did you? He's not me. That was enough, wasn't it? Well, you know what? He's more like me than you realised." He smiled, bitterly. "More than even I real-ised."

Marianne raised her hands in frustration. "There's no getting any sense out of him," she said to the prince. "Let's go."

Erik looked sharply at Wren. "Why don't you explain?"

Wren froze. She'd had no idea he'd even noticed her, but now his green-eyed glare locked her in place.

"Go on," Erik said, softly. "You know what I'm talking about. I've seen you before. Twice, I think: at my show, and in my cave. Which, by the way, I did not appreciate. Why don't you explain to them who Scott Lincoln is? They'll be-lieve you before they believe me."

"I have no idea …" Wren began.

"I was never the one you wanted," Erik said, although as he spoke there was such an electric hush around him that Wren doubted the truth of what he was saying. "It was him. It was always him."

"He's the Dark God? He's Thanatos?"

Erik shook his head. "He calls himself Hypnos."

"No," Wren shook her head, half-laughing. "Scott Lin-coln? The jock boyfriend from *Uptown Girls*? Leader of a cult? No."

"It's a good disguise, I know. Had you all fooled, didn't he? Had me fooled, too, until I looked him in the eye."

"So, you're saying Scott Lincoln has Bethany?" Wren said doubtfully.

"Who the hell is Bethany?" Marianne found her voice again.

"My sister," Wren replied, "and if Lincoln has her, I need to find him. Now."

After a few minutes' bickering, the only thing they all agreed on was that they'd rather be bickering with a drink in their hand. The cosy interior of the nearby Nag's Head pub seemed as good a place as any to argue. Erik went to the bar while the others found a table, and Wren watched him down two shots of whiskey and tell a couple of hovering fans to fuck off. The fans went away delighted and, sufficiently lubricated, Erik returned with a round.

He plonked the four bottles of beer in the middle of the table and sat next to Wren.

"You," he said, somewhat accusingly. "I don't remember your name."

"Wren," said Wren.

"Right. And you," he jabbed a finger at the handsome prince, "you're the one who phoned me up yesterday. Li's new partner."

"Tomas. And we've been dancing together for almost three years," the prince replied.

"Whatever. And you," he turned to Marianne, "obviously I know."

"Unfortunately." Marianne shot him a withering glare.

"You're telling me." Erik took a generous swig from his beer. "All right, now we're all friends, I've got questions. I want to know when you two last saw or spoke to Lia, and I want to know what you," he looked pointedly at Wren, "were doing looking for her."

"It was you I wanted to find, really ..." Wren began, but Marianne interrupted, turning to Erik.

"Hold on. If you saw Lia and Scott leave the party last

night, then you spoke to her more recently than either of us did. And who exactly do you think you are, talking to us like that?"

Erik leaned across the table until his face was close to hers. "Marianne. I am the person who knows what the fuck is going on here. If you want any chance of finding Lia alive, you're just gonna have to put up with me."

"Alive?" Marianne sat back and folded her arms, but Wren could see that she was just trying to cover up her alarm. "Is that some kind of threat?"

"I think I need to make clear who we're dealing with here." Erik looked at each of them in turn, deadly serious. "I know you all love Scott. Every fucking body loves Scott, right? Well, I don't know about you," he added, glancing at Wren. "I don't really know who the fuck you are. But anyway, you all need to learn to look past the pretty face. That is a man with more hidden depths than you could possibly imagine, and you do not want to cross him."

"If he is who you think he is," Marianne added.

"He is. I know him. He and I go way back. And I know how his fucked-up mind works. If he's even thinking about …" He stopped, clenching both fists and resting his forehead on them for an instant. When he looked up again, it was with renewed determination. "If you're not going to take this seriously, I don't have time for your shit." He downed his beer and stood. "Enjoy your drinks."

"Wait!" Wren said quickly. "You're not leaving?"

"I am leaving." Erik was already halfway to the door. Wren scrambled to her feet and caught up with him.

"What about my sister?"

"What about her?" Erik flung the door open and stepped outside. Wren followed, struggling to match his pace as he strode down the street.

"He's got her too. Scott … Hypnos. I thought it was you, it's true. I assumed … but if it's not, you can still help me, surely? We can help each other."

Erik stopped suddenly and faced her. "I really don't see what use you'd be to me." Somewhere beneath all his anger and arrogance, Wren sensed a thrumming terror. He fumbled in his pocket for a cigarette, taking several attempts to light it with shaking hands. "Now you're holding me up," he added, "so fuck off."

"You love Lia," Wren said. "I can see that. I love my sister. Just let me come with you. You don't have to do this by yourself. Hey," she went on, desperately, "I found your cave, didn't I? And I know what happened to Gade Sorensen. I can't be totally useless."

"You know what happened to Gade?" Finally, something seemed to have caught Erik's attention.

"You don't?" Wren was surprised.

"I've got my suspicions. I want to know yours."

"I'll tell you on the way." Wren grinned. She'd found a way in. "Where are we going?"

Erik took a long drag of his cigarette and let it out as a sigh. "Vegas."

32

Wren had never heard of anyone having a private sonic shuttle before, but Erik Dacre had one: a sleek, black cylinder as featureless as a bullet, parked up a siding at St Pancras station, with a driver sitting nearby eating sandwiches. He hopped into action when he saw Erik and Wren crossing the platform, stuffing his lunch away into a bag and hurrying to open the door for them. When he pressed his palm against the obsidian surface, it glowed white beneath his fingers, and Wren was irresistibly reminded of the Mark of Thanatos. Erik hopped inside and Wren followed, ducking under the low doorway.

The interior was as white as the exterior was black. Chairs, tables, walls, floors—all were white, either leather or gloss. Erik threw himself into a seat, reclining it as far back as it could go, and put his heavy boots up on the footrest. Wren sat down and curled her legs beneath her.

As the shuttle shuddered into motion, she cast around for something to look at other than the dark blot of Erik's figure opposite her. It was impossible, though—there were no screens and no windows, and her eyes slid off all the whiteness. She felt grubby in comparison, in her several-day old clothes, and desperately in need of a shower, but then Erik didn't look much better.

For a long while he lay motionless, staring at the ceiling. The capsule was eerily still, silent but for the low thrum of the motor. With no points of reference, it was impossible to tell where they were or how fast they were going. Wren fiddled with her phone, watching the minutes tick by.

"Are you all right?" she said, eventually.

Erik lifted his head and looked at her fuzzily.

"You want a drink?" he asked. "There's whiskey in that cabinet."

"No thanks." After a beat, during which he just stared at her, Wren added, "But I can get you one, if you want."

Taking his silence for assent, she opened the featureless white cabinet and took out one heavy-bottomed glass and a half-empty bottle of whiskey. She poured a generous measure and handed it to him. Erik knocked it back.

"Thanks," he said, hoarsely, putting the glass down on the table between them. Then he fixed her with a stare that was sharp even through the mist in his eyes. "I want to know how you found my cave."

"I've got a friend who's very good with computers. He was able to hack your Mark."

"Why? There's nothing in there you could possibly want."

"Seriously? Not even Gade Sorensen's control room? When I spoke to you back at your show, you said you didn't know a thing about what happened to Bethany." Wren jabbed a finger at him. "You lied. You could've found her all along."

Erik poured himself another drink. "Last I saw you were

headed in there yourself. So why didn't you find her?"

"I got pulled out of the system by a raid before I had the chance to do anything. But when I catch up with my friends … hopefully by now they've found a way to use Gade's control system. And if they haven't, you can help us."

"My powers in that place are more limited than you think. I can get into the control room. Doesn't mean I can use it."

"You are Gade Sorensen's heir, right? One of them, at least?"

Erik shrugged off his leather jacket, exposing arms covered in black tattoos, right down to his hands. He wore several leather bracelets around each wrist, and an array of weighty silver rings on his fingers. The same motifs were repeated again and again in both the jewellery and the tattoos: ravens, skulls, roses, snakes. Pretty typical Gothic stuff, but the art was well done.

"When Gade knew he was gonna die," he began, "he wanted someone to take on his legacy. But Gade being who he was, he couldn't just give away all his secrets to one single person. So, he chose two of us."

"You and Scott."

"That's right."

"But why? I mean … a rock star and an actor? Neither of you are exactly the obvious choice, if you don't mind me saying."

"Back then, I wasn't a rock star. Not much of one, anyway. I was just a kid in a struggling band, spending all his free time Scaping. I was an early adopter, and I learned a lot: how to code, how to manipulate environments." Erik fixed Wren with his piercing gaze. "I may not look like your obvious candidate, but I'm good at what I do. Good enough to have attracted Gade's notice."

"And Scott?"

"I'm just putting that together myself. I guess it must've come down to money. Hypnos always seemed to have the means to do whatever Gade needed—keep the servers safe, that sort of thing. For the sake of security, neither of us was supposed to know who the other was in the Mono. That was the plan, anyhow. But Hypnos—Scott," he added, with a snarl, "he got close to Gade, found out where he was hiding in the real world, and manipulated him into handing over most of the control to him. Gade talked about Hypnos as though he was some kind of long-lost son. The two of us were supposed to balance each other out, but I soon realised he'd locked me out of just about everything important."

"So, Scott's been out there, doing what the hell he wanted, all this time?"

"Building up his cult of brainwashed followers." Erik took another swig of whiskey. "Sacrificing one soul after another to his fucked-up experiments. Li wanted me to quit Scaping. How could I? I was the only one who knew what Hypnos was really doing."

"And he blamed everything on you. All those ruptures in the Scape. All the lost souls who fell through them."

"Every god needs a devil, right?"

"Sure. But how did the two of you convince everybody that you were gods?"

Erik thought for a moment. "People just really, really want there to be something more, you know?" he said, at last. "Something more than themselves they can pour their emotions into. Everybody wants a deity, whether they realise it or not. And the DreamScape is full of very receptive, very imaginative people. All it took was a little push in the right direction, and they started to believe what Hypnos was spouting. Add in a few churches, priests, that sort of shit, to give it some weight, and suddenly you've got a full-blown religion. Or two."

"I can't believe people are that easily led."

"Can't you? You were starting to fall for it, I think."

Wren shook her head. "No. I never believed in any god."

"Sure, you did. You came looking for me."

"I never thought you were a god."

"Never?" Erik leaned in close, fixing her with his laser-like stare. "Not even a little bit?"

When Wren squirmed under his intense gaze, he broke into a grin that bubbled into a burst of manic laughter. Throwing himself back into his seat, he clapped his hands together.

"I have that effect on people," he said, between gales of laughter. "I can't explain it."

"Must be nice," Wren muttered sarcastically.

"You think?" Suddenly Erik was serious again. "You fucking think? Everybody has this hole in them that they want filled and they think I can do it. They've got it back-wards. I *am* the fucking hole. I am empty space. I am nothing. You came to me wanting something and I sent you away, because I can't give you anything. I see that hole in you," he jabbed a finger at the centre of Wren's chest, "I see it, and let me tell you: I will make it worse. You spend too much time with me, and you'll soon see what I mean. The people who follow me—the Dravens, the ones who worship the Dark God—they get obsessed because they think I can fill that space and instead I take their adoration and I take their obsession and I pull it all into this emptiness and I just keep on taking." He stopped, flexing his fingers into tight fists, and took a deep breath. "They think the way to get what they want is to get closer," he went on, more quietly, "but you try getting closer to a vampire and see how well that works out for you. Just ask Lia."

Wren was silent. The whisper of the engines filled the space between them.

"When we get to Vegas," said Erik, "I'll give you some money, and you get off this shuttle and go home, all right? If I find your sister, you'll be the first to know."

Wren shook her head. "I can't just do nothing. Besides, you need me."

"Is that right?"

"You said you can't use the control room. Well, I think I can, as long as I can get back in there. My friend worked out what Gade's master credentials are."

"That's impossible."

"Nope." Wren grinned. "See? You can't just get rid of me that easily."

Erik rubbed his temples. "You're fucking tenacious, you know that?"

On arrival in Las Vegas, they moved to a black passenger pod that ferried them down the strip. It was late evening in London by now, so mid-afternoon in Vegas, and the unrelenting desert sun blazed through the pod's windows. Wren gaped as they passed hotels shaped like castles, sphinxes, and pirate ships, heading for the sleek glass monoliths at the newer end of the strip.

"This place is worse than Reverie," she said. Blinking,

neon advertisements swooped past the pod, carried by drones that paused in mid-air to make sure they had her attention, before flitting away to the next potential customer. On the streets, feathered chorus girls walked alongside tattooed cyborgs and Elvis impersonators in glitzy suits. Erik ignored all of it, muttering into his phone in a voice too low for Wren to hear.

They pulled up in front of a cylindrical glass tower, reaching dozens of storeys into the sky. Erik climbed out of the pod, and Wren followed, stepping into a wall of heat. A dark-suited bellboy greeted Erik by name as they headed into a vast marble foyer. Erik's appearance caused a buzz at the packed check-in desk, tourists turning eagerly to catch a glimpse of him. Wren did her very best to disappear, which wasn't hard. Nobody cared much about a mousy-haired girl in a hoodie when they had the world's biggest rock star to look at.

"You live here?" she asked, following Erik to an elevator with a gold-plated door.

"I own here," Erik replied.

Wren tried not to look impressed. She stepped into the elevator as though hanging out with rock stars was just an everyday occurrence for her, and soon they were shooting up the centre of the tower. At the top, they emerged into a marble entrance hall, and beyond that, a garishly opulent sitting room in shades of silver and purple. A black chandelier hung over a sunken sofa. It was not, Wren thought, what she would have chosen, but it seemed to suit Erik.

Outside the window was a pool area, high above the city, where a couple of bikini-clad girls with Draven tattoos lounged, drinking cocktails with a man in a hideous floral shirt. Wren recognised him as Kent Austin, the manager who'd introduced her and Delphi to Erik backstage at the concert. When he noticed Erik, he almost spilt his drink in his hurry to get up. Erik headed outside, Kent made his way over to their side of the pool, and they met on the windswept terrace, close to the sun, the city far beneath them.

"You," Kent jabbed a finger at Erik's chest, "you are going to fucking drive me out of my mind one day. Where the fuck have you been this time? No, don't even tell me. I don't wanna know."

Erik cast a glance over Kent and the two Dravens, who had approached eagerly but were now hanging back shyly a few feet away, shooting evil looks at Wren. "You look like you're doing pretty okay without me."

"I had to take my mind off your shit." Kent waved a dismissive hand. "You look like hell, by the way."

"Thanks."

Kent rolled his eyes. "Sit down." He indicated a sun lounger. "Just sit the fuck down and don't go anywhere. I'll get some food sent up."

"What I need is a drink." Erik collapsed onto the lounger and put both hands to his head. "And my dealer's on his way. You gotta meet him for me."

"No. No. No fucking chance. You're gonna eat, and then you're gonna sleep, and tonight you've got an interview with that music webcast. You know, the one with the asshole presenter. I want you sober for that." Looking closely at Erik he added, "But if that ship has already sailed, I'd settle for coherent."

"Don't fucking baby me," Erik snapped. "Fuck sleep. Fuck the interview." He leapt up again and stormed through to the sitting room. When Wren and Kent followed, he was rummaging frantically under the couch. "Where's my

Corona? I left it here somewhere …"

"I threw it away."

Erik stood, his fists clenched. "Away where?"

"We talked about this. You agreed …"

"It doesn't matter what I agreed! Everything's changed. You need to get that fucking Corona back." Erik took a breath and started again, more calmly. "Look, Lia's in trouble. I've gotta get into the Scape—it's the only way to find her. Ask her," he added, gesturing to Wren, "she'll back me up."

"It's true," Wren nodded. "We've got to find Lia, and we might not have much time."

Kent looked at Wren properly for the first time since she'd arrived.

"Look, lady," he said, putting a hand on her shoulder, "I know you like Erik, hey. Who doesn't? But what you gotta understand is, he talks a load of shit. A *load* of shit." He started to gently steer Wren toward the door. "If they gave out prizes for talking shit, he would be a multi-award-winning act, you know what I mean? So, you go on home and maybe he'll call you in the morning, all right?"

Wren stood her ground. "I'm not leaving."

"She's not leaving," Erik echoed. His phone buzzed, and he glanced at it. "Dealer's downstairs. Go and make yourself useful, Kent. Ask him if he can get us two more Coronas as well as the Slip. Go."

They stared each other down. Kent bristled with determination, but Erik had on his side the full force of his desperation to save Lia, not to mention his unholy green-eyed glare that seemed able to reduce anybody to rubble. Eventually, Kent relented. He turned away without a word and disappeared out of the door. Erik turned his biting stare on the Dravens, who tugged on their beach dresses and grabbed their bags without even needing to be told to leave.

Once they were alone, he caught Wren's eye across the room and nodded to another doorway.

"Go get a shower or whatever," he said. "Be quick. We'll get started the moment Kent gets back."

33

Kent Austin had returned, and Erik was already fitting his Corona onto his head, when Wren emerged from the shower. She'd found a spare black t-shirt in one of the drawers in the bedroom, which she'd put on along with her jeans. It was baggy on her and clearly one of Erik's, which made her feel weird about wearing it, but she was well overdue a new top, and if he noticed he didn't bother to say anything.

Wren couldn't figure out what to make of him. She'd stood in the shower with the heat turned up high, trying to blast away the detritus of the past few days and mulling over everything Erik had said to her during the shuttle journey. He seemed on a knife-edge, at times wound up so tight he might snap, and then, in the next breath, lethargic, drawling, half-drunk. Wren realised she had to tread carefully. She was dealing with a volatile substance; one she knew nothing about.

"You ready?" Erik looked at her sharply, then popped a couple of Slip pills in his mouth. Wren nodded and sat on the couch opposite him. There was a second Corona on the table which she picked up and fitted onto her own head.

Kent began to hand her the pillbox full of red tablets, then withdrew it at the last moment.

"You could just go home, you know," he suggested.

"I know what I'm doing." Wren snatched a pill, impatient to get started. She tossed it down her throat and, with one last confirming glance at Erik, lay back on the couch.

For the longest time, Wren hovered between reality and the DreamScape, trapped in a kind of holding pen of white, empty space. She'd paused here before, each time she entered the Scape, but usually for no more than a few seconds as she chose her proposed destination and her avatar's appearance. Now, with Erik Dacre in charge of the system, she found herself drifting in nothingness for long enough that she became anxious. Had something gone wrong? Was her Corona malfunctioning? Had she been a fool to trust Erik, after all?

She couldn't log out, not having properly logged in yet, and she was beginning to panic when, finally, she was standing on solid ground in a grim half-light. As her eyes adjusted to the semi-darkness, she realised she was in the middle of an empty road. Crumbling buildings towered above her on every side, coal black and ravaged by flames. Ahead, a blazing dumpster fire spat white-hot cinders into the road.

It was what Las Vegas, or Los Angeles, or any large city, might have looked like after the Apocalypse. The devastation continued in every direction, fires dotted throughout the city pumping so much black smoke into the atmosphere that it was impossible to tell whether it was day or night.

Wren sensed a presence and turned to find Erik at her side, watching her.

"Is this what it looks like inside of your head?" she asked

him, only half joking.

He cocked his head a little to one side and stared at her, much as a raven would. Here in the DreamScape, he looked very much as he did in life, but there was an almost imperceptible difference in his bearing. Whereas in the Mono he had struck Wren as a person at war with everything both within and without himself, here in the Scape he had the air of someone entirely in his element. He strode on ahead, seeming confident, assured, even relaxed. It was the same Erik she'd seen on stage at the concert, completely in command of his surroundings. This was *his* place, after all.

They passed a burnt-out car, still ablaze in the middle of the road, and as they walked through the thick cloud of smoke, a building came into view up ahead. A cathedral, but one that looked as though it had forced its way up from the depths of hell. Twisted, blackened, and gnarled, its spires rose high into the air like the trunks of diseased, ancient trees. Between them a vast, circular stained-glass window glowed in flame orange and blood red, and beneath that was a black wooden door twice as tall as Wren and several times as wide. She felt as though she had stepped into a nightmare.

"You seemed to like my cave so much," Erik said, with an unhinged grin, "I thought you might enjoy this even more."

He stepped up to the door and it slammed open as if blasted by a gust of strong wind. It was all an illusion, Wren reminded herself. Just showmanship and empty special effects, like at the concert. Nevertheless, she crossed the threshold with trepidation.

The moment they stepped into the cathedral they were mobbed by people. At least, some of them were people—men with crazed looks in their eyes, women in elaborate, ragged dresses. Others were creatures that could only have been dreamed up by the most warped of minds. Deformed things with dozens of eyes clawed at Wren with long, bony fingers. Soft, spidery legs brushed against her thighs, then scuttled away. A harpy with a woman's body and bird's wings flew at her, bare-breasted and screeching. Wren ducked and stumbled, and would have found herself on the floor among trampling feet if Erik hadn't grabbed her arm to keep her up. All of them were screaming, wailing, throwing themselves at Erik and making incomprehensible demands, and he walked through them without losing a beat, dragging a terrified Wren along behind him.

Eventually, as they reached the altar and began to ascend the steps, the hideous crowd melted away, and when Wren looked back, they were huddled at the base of the steps, dozens and dozens of them, staring up expectantly like starving dogs waiting for scraps.

"Lost souls," said Erik, in a low voice. "I didn't make them this way. *He* did that."

"He? As in, Scott Lincoln?"

"Exactly." He looked down for a moment, thinking. "What was your sister's name?"

"Bethany. Bethany Silver."

Erik turned to address the assembled creatures, looking like some kind of demonic preacher beneath the high arched ceiling of the cathedral.

"Is there a Bethany here?"

A murmur ran through the crowd. The creatures looked at one another, wringing their hands or blinking their wide, insect eyes, but nobody stepped forward.

"That's a good thing," Erik told a disappointed Wren, with a gentleness she hadn't seen in him before. "By the time they get here there's not a whole lot of hope for them."

"How do they get here?" Wren whispered.

Erik sat down at the top of the steps, seemingly oblivious to the rows of eyes watching him.

"Sometimes I try to guide them," he said, as Wren joined him, "seek them out, but most of them just wind up here somehow, like leaves on the wind. Maybe it takes them a few weeks, maybe it takes them years, but they end up here eventually. I'm sorry," he added. "I should've checked whether your sister was here weeks ago when you first asked me. But I figured, if she was here, you wouldn't want to know. These people—what's left of them—will never go home, you know? They can't. Their bodies are dead, or they don't know their way back. I try to give them somewhere to be. It's all I can do."

Wren looked sadly at the rows of pitiful faces, and then a thought occurred to her. She stood.

"Is there anybody here named Reza?"

The creatures whispered to one another, looking this way and that, until the crowd parted, and a figure was gradually nudged forward. He was human, or at least shaped like one, but his skin had turned to wood. He limped into the space created for him, moving awkwardly. Behind the moss covering his face, he looked as though he had once been handsome, with dark, sad eyes and a sharp jawline.

"The code gets a bit funny after a while," Erik said. "It deteriorates, mixes up with other things. That's why they look so strange."

"Are you Reza?" Wren asked.

The wooden boy nodded. "I think so," he said, in a voice that creaked like an ancient tree being bent in the wind. He looked back at the creatures who'd pushed him forward.

"They tell me so."

"You don't remember?" Wren made her way down the steps to face him. "My friend is looking for you. Andromeda. Do you remember her?"

Reza gazed at her, his expression blank. "I don't …" He frowned, thinking hard. "Andromeda … I don't … I can't … Who is that?"

"She was your girlfriend. She's been looking for you for years."

"He won't remember," Erik cut in, from his place on the dais above them. "He's been here a long time. His consciousness is disintegrating."

"Can't we do anything?" Wren thought of how badly Andromeda had wanted to find her boyfriend.

Erik shook his head. "I don't know any way to fix them. If I did, I would do it. I *would*," he repeated, as Wren shot him a tearful glare. "I'm not what you think I am."

"You're a liar," Wren shot back. "You said you couldn't help. You said you didn't know anything, when you knew about all this! If you'd been honest with me when you first met me …"

"Will you be honest with your friend, Wren? Will you tell her about him?"

Reza stood slumped just where she'd left him, staring straight through her.

"Do you think that'll make her feel better?" Erik went on. "I told you to accept your sister was lost and move on, because knowing that she'd ended up like this … it would haunt you."

"But you don't know this has happened to her. It wasn't your decision to make. And I don't see you accepting that Lia's gone."

Erik's expression hardened. "No. No, I won't accept that." He turned and walked back to the altar, leaning on it with both hands, head bent. "Call your friends," he said, at last. "Tell them to meet us. I want to know how to use the control room. And I want to know what you think happened to Gade. Because I always knew there was more to that story than Hypnos was willing to tell me."

34

Bethany wakes in the doll's house, in a four-poster bed with pristine white curtains. She can't tell how many times she's woken here before. She can't tell whether she was ever really asleep. The sun is already shining, although she's not sure that it ever actually went down. Every moment is the same as the next, and the next, and the next. She goes to the dressing table, brushes her hair, looks at her reflection in the mirror. It stares back at her, blank-eyed and strange. She lifts her hand. The reflection lifts one too. She flexes her fingers. The reflection flexes hers too. Bethany leans in, peering at it, pressing her finger to the glass, mirror-image fingers touching one another. Then she whips her hand away, sharply, suddenly, and the reflection does the same, but with the slightest delay. Almost imperceptible, but enough to make Bethany shudder.

She turns from the mirror, overcome with a disgust that she can't quite understand, and walks out of the room, down the stairs, out of the house. She wants to feel the warmth of the sun on her skin. No, she wants to feel cold. She hasn't felt cold for … for how long? Here it is warm, always. The warmth prickles her bare arms in just the same way as it did yesterday, and the day before, and the day before that. If they were days at all. How can there be days if there are no nights? How can it be warm if there is no cold? How is it that she never feels tired, or hungry, or in pain? How many times has she had these thoughts already?

Bethany walks down to the stream, straining her mind, trying to remember where she came from. There was the canyon, and before that the train with the kind woman, and before that, the palace, and all those decaying people. Is she just waiting now, like them? Waiting to die?

"I want to go home," she says. Her voice floats away on the breeze, heard by no-one. She says it again, more firmly this time. "I want to go home."

But how? Bethany walks along the edge of the stream. She walks and walks, passing the occasional tree, until the doll's house is out of sight behind her. The sun blazes high in the blue sky, unmoving, but she counts her steps and so she knows time is passing. The landscape never changes. Grass, trees, the stream trickling peacefully alongside her. More grass. More trees. And then she sees it. The doll's house, up ahead, coming back into view. She comes to a halt right where she started from—next to the tree with the swing.

Bethany tries another tactic. She walks up the hill to the house and back down the other side. Sure enough, she winds up standing next to the stream. It must run all the way around the house like a moat. There's only one option left. She hitches up her white dress and steps into the water.

As she walks, the stream becomes wider and deeper. She's moving forward, water covering her ankles, then her calves, then her knees, but the other side isn't getting any closer. Eventually, when she's waist deep, she stops and looks back. The shore is right there behind her, as though she hasn't moved at all.

Bethany slams her hands against the water's surface and screams in frustration. This is a prison. She is trapped.

"Let me out!" she screams. "Let me out of here! I want to go home!"

Nothing happens. The birds twitter. The sun shines high in the sky. The water burbles gently as it surges past her waist. And then she remembers something Boy told her. It's not really water. It can't drown her. She keeps walking. The water comes up to her chest, then her shoulders, and then, finally, she disappears below the surface.

For a moment, Bethany panics, imagining that she can't breathe, but she reminds herself of Boy's words and calms herself enough to push forward. It's gloomy down here. The sunlight flickers on the surface above her, but around her is nothing but cloudy water. Thick, like syrup. Her limbs grow tired. She feels as though she's trying to force herself to wake from a bad dream. *Keep walking. Just keep walking.*

35

Lia stared out at the blackness as the sonic shuttle sped through a tunnel deep beneath the ground. Scott, sitting beside her in the first-class carriage, was silent and sullen, and refused to answer any of her questions about where they were going. Not for the first time, Lia felt her life was being shaped by an invisible force too huge and too secretive for her to understand. She supposed this feeling was why some people believed in God, but she suspected something closer to home. There was a whole world out there, after all, that had influenced her life more than she cared to admit, but that she herself had never actually experienced.

She'd never once ventured into the Scape. It was not real, and so it was meaningless to her, and she'd never understood why Erik clung to it the way he did, and took it so seriously. It was a fantasy world, but it had become real to him, and where it had once been his escape, at some stage it had become his curse.

It was very late by the time Lia and Scott—and Scott's minders—disembarked from the shuttle. In the dark, near-deserted station Lia couldn't pinpoint exactly where they were, other than the fact that they were still in Europe—somewhere Eastern, judging by the unfamiliar language on the station signs. Scott had a car waiting for them at the exit, and in moments they were on the move again, speeding down silent, rain-sodden streets past hunkering old Soviet buildings that gradually gave way to a shiny new business district filled with skyscrapers. As Scott's car turned off the road and descended into an underground car park, Lia couldn't help dwelling on what Erik had said earlier that evening, about walking away and never troubling her again. It just didn't ring true. And yet he'd clearly meant it.

The car came to a halt in a parking space close to the elevators. Scott got out of his side, slamming the door hard, but Lia didn't move. An icy horror had gripped her chest and was spreading outward to her limbs, freezing her in place. She wasn't sure she was still breathing. He'd been certain he wouldn't trouble her again, because he was going to make absolutely sure he didn't.

She hadn't said it, though, had she? She hadn't told him to go.

Scott flung her door open impatiently and Lia climbed out of the car.

"I need my phone," she said, her breath steaming in the cold night air.

"Not now," Scott gripped her arm, steering her towards the elevators. "There's something I want to show you."

"It's important!"

"What's the problem? Want to call your other man? Don't you get it? You're never going to see him again." His fingers tightened around her wrist.

"You don't understand!" Lia shouted. "You didn't hear what he said!" She took a deep breath, trying to speak calmly, to appeal to Scott's rational side. "I think he's going to do something stupid."

"Well, it wouldn't be the first time, would it?" Scott said, referring to Erik's well-documented overdose several years earlier. As he dragged her into the elevator, he added, "Let's hope he gets it right this time."

"Please, Scott. I won't ring Erik. Just let me speak to Kent, to warn him. Just in case."

"Forget it. The world will be a better place without him in it."

The lift doors slid closed, and Lia faced him, gasping with fury and horror. "What happened to you, Scott? Who *are* you?"

His matinée-idol mask looked back at her, all charm. "Something more than you think, Li. You'll soon see. What I can offer you—it's so much more than he ever could. Before long, you won't even remember him."

They sped upwards, ascending over a hundred floors before the elevator came to a halt. When the doors opened, Scott nodded for Lia to get out ahead of him. She stepped into a vast, empty space that stretched across an entire floor of the skyscraper, full height windows looking out onto the darkened city. The only things in the room were a cluster of computer equipment, and four black leather couches, one of which was occupied by a pale, dark-haired girl in a white hospital gown. A man in a lab coat hovered over her, moving from one blinking machine to another, making notes and checking her pulse.

"How did the transfer go, Professor Gendry?"

The doctor looked up, widening his eyes in surprise on seeing Lia. "Er … Everything looks to be stable, Mr Lincoln. There was a moment when we almost lost track of the girl's consciousness, but we recovered her. She seems to be taking to her new environment well enough."

"Then you'll be able to start the severance process soon?"

"Soon enough. Yes, I think so."

Lia approached the girl's bedside. The sight of the Corona around her head brought back a flood of memories. She had that corpse-like look that Erik always had when he was Scaping.

"She's only a child." Lia crouched to get a better look at her. "Who is she? What is she doing here?"

"This child ..." Scott stood over them, arms folded, looking for all the world like a proud father. "This child is our key, Li. She's our way out. We don't have to be troubled by Erik Dacre, or anyone, ever again. You and I can be together, just the two of us, in our very own world."

Lia stood, numb with astonishment. "But who is she, Scott? Doesn't she have a family? Parents? What are you doing to her?"

"Her name is Bethany, I believe," Professor Gendry explained. "The girl became lost in the DreamScape. The parents have given us permission to do whatever we need to do to preserve her consciousness. In return for full payment of all medical bills."

"Everything's above board." Scott waved her concerns away, as if this was all just a game. "Nothing for you to worry about."

"Bethany." Lia looked at the girl, the banks of computers, the glittering cityscape beyond them all. She'd heard that name somewhere, recently. The girl who'd sought her out outside the Opera House, wanting to speak to Erik. This was her sister.

"He was right, wasn't he?" she whispered. "Erik. He recognised you from somewhere. From the DreamScape. You—you're not who I thought you were, so who the hell are you?"

"I'm exactly who you think I am—here. I'm Scott Lincoln. But in there," he indicated the Corona, "in there I'm so much more, Li. In there, I'm a God."

Exhausted, with nothing to do but watch Scott and Professor Gendry pouring over incomprehensible charts and computer readouts, Lia fell asleep on one of the couches alongside Bethany. When she woke, it was daylight, and someone had left a takeaway coffee and a couple of croissants on the table near her. Bethany was still there, still sleeping, but Scott and Gendry had gone.

Lia sat up, trying to stretch the crick out of her neck, and reflexively went to check her phone. The discovery that it was nowhere to be found reminded her, with a lurch of her stomach, why she'd wanted to contact Erik the night before. He had meant to kill himself. She was sure of that. It was nothing he hadn't tried before, but before it had been the impulse of a moment. This time he had planned it, even told her outright. "Tell me you never want to see me again, and I promise you won't." Of course, she'd assumed at the time that he only meant to walk out of her life and stay out. That was what he'd meant her to assume. But she knew Erik. As far as he was concerned, she was the only thing tying him to the real world. He would never have been able to stay away.

Or perhaps, tired and confused after the long trip with Scott, she'd let her imagination run away with her. Perhaps she just really didn't want to believe that Erik would let her go that easily. If only she could try and get in touch with him, put her mind at rest …

"Ah, you're up." Scott stepped out of an elevator, smiling broadly despite looking as though he hadn't slept. "Don't you want your breakfast? If the coffee's cold I can send for another one."

"I'm fine, thanks," Lia replied, coldly.

Scott frowned. "You should eat. I want you to keep your strength up."

"What for?" Lia scanned the room, the computer equipment, the medical monitors, and Bethany, lying in the midst of it all with the Corona flickering at her temples. "What are you planning to do to me?"

"Do to you?" Scott sat beside her, looking concerned. "Heck, Lia. I don't want to do anything to you. I want you to understand. I want you to choose me. I think if you understood what I can offer you, you would."

"I did choose you. I married you."

Scott shook his head. "But you were never really mine, were you? I love you, Li. I just want us to be together. Just the two of us, somewhere we can be alone."

"Somewhere in there?" Lia nodded towards Bethany's Corona. "In the DreamScape?"

"In there, we can live forever. We can be gods. You don't see it now, but you will when I show you."

"We don't need to be gods," Lia said, desperately. All she wanted was to get her phone back so she could contact Erik or, at least take a look at the news. "We have everything we could possibly want right here. Oh, Scott, let's just go home. Let this poor girl go back to her family and come back to London with me. You don't need to do all this."

Scott narrowed his eyes. "You think I'm crazy."

"No, no, I ..."

"You're trying to mollify me. I'm not stupid, and even if I was, you're a terrible liar." He smiled indulgently, but there was something chilling about the look in his eyes. "It's one of the things I love best about you. Or it was. Perhaps we'd both be a lot happier if you could lie to me and I could believe you."

"Scott," Lia put a hand on top of his and tried to speak as honestly as she could. "I have history, we both know that. You may not like it, but I come with a lot of baggage. I can't help it. The past is the past, but if you can't trust me then what do we have to build a future on? Does it really make any difference whether we're in the DreamScape or out here?"

Scott shook his head slowly. "You say the past is the past, so how come the past keeps showing up on your door-step?"

"I don't want to talk about Erik. I want to talk about us." Lia managed to keep her voice steady and looked him in the eye, forcing herself to ignore the clamour of anxiety that was reaching screaming levels inside of her head.

Scott pushed her hand away. "We've talked enough. It's time you understood. Who I am. Who he is. You once told me you never went inside the DreamScape, is that right? You never saw what this other life of his was really like, did you? Perhaps it's time you took a look. You might learn something."

36

There was one possible advantage to all this, Lia told herself as she sat on the couch and let Scott attach a Corona to her head: being in the DreamScape would at least connect her to the world outside this skyscraper. Perhaps if she could figure out how to work the thing, she could get a message to Erik.

"Do I have to take this?" she asked when Scott handed her a small red tablet. She had plenty of second-hand experience of Slip, and that had always been enough to put her off ever letting the drug pass her lips.

"I wouldn't recommend going in there without it," Scott replied. "It helps your body and mind deal with the experience."

Lia held the tiny pill between her finger and thumb. Perhaps it had always been inevitable that she would reach this point eventually. She'd just never imagined it would be Scott who pushed her into it. She popped the pill into her mouth and washed it down with a gulp of lukewarm coffee, then lay back with her hands folded over her stomach, and waited.

Professor Gendry bustled around them, fiddling with equipment and taking readings, while Scott fitted his own Corona and lay beside Lia. She looked over at him.

"Why didn't you ever tell me you visited the Dream-Scape?" she asked him.

Scott gave her an incredulous look. "Would you have married me if I had?"

"No, you're right." Lia sighed. "I married you because I thought you were worlds away from all of this. Because I wanted to be worlds away from it all. This place is the touch of death, Scott. It destroys everyone who ventures into it. It makes me so sad to think that it got you, too."

"You don't need to be sad. You just can't see, Li. It doesn't have to be destructive. There's so much potential, but nobody has ever truly managed to harness it. Gendry and I are close. Damn close." He turned to the professor. "Log us in, Gendry."

Lia stared at the ceiling, coloured lights dancing in front of her eyes. For a while, nothing much happened, and then her vision blurred, and the world slid sideways as a syrupy warmth oozed through her body.

Slowly, she became aware of murmuring voices. Shapes drifted though the emptiness around her, and gradually she made out figures. People in white, Grecian robes drifted through a space made of pure ice. Pillars stretched high above her, curving over her head. It was beautiful, but cold. She shivered.

"Hello, Lia."

She turned. Scott was there, himself but different. Younger, with longer hair, and smooth, expressionless features. He wore a toga draped around his muscular form. She, too, was dressed in a Grecian style, barefoot in a gold dress that cascaded to the floor like a waterfall. She touched her hair, to find it piled on top of her head.

"You look beautiful," Scott smiled. "Absolutely perfect."

"So strange." Lia turned her hands over. "They look like real hands, but not like my hands. It's like I've been swapped into a different body. How do you ever get used to it?"

Scott shrugged. "I guess I never thought about it much. Come on, let me show you around."

He led her through the great chamber, passing groups of people with candy-coloured hair, who watched them go by through blank, soulless eyes.

"What is this place?" she asked, as they passed into a narrow corridor lit by a white glow. "It looks like a church."

She trailed her hand along the ice wall, and it melted slightly beneath her touch, leaving her fingers damp.

"It is a church. I designed it myself," Scott replied.

"A church for who?"

"Hypnos."

"Hypnos?" She followed him through a doorway into a peaceful Japanese garden, cool stones beneath her feet. "And who or what is that?"

There were a handful of people already in the garden, talking quietly and drinking from small china cups. They looked up at the sound of Lia's voice.

"Apollo!" A woman with violet hair scrambled to her feet and bowed her head. "Your worship. Your visit is an unexpected honour. Will you drink with us? And your companion too, of course."

Lia cast a sidelong glance at Scott. "Apollo?"

"You don't expect me to go by my real name, surely?"

he said, in a low voice, before turning to the woman. "We would be delighted."

He sat down to join the group, and Lia followed suit, trying to avoid eye-contact with the strange, not-quite-people who stared at her.

"Will you have a drink?" One of the men filled a teacup with golden liquid and tried to pass it to Lia. She shook her head.

"No, thank you."

"You should," Scott said, and Lia recognised the tinge of impatience beneath his mellow tone. "It'll help you relax."

Lia accepted the cup and took the tiniest sip she dared. It tasted like mead, and it *was* relaxing. She had a little more.

"Hestia." Scott turned to the violet-haired woman. "My friend is new here. Can you answer her question? 'Who or what is Hypnos'?"

Hestia's eyes widened and she turned to Lia with a look of fervour. "You don't know Hypnos?" she said, in amazement. "I almost envy you. Having my eyes opened to Him was the most sublime experience of my life. Hypnos is the life-force of this whole world. He is everywhere, everything. He watches over us, protects us, shows us the way to freedom."

"Freedom?"

"To be in the Dream is to be free," Hestia explained, breathlessly. "Hypnos helps us see the way to shedding our mortal selves and becoming part of the Dream for eternity. That is what we all work towards."

"How many of you are there?" Lia asked, horror creeping up her spine.

"Oh, thousands, I'm sure. And more every day. There

are many churches like this."

Lia looked at Scott, who smiled benignly. His smooth, blank face betrayed even less than the mask he wore in real life. His eyes reflected her own surprise back at her, like mirrors.

"You see," he said. "Here, we believe that the Dream-Scape is the key to immortality. Hypnos has followers all over the world, researching and testing and doing whatever they can to forward our goal."

Lia shook her head in amazement. "A cult. You've started a cult."

"I started nothing. I am only a guide."

"I don't believe you."

Scott got to his feet. "Come with me. Let's talk in private."

"No, let's talk here." Lia stood, looking at the assembled fanatics. "Do they know who you are? Do they know what you're doing out there, in the real world? That girl, Bethany—was she one of your followers?"

Scott put a hand on her arm. Lia shrugged it off.

"I helped Bethany," he said. "She was lost, and I found her. Tell her what happens to the lost people, Hestia."

"When somebody becomes lost in the DreamScape," Hestia recited, as though from a script, "the connection between their mind and body severs. Their body remains outside in the Mono—the real world, as you call it, although we don't like that term here, since the Dream is as real as anywhere else. The lost one's mind is left as part of the Dream's code, gradually disintegrating and becoming confused with the rest of the program until there is nothing left to distinguish the person from the world around them. They lose the power of independent thought, their memories, their sense of self. But if we could prevent that from happening," she glanced at Scott, who nodded, "if we could prevent that from happening, we would be able to upload souls to the DreamScape and allow them to escape their corporeal bodies and live for ever."

"And that," said Scott, "is what I've been able to do with Bethany. I have tracked down the code that makes up her mind and isolated it. Her mind can be returned to her body, or, if our experiment is successful, it can be released from its physical bounds and become pure code—but thinking, feeling, intelligent code. It will retain the essence of Bethany. Her soul, as it were."

"If your experiment is successful."

"The severance process is a delicate one, but we've learnt from our mistakes. Gendry thinks he can make this one work."

"You're deluded," Lia said, softly. "My God, I always thought Erik had lost his grip on reality, but you … What you're doing is evil. Can't you see that?"

"What we're doing is securing the future of humanity. Our planet is dying, our world is crumbling. This place …" Scott spread his hands, encompassing the whole of the tranquil garden and everything beyond. "This is heaven. This is where we're meant to be." He paused, and perhaps this would have been the moment when he sighed, or took a breath, had he been real. But he was not, and his avatar remained eerily still. "This is a lot for you to take in all at once. I must be patient." He raised a hand, moved his fingers in some mysterious way, and all of a sudden Gendry's voice floated into Lia's consciousness.

"Mr Lincoln, what can I do for you?"

Hestia and the others didn't show any reaction to the

disembodied voice, and Lia concluded that she and Scott were the only ones who could hear him. Nevertheless, Scott took a few steps away from them all before answering.

"I want you to start the isolation process on Lia," he said.

"Are you sure? There are a few issues to be ironed out. Bethany's mind is still fighting the severance. I may need to start the process over again."

Scott glanced at Lia, and she saw a jealous determination in his eyes. "Just do it," he said, dismissing Gendry with a sweep of his arm. He put a hand on Lia's shoulder.

"I wanted to let you come around to my way of thinking in your own time, Li, but I can see you're going to take a while to convince. I *will* convince you, I promise, but we should really get started. I can't risk Thanatos … Dacre, I mean … interfering before I've shown you what eternal life is like."

"I don't want to live forever. Not like this." Lia looked at her blemishless, puppet hands. "This isn't life."

"You never need to feel pain again, Li. Just think about that. No pain, hunger, illness. No growing older and watching life slip away from us. We can live in any paradise we can dream up, create a perfect world. Hell," he smiled, "we could create a couple of kids if you wanted."

"No," Lia shook her head. "No, you just don't understand. That's not what I want. It was never what I wanted. You've been trying to tie me down ever since I married you and I don't … I can't be that person. You talk about having a perfect world, a perfect life, but it's all so flat, so false. This is not living. Let me go, Scott. I'm not what you want. You need to realise that now, and not when you've trapped us here together for eternity."

Scott's glassy eyes stared back at her. She couldn't be

sure he was even listening. Desperately, she wondered whether Erik was in the DreamScape right now—if he was even still alive. If she thought hard enough, could she find some way to connect with him? But she was out of her depth entirely. This world was vast, and she had no idea how any of it worked.

"I'll see you soon, Li," Scott said, without emotion. "The isolation process will seem strange, perhaps even scary to you, but try not to panic. You're perfectly safe. Gendry and I will be keeping a very close eye on you."

Lia wasn't sure if that was supposed to be comforting or threatening. It certainly felt like the latter.

Scott led her out of the Japanese garden and back into the ice corridors. They walked for some time, weaving their way through tight spaces and around corners until Lia felt she was in a maze. And then, all of a sudden, she rounded a corner to find herself in a dead end. She turned around, but Scott was nowhere to be seen, and neither was the entrance she had just come through. She was entirely surrounded by walls. Encased in ice. She ran her hands across its surface, searching for a handle or a button or anything that would let her out, but the ice was relentlessly smooth and featureless.

"Scott! Scott!" she screamed. "Let me out! For God's sake, let me out!"

37

"Well, we're screwed."

Wren looked at Kazuo, who had spoken, and then out at the empty black void in front of them. She and Erik had met Kazuo, Andromeda, and Delphi on the beach, ready to head underwater and back into Erik's cave, and it didn't take a genius of Kazuo's level to spot the glaring problem with their plan. The rampant code that had once been Gade Sorensen had finally engulfed the sky and the sea, and a huge chunk of the beach itself. It was growing by the second. There was no way they could reach the control room now.

"Now what?" asked Delphi in a quiet voice, backing away from both the cliff-edge where the beach met the void, and from Erik, who seemed to intimidate her here even more than he had in the Mono world. Erik, however, didn't seem to have noticed her, or the others. He stared at the darkness, deep in thought.

"We tried to use the control room to find Bethany," Andromeda said, placing a gentle hand on Wren's arm, "after you disappeared. But the virus got in. It tore the place apart.

We had to leave. I'm sorry."

All Wren could think of was Reza, or what was left of him. Andromeda had done so much for her—Wren owed it to her to tell her the truth. But even as she opened her mouth to speak, she found she couldn't. Perhaps Erik was right. Would Wren have wanted to know if Bethany had ended up like that? It seemed a fate worse than death. She couldn't bring herself to destroy Andromeda's hope, but that didn't stop the guilt from gnawing at her.

She felt like crying. The control room had been their only chance. Their only lead. And now it was gone, or as good as. What could she possibly do now?

"Is there another way into the cave?" she asked. "What about the other Marks?"

Erik shook his head. "It's not just that the portal is gone. The cave is gone, too. When you entered the credentials to get the control room up and running, you let that … thing in, too. The code for the cave has been completely destroyed. Even the control room itself may not exist anymore. Nice work," he added, bitterly.

Wren looked at Kazuo. "The virus …"

"It tricked us," Kazuo finished. "Me. It tricked *me*. All it needed was for somebody to enter those credentials, so it made it easy for me. I thought I was such a genius, but it was leading me by the hand the whole time. Jeez, Wren. I'm so sorry."

Wren shook her head. "Not your fault. Not at all."

"You said you had a theory about what happened to Gade," Erik said. Wren could see that he was already putting two and two together, and as Kazuo explained about Sorensen uploading himself into the DreamScape and spreading his consciousness like a virus, Erik listened closely.

"Sounds like Gade," he said, nodding. "Or, rather, sounds like the way Gade was starting to talk towards the end of his life. He wasn't a bad guy, you understand? He meant this place to be some kind of utopia. A place where humanity could co-exist peacefully, without the fear of war, famine, pain, or environmental disaster."

As he spoke, Erik led the way up the dunes, out of the reach of the encroaching darkness.

"He had a plan to create a huge mine shaft in Venezuela and bury the servers deep beneath the Earth, where they would remain unharmed by anything that happened to the planet. Then we could all upload our consciousnesses to the Scape and live forever. Just as soon as he figured out how to keep us all alive."

"That's insane," Delphi said.

Erik gave a half-shrug. "Pretty much everything in here is insane. You get used to it, or you get out."

"You didn't subscribe to this craziness, did you?" Wren asked.

"I don't believe in heaven. I sure don't believe this place is it. This place is a curse. It chips away at your sanity bit by little bit until you hardly know who you are anymore, much less what's real and what's not. Nobody could survive in here and remain the same person they were outside, not even if Gade had perfected the system and found a way to keep a mind intact without the presence of a body. It's too batshit crazy in here. There's nothing to keep us rooted."

"If you think it's so bad, why keep coming back all these years?"

Erik sat down on one of the dunes, and the others joined him.

"At first, it was fun. I just wanted to escape my life. But after a while, you get to the point where this is the only place you feel real. I can't stay in the Mono for more than a few days at a stretch or I lose my mind. I never sleep. I see all sorts of shit that's not there. I get paranoid; I forget who I am and what's really happening." He shook his head. "It's withdrawal. I know it. But I can't do it, and even if I wanted to, there are people here who need me. Thanks to Hypnos. He always believed in Gade's bullshit. I think he got impatient, pushed Gade into trying to upload himself before they knew it would be a success, just so that he could see what happened. Now he's trying it with all these other poor suckers, getting closer to what he thinks is the holy grail of immortality."

"What do you think he wants with Lia?"

"I'm not sure. Perhaps he knew who I really was all along. It wouldn't've been difficult to figure out that if he kept Lia away from me, I would start to fall apart. Maybe he was trying to push me into destroying myself so that he could have total control. Or maybe he really does love her. Fuck knows, and frankly I don't care. But when he took her—and I'm sure he's taken her—there can only have been one thing on his mind. I've got no doubt that he intends to upload her into the Scape."

"So, what do we do now?" Wren asked. "The control room is gone. I'm out of ideas."

"There's only one thing we *can* do," Erik replied, darkly. "We need to speak to Gade. We need to go into the void."

"We can't do that!" Delphi spoke up. "We'll all get lost. That's right, isn't it, Andromeda? That's how Bethany and all the others got lost, by falling into these voids."

"That's what I believe happened to them," Andromeda

replied. "I could be wrong."

"No, you're right," Erik said. "You venture in there and the system won't be able to keep track of you. I wouldn't ask you to do that. Any of you," he added, looking pointedly at Wren. "I'll go in. I'll do whatever I can, for Bethany as well as for Lia."

"It's a suicide mission," Kazuo pointed out. "We might never be able to get you out."

Erik shrugged. "I'm living on borrowed time now. I should be dead already. Who the hell cares?"

He got up, heading for the blackness with grim determination, almost as though he wanted to be a part of it.

Wren fell into step beside him. "I want to come too."

Erik stopped. "There's just no getting rid of you, is there? Fuck's sake, go home. Or, hey, if you want to be useful, try and find out where Lia and your sister are in the Mono world. There's no use us releasing them from the Scape if they wake up still in his hands."

"Kazuo and the others can do that," Wren replied. "Right Kaz? Can you find a way to track them down?"

"I am offended that you even have to ask," Kazuo said, in a haughty tone. "It'll be a piece of cake. Getting to wherever they are might be another matter, though."

"I'll transfer you some credits," Erik said. "Enough to get all three of you to wherever you need to go."

"All *four* of us," Delphi said. "Right, Wren? You need to be there when your sister wakes up."

Wren looked at her friends and then back at the rupture. "No, I've come this far. I want to go in."

"There's no point arguing with her," Erik said. "Believe me, she doesn't quit." He started walking again.

Wren was about to follow when Delphi darted over and

hugged her tightly.

"Good luck," she said.

"Don't worry about me. I'll see you guys on the other side, all right?"

"I'm tracking you as best I can," said Kazuo.

Andromeda smiled sadly. "I'd tell you I'd pray to Hypnos for you, but …"

"We don't need him," Wren grinned. "Not with the Dark God on our side." She turned to hurry after Erik, who was already halfway down the beach. Where she met him, sand poured into the void, turning back into pixels as it vanished.

Erik held out his hand. "We'd better keep hold of each other."

Wren nodded, took his hand, and they stepped into the darkness together.

38

First, there is darkness. Then something moves. The slightest flicker, accompanied by a tiny crinkling sound, like the beating of a moth's wings. A second later there is another movement, and this time there is enough light for Bethany to see, faintly. A pair of black, blinking eyes stares back at her. To her horror, as she creeps her way into the emerging light, still dripping with water, she realises there is not one, not two, not even a dozen, but hundreds of pairs of eyes watching her.

Worse are the outlines of the bodies connected to the many eyes. Strange, half-human things with spiders' legs, and wooden heads, and sprouting vines growing out of their ears. Bethany is ready to turn straight back to where she came from, but when she spins around, she finds yet more of them clustering around her, clawed hands reaching for her, twisted faces gawping, fascinated. Incomprehensible sounds rise from their throats—a babble of subhuman squawks and clicks, and the remnants of language, long forgotten.

"Get off me!" She pushes through the rabble in a rising

panic. "Don't touch me!"

Her voice echoes off the high ceiling and bounces around, mockingly. *"Touch me ... uch me ... uch me ..."*

Crooked stone pillars stretch up and overhead. Tall windows stain the hall with a blood-red hue. A cathedral, but one straight out of her worst nightmares.

Up ahead is a stage of some kind—an altar rising out of the sea of deformed creatures. Bethany elbows her way towards it, thrusting feathers and fingers out of her face, tugging her skirt from the grip of some rabid, dog-like thing, before clambering onto the relative safety of the dais. She stumbles back against the altar, looking down at the monsters, and to her surprise, the noise of their chatter dies away. They stare up at her in rapt silence, as if waiting for her to speak.

"Where am I?" she asks, in a voice that is little more than a whisper, but which rings out crystal clear through the cathedral.

The creatures look at her, and then at one another, and then a wooden figure steps forward, nudged by some of them, like an elected spokesperson. He moves slowly, dragging one heavy leg along behind him.

"This is the Dark God's place," he says, in a creaking voice.

"The ... Dark God? How did I get here?"

The wooden creature shakes his head. He does not know.

"You're Bethany," he says.

"Yes. How do you know my name?"

"They were looking for you."

"They?"

"The Dark God and ... and a girl."

Bethany raises her eyebrows. "A girl?"

"He called her …" The wooden creature frowns. "He called her Wren, I think."

"Wren?" Bethany's world switches from black and white to full Technicolour. "Wren's here? She's looking for me?" For the first time since she's been drifting here, there's some real hope. Something to focus on. "Where did she go? How can I find her?"

"She was with the Dark God," the wooden creature says, as if this is a satisfactory answer. "They went … elsewhere."

"Great." Bethany sits down on the edge of the dais, her hope crashing down all around her. "So, Wren came in here to find me and now I'm here and she's gone. That's just great."

"Use the raven," the wooden creature suggests. For a moment, Bethany is puzzled, then she notices the statue in the middle of the altar: a black raven with spread wings. She gets up and approaches it with trepidation.

"What does it do?"

"The Dark God uses the raven symbols to move about the DreamScape. Where it will take you … I'm not sure."

"Well …" Bethany holds a hand above the raven, hesitating. "Better than hanging around here, I guess."

"You really don't like to make things easy for yourself, do you?"

Bethany recognises the voice at once, and knows that something has gone badly wrong. Boy crouches in front of her, handsome as ever, his expression sorrowful, almost pitying. Around her is nothing but ice, as far as the eye can see.

"Where are we?" Bethany shivers. "What are you going to do to me?"

"I had to isolate your signature again." Boy sounds older than he should. "You shouldn't have left. You've only made him angry."

"Who?"

"You know who."

"Hypnos? Sorry, I can't keep up with all these crazies. It was the Dark God everyone was going on about a moment ago."

Boy looks taken aback. "The Dark God?"

"My sister's with him." Bethany grins, enjoying knowing something that he doesn't. "They'll find me, I'm sure of it."

Boy looks puzzled for a moment, then gets to his feet.

"Nevertheless," he says, "it doesn't matter right now. I've got to perform the severance process right away. Do you know what that means?"

Bethany shrugs.

"We sever your consciousness from your physical body completely. You'll continue to exist here, in the Dream-Scape, but your body in the Mono? That will die. Brain death. A ventilator could keep it alive, but why bother? It'll be a vegetable, nothing more. But don't worry." Boy raises his eyebrows at Bethany's alarmed expression. "You will be fine. You'll be here, just as you arc now. You probably won't even notice the difference."

Bethany launches herself at him, grips his arms, frantic. "I don't want to die! I don't want to be here! I want to go home."

"Don't worry," Boy repeats, infuriatingly calm. "You'll be fine." Gently, he prises her hands off one of his arms, then the other. "Don't go anywhere. You'll only make the process more difficult if you do."

He takes a few steps back, turns away, and vanishes. Bethany is left looking at the blank ice wall. Despair floods her, leaving her limbs heavy as lead. She sinks onto the cold ground, her legs curling beneath her, and just as she starts to cry, she hears a voice say her name.

"Bethany?"

It is a kind voice. A familiar one. Bethany turns to see the beautiful woman from the train, only this time Bethany is sure she's is a real person, not just part of a game. Something about her eyes is different. More alive. She sits on the floor, leaning against the wall, looking exhausted. She smiles, but sadly.

"Are you all right?" she asks, and when Bethany shakes her head, she adds, "I'm sorry he brought you back."

"Who are you?" Bethany asks.

"My name is Lia. That boy you just spoke to—he's not really a boy. His name is Professor Gendry. And the person telling him what to do is, I'm sorry to say, my husband."

39

The darkness was total. It took a while for Wren to realise she'd stopped falling. She sensed that the blackness surrounding her was not mere empty space, but a living creature, dispersed like atoms into the air. With each breath in, she inhaled it. With each breath out, she exhaled some, but not all. It was slowly filling up her lungs. Filling up her body. She was almost part of it.

Remembering where she was, Wren stopped breathing. It didn't help. The need to breathe was all in her mind, but so was her illusion of control over the invader. It carried on seeping into her skin, crawling up her veins, muddling its thoughts with hers. She sensed a deep, unfathomable anger, bitterness, disappointment and, above all, confusion. A wild, furious confusion, like a caged animal. *Why is this happening? Why, in this place where I, above all others, should belong?*

"Wren?"

Erik's voice was a handle Wren could grasp, holding herself firm against the ebb and flow of the creature's emotions.

"I'm here," she said, thinly.

"Okay. Just … hold on, all right?" Erik was trying to sound reassuring, but his voice was strained. Despair lapped over Wren in icy waves. She'd stepped into this black pit with someone who, just a few short hours ago, had been seriously considering taking his own life. Someone who had spent so much time in the DreamScape already, with Gade's code eating away at his mind, atomising his sense of self. How stupid she'd been to expect him to hold it together here, in the black heart of the beast.

"How do you feel?" she asked. She turned around in the darkness, but there was nothing to see, no way to figure out where he was—if he was anywhere at all.

"I hate the night," he said, in a dull voice. "I always felt like it was alive. Breathing. Creeping under my skin, twisting my thoughts, driving me insane. I hate it. I fucking hate it."

"Erik …" Wren began, but he cut her off. Wren wasn't sure he was even talking to her, exactly.

"Why do I have to live here, when other people live in the light? Lia … She always lived in the light. She was like the light at the end of the tunnel, and I could never quite reach her. I never could … The harder I tried, the further away she seemed to get."

"Erik, you have to focus. We came here for a reason. We need to find Lia, remember? We need to figure out if Gade knows where she is. How do we talk to him?"

"We don't need to talk to him. He's here. Everywhere."

The sickness. The pain. The ache, so deep in his muscles that it became him. His joints pooled with acid. His tongue was dry, his skin bruised and punctured with the pinpricks of so many needles.

Cancer. Gade's body was eating itself from the inside, the black dread multiplying, feeding on his cells, consuming everything.

And along with it all, the fear. Fear of dying. It would hit him at some unexpected moment, kicking the ground out from beneath him. making his stomach lurch. To cease to exist? To become nothing? It was incomprehensible. How could it all end like that, when there was so much more to do? So much to learn, so much to experience?

He stood on the brink of a cliff, and all he saw below was emptiness.

It could not be. It would not be. He would not end. Not now. Not like this.

"Erik?"

"Do you feel that?" Erik sounded far away. "The thoughts?"

"We need to get out of here. This is … this is too much."

"This is Gade. His feelings, his thoughts. When he came here, he was dying. He wanted to cheat death. That's what preoccupied him when he uploaded his consciousness. We have to ride it out. The answers we need are here some-where."

"That's easy for you to say." Even as she said it, Wren knew she was being unfair, but still she went on, "You wanted to die. I don't want to die. I can't."

"You're not gonna die, Wren. This is Gade, not you. Ride it out. The sun always comes up eventually, right? That's what I tell myself."

"Then why were you going to do it?"

Silence fell between them like a heavy velvet curtain.

It was Hypnos who gave him the answer. The golden son. The one Gade had always loved best. He brought the solution.

Too soon, though. Too soon.

Had love made him suggest it? A desire to save his patron before it was too late? Or was it malice that made him tell Gade the technology was ready when it was not. Did he hope for a miracle? Or did he truly want to tear Gade's soul to shreds?

Perhaps he was simply indifferent.

That seemed the worst answer, somehow. The idea that Hypnos just did not care. For himself, Gade could almost have forgiven that, but for his world, his baby, his creation? It was not ready. It had rejected him, and now he had been made the agent of its destruction. He could feel it falling apart everywhere he turned. Everything he did made it worse. He had been destroyed by cancer, but now he was the cancer. He couldn't forgive Hypnos for that.

"Do you ever feel," came Erik's voice, "that you're battling to put one foot in front of the other, fighting to keep moving, all to get somewhere you don't even want to be? Aren't there times when you wish it would just … stop?"

Wren thought about this, as the blackness that was Gade Sorensen's mind crawled over her like a flood of spiders. There was something oddly comforting in Erik's bleak view. Like a huge grey blanket that she could just crawl under and hide beneath—hide from the world, from everything that was hard.

"I guess," she said. "Sometimes, when things with Jared got really bad, I wished it would all just stop. But there was always somewhere I wanted to be, and that was away."

"Imagine if the thing you wanted to get away from was inside you. You can stretch away from it for a bit, maybe forget about it for a day, a week—a year, even—but it's always there, and there always comes the day when you feel it turning over in your stomach, black and feathery. I can't rationalise what I was going to do, because that thing's not rational. It made sense to me, clear as day. It was like I could see a truth that no-one else had noticed. I could never give Lia up. Never, as long as I live. But she deserves better, so if I was ever going to stop dragging her down alongside me and let her get on with her life …"

"You had to go."

"I don't see any other way out of this. Do you think I'm going to fucking settle down and live to a ripe old age? I'm just staving off the inevitable, one goddamn step at a time."

"Think of Lia," Wren said. "Concentrate. How are we going to find her. Where has Scott taken her? Perhaps if we think hard enough, focus our minds on what we need, Gade will respond in some way."

Balance.

There had been a need for balance. Hypnos might have been made of gold, but he was cold, hard, like the metal. He was an optimist. He saw the potential in the DreamScape, but his need to realise it was insatiable, unfettered by any sense of morality or, indeed, reality. Thanatos, on the other hand … He saw the world for what it was, not what it could be. Locked in an unending dream, yet a pragmatist all the same. Or a pessimist, perhaps. He was emotional and filled with anger, a burning coal smouldering in the heart of Gade's creation. But he cared. He cared enough to make a home for all those who did not fit in the real world. The directionless, the dispossessed. All he wanted was a place to escape to.

It is clear to Gade now. This must end. He struggles to form thoughts, scattered as he now is, but this one is clear to him. This must end.

He cannot go on this way, a parasite eating away at his own creation. He can sense Thanatos here, though he cannot see or hear. All his input comes through code now, and he recognises the unique signature of Thanatos' consciousness. It is a comfort to him. The charismatic boy he once took on as an apprentice, whom he has grown to love, in as much as he, through his lonely existence, ever loved anyone. Ever since he found himself here, lost and alone, Gade has been trying to speak to him. The Dark God, with his ability to create or destroy. The Dark God must release him.

He lets his consciousness crawl into Thanatos' code, encircling it, changing it here and there. Just enough to make him understand. The thought will come to him, as if it were his own.

"We have to kill him," Erik said. "This is no existence for anyone. And once we do, we should be able to get back to the control room."

"All right. But how do we do it?"

"We need to overwrite his code."

"With what?"

"With ourselves, I guess. We're all we've got." He paused. "You seem like you'd be good at this. You know who you are. Where you feel him creeping in, push back. Just keep pushing back, all right? Make yourself bigger, stronger. Take that light inside of you and push it outward."

At first, Wren thought he was talking nonsense, but she pushed all the same, wedging her thoughts against the creeping darkness, trying to force the light through. And then she saw it. A brightness where her fingers ought to be. She focused her thoughts on the faint glow, and it grew stronger, more powerful, flooding up her hands, up her arms, into the centre of her body.

"You've got it!" Erik said. "I see you." His own light was getting brighter, too.

Wren mustered all her strength and kept forcing her way outward, taking up the space she deserved. She thought of Jared, who had tried to crush her, and imagined he was the force of darkness holding her back. But Gade was no Jared. He wanted this. He yielded in the face of her determination, and before long she could see not just her own body, but the water around it: the sea they would have walked into if the void had not been there.

Alongside her, Erik was becoming more solid, too, his outline filled with black light. He was growing by the second now that he had gotten hold of Gade's code, and Wren, weak with effort, let him take over, watching as his light flooded her entire vision. It was dark and bright all at once. She was blinded, her mind burning with the sensation that she was being pulled apart, atom by atom, stretched out in every possible direction, across all possible planes of existence. And then she snapped back in on herself like a rubber band let go, and there was nothing.

40

"Well, this is interesting."

Wren's vision flickered like a broken-down image on a computer screen. One moment, a blurred face was looking down at her, and then, all of a sudden, a shadowy figure was coming toward her from much further away, before the scene switched back to the close-up. It was as if she were re-living moments in the wrong order.

"Fuuck."

The groan was unmistakably Erik. Wren tried to turn her head, but the movement made her vision lurch. She saw the inside of an old-fashioned train, tables set for dinner. Her gaze lingered on the silverware, and then the image flickered again—a beautiful, blue-eyed face. Lia's face, sort of. A bland, avatar Lia. Her lips moved but Wren couldn't make out a word. Another jump, and she was looking into a vast canyon. Another, and she was studying crazed, dancing paintings on a cave wall. Another, and she was being dragged down a corridor made of ice into this cold, bare room. Here, now.

The present moment finally settled down, her vision

cleared, and the face watching her became recognisable.

"Apollo?"

"Is that what you're calling yourself these days?" Erik struggled to sit up, propping himself on his elbows. He looked as though he was coming round from the worst hangover ever. Wren was sure she didn't look much better.

"He's a priest," said Wren. "A priest of Hypnos, apparently. I met him before." And then she looked at Apollo and Erik—their eyes locked across the frozen room—and the bland smile that spread across Apollo's smooth features, and she understood.

"Or more than just a priest." She scrambled to her feet to face him. "You! It was you all along, and you stood there and lied to my face!"

Apollo—Hypnos, Scott, whoever he was—shrugged. "I told you what was true."

"Oh yeah, well tell me now, you arsehole: where is my sister? Where. Is. My. Sister?"

Scott turned to Erik. "I'm really fascinated," he said. "I've got to know. What did you do? I picked up some weird readings coming from the middle of damn near nowhere, and all I could see was a load of Gade's messed up code. Then, next thing I knew, it was all being written over by you two. You wiped him out, just like that." He clicked his fingers. "But you left yourselves completely vulnerable. So, I isolated your signatures and brought you here because, well, how could I resist?" He crouched close to Erik, spitting the words: "You're lost, Dark God. Your connection to your body has been severed. You're not going back to the Mono. Either of you. The only person who knows where you are is me."

"Do you think you can keep me here?" Erik sprawled on

the icy ground, propped up on his hands, yet somehow, he had more presence in that room than Wren thought she'd ever manage to muster in her lifetime. He raised his eyebrows lazily, as though the answer to his question was so obvious that it was a waste of energy for either of them to contemplate.

"You're not in the Scape, Dacre. This is my private server. You have no power here."

"Don't I?" Erik ran a hand across the ice and examined his damp fingertips. "The code's not bad. Who wrote that? Not you, obviously. We both know you don't write code."

Scott turned away, irritably. "You sit here and ponder who built the place, if that's what you want. I've got work to do."

"Work. Is that what you call it? Kidnapping people and severing their minds from their bodies? Isn't that more like a hobby for you? Must be an expensive hobby, but I guess Gade's fortune helps with that, right?"

Scott faced him. "What makes you think Gade left me anything?"

"Well, he sure as fuck didn't leave it to me, and last I checked he didn't have a lot of close friends or family around him. But, hell, I don't give a shit about his money. I give a shit about the fact that you betrayed him. He gave you everything and you tricked him just to get your hands on his cash. What did you tell him, that you could keep his mind alive as long as you had the funds to keep your project running?"

Scott shot him a chill glare. "You'll have to excuse me. I need to see to Lia."

He let this last word hang in the air, heavy with gloating significance. Erik bounded to his feet and took a few steps toward Scott. Here in the Scape, they were equals in height—Scott had made his avatar a little taller than his real-life self—and they could have been two sides of the same coin, Scott as golden-haired and glowingly handsome as Erik was dark and sharp-featured.

"I gave her the chance to tell me to leave for good," Erik said, in a low, calm voice. "I told her she only had to say the word and she would never see me again. You know what?" He spread his hands. "She couldn't do it. You can marry her, fine. Keep her here in one of these little cells. Lock her up in the DreamScape for eternity. It doesn't make a difference. You'll never have her. Not really. Not," he jabbed a finger at Scott's chest, "in here. But you know that, don't you? Deep down. Why else the rush? You know your procedure isn't ready. You know you have as much chance of destroying her as you do of capturing her, so why do it now? Because you know it might be your last chance, don't you?" He shook his head, half-smiling. "Go and see to Lia, then. Go and try and tie her to you. Go and just fucking try it. You won't do it. You never will. I hope you enjoy your fucking eternity with her, because every time you look into her eyes, you're gonna know she's thinking of me."

Scott sucked in a long breath through his nose. "Are you done?"

"Oh, yeah. I think I've done enough here. Wren?" He held out an arm, and Wren took it. "See you, Scott."

The ice cracked beneath their feet, dark fractures spreading across the room, opening up into a chasm between them and Scott, who backed into the doorway. As soon as it was wide enough, Erik gave a tug on her arm and they jumped, in tandem, straight into the gulf.

Wren emerged into consciousness slowly, knowledge of her real-life body returning like blood to a tingling limb. She lay with her eyes closed, feeling the pressure of the sofa beneath her, the softness of the cushions, the thud of her heartbeat. For the first time since she'd been making trips into the DreamScape, she appreciated the difference between being a drifting thought in a virtual body, and being a living, breathing, physical being. It was like returning to a home she thought she'd never see again. She took a deep breath of stale, smoky air, and slowly opened her eyes.

It was dark in Erik's hotel suite, the room bathed in the faint silver glow of moonlight and the distant flicker of lights on the Vegas strip. A slight, warm breeze wafted through the open door that led to the pool. Wren sat up, feeling as though she were bobbing on a sea of dreams. For a moment she forgot that she was not sleeping and marvelled at the detail in the scene: the way the starlight refracted through the windows; the droop of a tired lily in the vase on the coffee table. And then she remembered that it was all real, solid, and ran her hands over the fabric of the sofa and onto her jeans, noticing the signals shooting from the nerves of her fingers, up to her brain.

"Yeah, it gets that way."

Erik leaned on the back of the sofa, looking down at her with an expression of concerned amusement. Moonlight fell on the contours of his face, mapping the depth of his eye-sockets and the peaks of his cheekbones.

"What way?" she said, and her voice came out as a croak. She coughed a little and repeated her question more clearly.

"Hard to tell if you're awake or dreaming. It'll drive you mad, in the end."

"If I ever wondered, I'd be able to tell just from looking at you," Wren said. "You're like a different person here."

"Am I? How?" Erik looked surprised.

Wren shook her head, searching for the right explanation. "There … you belong, I guess. You seem to own the place. You're unshakable. Here, I'm not sure you're here at all. I could blink and you'd be gone. It's like you're on a different plane. Except when I saw you on stage," she added. "Then you were pretty damn solid."

Erik stared at her for a moment, then shook his head. "You need to lay off the Slip, kid," he said.

Wren ran a hand through her hair and sighed. "Maybe. Maybe I do."

"Take it from me. The moment you start wondering whether people are real is the moment you need to turn back."

"And if I don't?"

"You'll lose everyone you really cared about." As Erik spoke, the door from the corridor opened and Kent Austin appeared in the wedge of yellow light, wearing a silk dressing gown.

"You're awake!" Surprise turned to anger in an instant. "Jesus Christ, Erik, what the fuck? I thought you were a gonner. Do you have any idea how long you've been out?"

"Not a clue," Erik replied.

"Well, I sure can tell you you're talking about days rather than hours. I was gonna call somebody. One of those Scape experts or something. I didn't know how to get you out."

"Well, you can quit worrying now. Go back to bed. Or better yet, get us pizza. I feel like I haven't eaten in days." Erik turned to Wren. "Can you get hold of your friends? Now we know where Lia and Bethany are in the Scape, we need to find them in this world, the sooner the better."

Wren turned on her phone and put through a video call to Delphi. She answered quickly, and Andromeda and Kazuo squeezed into the view beside her. It looked as though they were on a shuttle.

"Wren!" Delphi grinned. "Hoo boy am I glad to see you! Nothing can keep you down, can it?"

"We didn't think we'd see you again," Andromeda said, her gaze focused vaguely on a point just to the left of Wren's head. "How did you get out of the void?"

"It wasn't really us," Wren replied. "Gade kinda let us go. And then we got captured by Scott, but we got out of that one by … Well, actually, how *did* we get out of that, Erik?"

Erik sat on the sofa beside her, bringing him into view of the video screen. "The guy's a moron, what can I say? He can't code himself, so he built his little world out of some patched together bits and pieces of Gade's code. What he doesn't realise is that Gade left back doors all through everything he coded—a means to get straight from any area of the DreamScape to any other. When Scott copy pasted the code he needed for his ice prison, he also copied a bunch of Gade's back doors. They're not easy to spot, unless you know what you're looking for."

"Which I guess you do," Wren said.

"I've been using them for years. My own network, linked together by the raven symbol. I never told anyone how I did it, although your friend Kaz started to figure it out pretty fast," he added, with a respectful nod to Kazuo. "But Scott … it always really wound him up that he couldn't work it out. No matter what he did, however many clever brains he got working for him, I was always able to move around the Scape safely and anonymously. Otherwise, he probably would've had me in that ice cell long before now."

"How'd he get you this time?" Kazuo said. "If you don't mind me asking?"

"When Wren and I jumped into the void, the system lost track of our signatures, just like it did with Bethany. I can't say for sure, but I'd guess Scott has a way of pinpointing rogue signatures and linking them back up with the Corona they logged in on—returning them to their bodies, in effect. When he saw our signatures floating loose, he connected us back up and downloaded us onto his private server." Erik gave a wry smile. "He did us a favour, really. I've got no idea how we'd have made it back to our bodies otherwise. Because we were on a private server, not in the Scape, the only place I could take us when I got hold of one of Gade's back doors was out. So here we are."

"Wow," Delphi breathed. "You're much smarter than I expected. I mean, not that I didn't think you were smart. I mean, oh, hell, that came out wrong. Sorry."

"Take it easy, kid. You'll strain something." Erik sat back against the sofa cushions. "You guys look like you're going someplace."

"Budapest," said Kazuo. "We were able to follow the trail Scott and Lia left when they left London. Shots on CCTV, borders where their passports were scanned, that sort of thing. They're in Budapest, so that's where we're headed, and then … well, I don't know what then."

"Hang tight," Erik said. "Find out exactly where they

are. We'll be joining you soon."

41

Lia watched Bethany prowl the perimeter of their ice cell, running her hands over the walls and muttering to herself. She slammed her fists against the ice, shouting up into the empty air.

"Hey! Hey! Let us out! Let us out!"

"How did you end up here?" Lia asked, from the corner. She was freezing cold in her thin dress, and she hugged her arms, trying to rub some life back into her skin. Then she remembered, with crashing despair, that this was not real skin, not real cold, and that the place she was a prisoner in was her own mind.

"Your guess is as good as mine," said Bethany. "This place is a bloody mind-fuck, is what it is."

Lia was growing to like her already. She was irritable and moody—who wouldn't be, in this position—but she had a vulnerable charm about her. The posturing was a defence mechanism protecting a fragile core.

Not unlike Erik, Lia thought, and sighed. When would she stop giving in to this urge to try and put broken people back together?

"What's the matter with you?" Bethany turned to face her, folding her arms, as though Lia's low mood had personally offended her.

"I was just thinking about someone."

"Who? Your evil husband?"

"No, I … it doesn't matter."

"Whatever." Bethany turned back to the wall and laid both palms against it, pushing hard. When nothing happened, she kicked it, swearing loudly. "Fuck's sake. I should've stayed in the last place. This one is so much worse."

"Where were you before?"

"A house. My doll's house, from when I was little. It was pretty creepy, but at least it was a nice place. And warm. Not that you have to be cold here," she added, watching Lia shiver. "It's all in your head. If you think yourself warm, you will be." She sighed. "The Boy told me that."

Lia frowned, concentrating on the idea of warmth. To her surprise, she did start to feel a little better. "You seem to know this place well," she said, smiling. "Like an old pro."

"I've been here a while. I think."

"You think?"

Bethany shrugged. "It's hard to tell. It's not like there's any clocks."

"Fair point. What happened? How did you end up here?"

"I can't really remember." Bethany leant against the wall with her arms folded. "I was just hanging out here with some friends I made, and the next thing I knew, I fell through one of those big black gaps and ended up in some random place and couldn't get back, couldn't log out. I was just stuck. So, I wandered around until I met the Boy, and he tried to take me to Hypnos. Who is your husband, I guess. Thinks he's some kind of god, did you know that? Bit of an egomaniac, is he?"

"It's starting to seem that way."

"But then I escaped and found myself in this weird cathedral that looked like it was off the cover of a heavy metal album, and everyone there was rabbiting on about the Dark God, or something. Seriously. Cannot keep up with these weirdos."

Lia rubbed her temples, trying to process this sudden flow of information. "So, who is the Dark God?"

"Some guy. I dunno. I never actually got to meet him. Sounds like he's pretty powerful though. He's got all these weird mutant people, like, worshipping him or something." Bethany made a face. "Anyway, then the wooden guy told me to touch the big black raven and … poof. Here I am."

Lia leaned forward. "Big black raven?"

"It's kind of like his thing, I guess." Bethany shrugged. "Apparently, he puts these ravens all around the place and they help him travel here and there. Didn't work well for me," she added, looking dolefully at the ice cell.

"But you didn't actually meet the Dark God?"

"No. Think we'd just missed him or something."

"Just missed him? As in, he was there recently?"

"Whatever recently means in a place like this."

Lia got to her feet. "We've got to get out of here." She pushed the hair from her collapsed up-do out of her eyes and scanned the featureless walls with a new sense of urgency. "You said you were trapped before in that dolls house? How did you get out of there?"

"I'm not really sure," Bethany said. "I got to the edge of the place, and it wanted to force me to stop but I just kept pushing and pushing until I got through."

"So why can't we do that here?" Lia put her palms on the wall and pressed. Unsurprisingly, nothing happened.

"I tried that," Bethany pointed out. "It doesn't budge. In the doll's house, the way out was through the water. It was like a weak spot. The thing you've got to remember is that none of this is real," she said. "You don't move. You are where you've always been, just the code changes around you. Your husband told me that himself. That's how he captured us. He had to, like, locate our signatures in the code, or something. But we never moved. We're still in our bodies, wherever they are. We're still in our brains—at least, I hope we are."

"So, the point is …" Lia hesitated. "What you're saying is, we should be able to just wake up, if we tried hard enough?"

"I mean … I guess so. That's what it felt like, like waking up from a dream, but I didn't actually wake up, I just ended up back where I started."

"Perhaps there's levels to it," Lia mused. "Say we're in a folder, like on a computer, and outside of that folder is another, bigger folder, and outside of that is the whole desktop. Does that make sense? I'm not very good at computers."

"We've got to get out of the little folder first," said Bethany.

"Right. We've got to find the weak spot in each folder." Lia turned in a circle, looking for anything that stood out as different, while Bethany examined the wall once more. Something moved, and for a moment Lia thought Bethany had actually broken through, but then she realised that it was the door opening—a shaft of vertical light appeared in the wall and grew larger until Scott's avatar entered.

And that was when Lia realised: the weak spot of their cell didn't have to be a thing. Perhaps it could also be a person. If they could just get out into the wider world of Scott's church, perhaps they could find one of these ravens Bethany had talked about, and use it to travel out of his reach. She had never been a good manipulator—she was a terrible liar, as Scott had already noticed—but what she was good at was people pleasing. And she was determined to use all the people-pleasing power she had in her to make Scott let them out of their cell.

"How are you, Li?"

She looked into his glassy eyes and wished she could see some sort of expression that would help her attune to his mood. What did he want from her? Who did he want her to be? She had to be honest to be convincing.

"I'm cold," she said at last, glancing down at her gauzy dress. "Can you magic me up a warm jumper or something?"

She thought she saw the faintest flicker of a smile on Scott's lips. "I'm so sorry," he said. "I'll change the ambient temperature. There, is that better?"

"Much better." Lia stopped hugging herself and let her arms drop to her sides. "Thank you. I don't understand how this place works at all."

"You'll get used to it," Scott said. "Give it time."

"Will you stay for a bit? Talk to me? I feel so lost here." She glanced at Bethany, hoping the girl would understand what she was trying to do.

Scott came a little further into the room, leaving the door open behind him, and took Lia's hand in both of his. "This wasn't how I meant things to be, Lia. I wanted to ease you in gently. I wanted you to choose for yourself."

"I know," Lia nodded. "I know. I want to understand, Scott. I'm going to be here forever," she took a deep breath, "and I can accept that. But I need to understand this place better, and then maybe I can choose for myself. We can start this off on a positive footing, can't we? Put everything else behind us?"

Scott regarded her seriously. "I'd sure like to."

"I can't learn about the DreamScape from this cell."

"I need you here. I need to keep you contained until Gendry can do his work."

"Where do you think I'm going to go, Scott? I don't know how to work this place. I wouldn't know how to get anywhere even if I wanted to, and I'll be with you, won't I? Please. I just don't want to stay in this cell any longer. Treat me like your wife, not a criminal."

Scott shook his head. "Goddamn, Lia. You know, when I met you, I never meant … I never expected to feel this way."

"What do you mean?"

"I only wanted to wind him up a bit. Dacre. Get a few photos with his ex, just to piss him off. But you got into my head, and now look at me." He sighed. "Come on, then. I'll show you around some more."

As he took her arm, Lia forced down the horrified realisation that he had deliberately targeted her and tried to rearrange her features into a mild expression.

"What about her?" She indicated Bethany, who had slunk into a corner, looking wounded at the idea Lia might leave without her.

"What about her?"

"Why not let her come with us?"

"No," Scott's voice was firm. "I don't think so."

"She's just a kid, Scott. Don't leave her locked up in here."

But on this, Scott refused to be swayed. "Gendry's about to perform the severance procedure," he said. "I can't move the girl now."

Bethany bolted. Like a shot, she flung herself at the door, and before he could even react, she was gone. Lia took advantage of his surprise to pull her arm free and flee herself. She threw herself into the white light, and the next moment she was running down one of the ice corridors, Bethany just ahead of her, feet slipping on the damp floor.

"We don't have much time," Lia gasped. "We've got to find a way out of here."

"Where?" Bethany shouted, still running full pelt with apparently no clue what direction she was leading them in.

"The hall."

"What?"

"There's a big central hall," Lia said. "A gathering place for all of Hypnos' followers. If the Dark God's hidden one of his raven symbols somewhere here, it'll be there."

"How do you know that?"

"Because," Lia rolled her eyes, "because it's what would annoy Scott the most if he knew. Come on, let's try this way."

"Lia!" At the sound of Scott's voice bellowing her name, Lia sprinted off down another corridor, banking on the chance that every route would eventually lead to the central hall.

"We're never going to find it," Bethany panted, struggling to keep up. "Everywhere looks exactly the same."

"We've got to. We're never going to get another

chance." Lia glanced back over her shoulder, but there was no sign of Scott behind them. She hoped he'd lost track of them in the maze. She took a sharp left and rushed straight through an open pair of double doors into the hall. Reaching behind her, she grabbed Bethany's hand, and the two of them made straight for the fountain in the centre of the room, barrelling past the surprised worshippers.

Desperately hoping that her instincts were correct, Lia leapt over the edge of the fountain and straight into the water, wading up to her calves, her gold dress billowing out around her ankles. She made for the gold statue in the centre, hunting high and low across its smooth surface until she found what she was looking for. Tucked away behind the curling edge of a gilded leaf was a small, hidden, taunting black raven.

"Lia!"

Lia froze. The crowd scattered as Scott's avatar rushed toward them. Bethany, still gripping Lia's hand, pressed her fingers to the raven hopefully. When nothing happened, she tried again.

"It's not working!" she shouted.

"Lia, stop!" Scott was closing in, almost within reach of them. "If you do this, it's all over, do you understand me? It's over!"

"It's not working," Bethany repeated, frantic. "We're stuck here!"

"Let me try." Lia pressed a finger against the ink-black shape. There was a breathless pause, a sense that it was somehow reading her mind, and then it glowed gold, and the world around them—the fountain, the hall, the crowd, and Scott's furious face—all dissolved.

They emerged in a cave. Stalactites hung above rows of stone seats, like an auditorium. A heavy calm rested over the cavern, the air thick with a reverent silence. Lia leaned on a misshapen stalagmite, taking a moment to get her breath back.

"Bethany?"

"I'm here." Bethany stood at the edge of a vast lake, staring out across the water, as still as if she were being held by an enchantment. A huge raven shape was burnt onto the wall of the cave, at once threatening and somehow protective, and below it, moving slowly, silently across the water, was …

"Is that you?" Bethany asked.

"Yes." Lia watched the ghostly dancer create ripples across the lake, the steps so familiar that they were ingrained in her bones. The *Swan Lake* solo she'd danced the day she and Erik had first met. "Yes, that's me." She sat down heavily on one of the steps, the sadness of the place bleeding into her skin.

Bethany turned to her. "What do we do now?"

"Stay here," said Lia. "For now. I have a feeling we'll be safe here."

42

By early morning, Vegas time, Wren and Erik were back on the shuttle heading for Budapest. Erik was in an abysmal mood. Wren didn't blame him. The thought of Bethany trapped in one of those ice cells made her so anxious she wanted to scream. To distract herself, or at least to feel as though she was doing something, she patched a call through to Delphi.

"What are you doing?" she asked, as her friends appeared on the screen.

"Waiting for you." It was sleeting in Budapest, and Delphi hugged her coat around her. "We think Scott's got your sister and Lia in a skyscraper just north of here. Trouble is, the place is crawling with these burly secret service-looking types. His minders, I guess. Not sure if they're armed but I wouldn't like to risk it. We were just going to get coffee while we figure out what to do. There's this really quaint looking place just across the road and …" Delphi caught Erik's eye and trailed off.

"Oh, hey, yeah, enjoy yourselves," he said. "Why not do a bit of sightseeing while you're at it?"

"Ignore him." Wren shot him a sharp look. "He's a bit tense." To Erik, she muttered, "They don't have to help us, you know."

"Sure. All right. Sorry."

Wren glanced at her watch. "We've got hours 'till we get to Budapest," she said. "We might as well go and see if we can get into the control room. It's better than doing nothing. See you guys soon."

"Wren!"

Wren heard her sister's squeal of delight before she'd even managed to work out where she was, and before she knew it Bethany was on top of her, flinging her arms around Wren's neck and pressing her face to her chest. Just as Gade had promised, Erik's cave had been restored. Erik had transported them both straight there, intending to do nothing more than pass through on their way to the control room, but no sooner had they arrived than, to Wren's astonishment, they'd stumbled upon the very people they were searching for.

"Oh my God, Wren! I never thought I'd be so happy to see you!"

"Er …" Wren shook her head, then burst out laughing. "Well, it's good to see you too, brat-face. How on Earth did you get here?"

"They must have found one of the Marks." Erik's voice was taut.

Bethany craned her neck to peer over Wren's shoulder. "Oh my God, is that Erik Dacre?"

It was only then, with her sister distracted, that Wren had the chance to look around. They stood in the aisle between the stone seats, and the ghostly dancer was still endlessly retracing her steps across the lake. But this time, her real-life counterpart stood there too, barefoot and bedraggled in a torn Grecian gown, her honey-blonde hair hanging half-collapsed out of its up-do. Wren glanced back at Erik, and figured she had a pretty good idea, standing between the two of them, how it felt to be invisible.

"I touched the raven, and it brought us here," Lia said quietly, hitching her long skirt up with one hand as she made her way up the uneven steps.

"When I designed the pathways I put a little extra clause into the code," Erik replied.

"Just in case." Lia smiled faintly.

"I knew you'd never come to the DreamScape, but I couldn't help myself. I thought, if you ever did …"

"You'd want me to see this?" Lia glanced back at her ghostly echo.

"I'd want to see you."

"Come on," Wren muttered to Bethany, dragging her towards the back of the amphitheatre.

"Is that really Erik Dacre?" Bethany carried on, loudly, as they passed him. "What is he doing here? Do you know him, Wren?"

"Just shut up, will you?" Wren bundled her into a seat. "Give them a moment."

"Well?" Lia's voice was shaky. "Is it really you?"

"Last time I checked," Erik grinned unconvincingly. Lia raised her eyes to the heavens, looking like she was trying not to cry.

"What kind of an idiot are you?" she burst out, striding

forward and giving Erik a sharp push to his chest, which didn't affect his balance in the slightest. "What on Earth were you thinking? Do you know how worried I've been? I thought …" She trailed off, wiping her eyes.

"I didn't mean to upset you," Erik began.

"Really? You didn't think I would be upset? You thought I'd just turn on the news the next morning and think 'oh, Erik's finally gone and done it, never mind, what's for breakfast?'"

Erik grimaced. "You weren't supposed to guess …"

"What you were planning?" Lia finished. "I know what you were thinking. I know you, remember. God," she put her hands to her head, turning away from him. "It never ends, does it?"

"I wanted to let you go. I wanted you to live your life and be free of this. You never deserved this … all this shit that comes along with me," he finished, apologetically. Lia looked as though she might scream. She rounded on him.

"You've spent too much time in this fantasy world, Erik. You think these high-flown sentiments and insane gestures mean something? Well, they don't. You might have Dravens falling over themselves to hear that kind of madness from you, but you know what? If you really died, they'd be so busy enjoying indulging their over-the-top grief, they'd forget to actually miss you."

"And you?" Erik said, quietly.

Lia looked up into his face. "I'd miss you," she said. "I love you. God help me, I must be mad, but I do. I don't want you to die, Erik, for me or anyone else. I just want you to live. That's all I ever wanted."

Erik, for once, was speechless.

"You bloody idiot. I missed you so much." Lia took a

deep breath, stood up on her tiptoes, wrapped her arms around his neck, and kissed him.

Wren looked away, feeling awkward. Beside her, Bethany hugged her knees to her chest and continued to watch them with overt fascination.

"How are you?" Wren asked her, in a low voice. "Are you okay?"

"You mean apart from being trapped inside an insane computer simulation?" Bethany whispered back. "Apart from that, I'm peachy."

"You don't need to be sarcastic. I've been looking for you for weeks."

"Weeks? Is that all?" Bethany looked at her hands. "I thought I'd been here for years," she said, in a small voice. "I thought I'd been here forever. There's no way to tell, you know. No day, no night. You don't get hungry or tired. You just drift, here and there, forever." She bit her lip. "I thought I'd never see you again. I thought I was probably rotting away in that park, and nobody knew where I was, and then that cowboy got hold of me and said he was going to kill me, and …"

"Bethy," Wren pulled her into a hug. "It's okay. You're gonna be okay. I know where you are. Erik and I are on our way to get you."

Wren noticed a small alert flashing at the edge of her vision. She looked at Erik and Lia, who were still oblivious to the world around them, and coughed loudly.

"Erik, I'm sorry, but the shuttle's about to arrive. We need to go."

"Sure. Sure." Erik turned back to Lia. "I'll be there soon, all right? When all this is over, I'm gonna give all this up. The drugs, booze, the Scaping. I'm done. I swear."

Lia smiled faintly. "I'll believe that when I see it."

"I mean it."

Lia put her palm flat on the middle of his chest. "I know you do. Now. But what about tomorrow? Next week? Next year?"

Erik looked as though he was about to protest, but Wren cut in, "Guys. You can talk this through when we're back in the real world. Right now, Scott's still got you, and I bet he's pretty pissed off. We've got to go."

"She's right." Erik stepped away from Lia, reluctantly. "Whatever you do, don't go anywhere. You're safe as long as you stay right here, got it?"

"Got it."

"See you on the other side."

By the time Wren woke up, the shuttle had already come to a halt in Budapest station. She and Erik disembarked and hurried through the station, hunting for a place where they could catch a taxi pod. Neither of them said anything much until they were securely in a pod and well on their way to the skyscraper. Erik was obviously distracted, gazing out of the window as the city passed by. Wren sat back against the seat, jittery with nerves and relief.

"That seemed to go well," she said.

"I feel like my heart's started beating again after a long time dead," he replied, more to himself than to her. Wren raised an eyebrow.

"You should write that down," she said. "It'd make a good song lyric."

Erik narrowed his eyes. "Are you jerking me around?"

"Would I?" Wren tried to look innocent, and then broke down laughing. After a moment's pause, so did Erik. When he smiled—truly smiled—his face lit up like a sunrise. Wren thought she was beginning to see what Lia liked so much about him.

"I'm happy for you. Seriously."

Erik's smile faded. "We're not out of the woods yet."

Wren and Erik met Delphi, Kazuo, and Andromeda in the quaint coffee shop that Delphi had been keen to visit. The place was a clutter of mismatched crockery and Art Nouveau posters; antique chairs upholstered with threadbare printed cushions. It was directly opposite the blue glass tower where Scott was keeping Bethany and Lia, but with its musty atmosphere and piped accordion music it could have been a million miles away. Wren spotted her friends and grabbed a chair. Erik was mobbed the moment he stepped through the door, by a group of excited Hungarian teenagers trying to take selfies. Delphi sat bolt upright in her seat, watching, and Wren got the feeling she would have quite liked to join them.

"What's he really like, then?" she whispered to Wren.

"Monumentally fucked up," said Wren, but then, lowering her voice a little, she added, "But, I don't know, underneath it all I guess there's something quite sweet about him, in a way. You've just got to dig pretty deep to find it."

"Find what?" Erik slid into the seat beside her, leaving a trail of disappointed fans behind him.

"Your redeeming feature. I assume you have one some-where."

"Fuck knows." Erik reached into his jacket pocket for his cigarettes. "If you find it, let me know. Better yet, let Kent know. Pretty sure the guy curses the day he met me." He lit a cigarette, waving away the waitress who'd come to offer them drinks. "Right. We don't have a lot of time. I saw Scott's minders buzzing around the front of that building, so how the hell are we going to get in there?"

Kazuo flipped open his tablet to display a detailed blue-print of the building. "You can thank me later," he said, grinning at Wren.

"You're a bloody genius, Kaz."

"There's the front door here," Andromeda said, leaning over the plans, candy-coloured hair trailing on the table. "And a service entrance back here, but we assumed Scott would've put someone there."

"So, then we looked closer," Kazuo said, "and we found this." He jabbed his finger at the plan. "A garbage disposal hatch leading from the kitchens to the dumpsters. You don't mind getting dirty, do you Wren?"

"I take issue with your tone," Wren said, "but I can climb into a dumpster if that's what I need to do."

"Once we're inside," said Delphi, "we can get up the emergency staircase right here, and we think, judging by the amount of electronic activity coming from this room ..." here she looked at Kazuo for confirmation, who nodded, "we think this is where they are."

"The main way in is via the lift," Andromeda added, "But if we can come up the stairs—it's twenty floors, so I hope you're feeling fit—we're hoping the minders won't notice us. At least, not until we're more or less on top of them."

"There's probably one by the door," Kazuo said. "But we were hoping we could take him by surprise and, you know, take him out."

"Not a problem." Erik was already on his feet. "Let's go."

43

"We-ell," said Bethany, a half-amused, half-quizzical look on her face.

"What?" Lia sat on one of the stone seats, absent-mindedly watching her monochrome twin on the lake. It was impossible not to pick flaws in her performance.

"Well, you didn't tell me about your *boyfriend*," Bethany continued, with a grin. "No wonder your weird old husband is in such a bad mood with you."

"It's complicated …" Lia began, but whatever Bethany imagined her transgressions to be, it was clear they were already forgotten. The teenager leapt up from her seat and began pacing once more, shuddering with nervous energy.

"How long do you think they'll be?" she asked, rubbing her hands together.

"I'm sure they'll get to us as soon as they can," Lia replied.

"How can you stay so calm? God, it's really irritating. Don't you even care if we get rescued?"

"Of course I do. And trust me, I don't feel calm underneath. I suppose I'm just used to putting on a front," she added, glancing at the ghostly dancer. "Besides, Erik said we'd be safe as long as we stay here."

"I don't know if I'm so sure about that," said Bethany. Something in her voice made Lia look round. Behind her, an all-too-familiar figure in a toga made his way up the aisle towards them, followed by Boy.

"Scott." Lia scrambled to her feet as if preparing to run, but she knew there was nowhere to go. Instead, she stood her ground, trying to ignore the rising panic in her throat. "How did you get in here?"

"Gendry here is really very resourceful." Scott smiled. "He's been watching that Wren girl and her friends for a while now, and he took note of the method they used to break in here."

"You again!" Bethany lunged at Boy, but stopped dead in mid-air as though she'd hit a force field. Thrashing impotently against the thin air, she shouted, "Why are you doing this to me? Why can't you leave us alone?!"

Ignoring her, Scott walked down the steps to Lia. He stopped close to her and ran a hand down the side of her cheek. Lia flinched.

"Gendry tells me Dacre is on his way to us in Budapest," Scott said. "We need to move, and that means I'm going to have to wake you up."

"I don't know much about the DreamScape," said Lia, "but if you wake us now, don't you risk …"

"Brain damage?" Scott's look of concern was unconvincing. "It's true, we do. Especially for her," he added, indicating Bethany, "but what else can I do? I can't take you out of here—Dacre's security makes it impossible, I'm afraid. So, if he tracks us down in the Mono, you're lost to me, Li. I just can't have that."

"I'm already lost to you," Lia replied. "Do what you like."

"I'm sorry it's come to this," Scott said. "But try not to worry. Gendry knows what he's doing." He nodded to Boy. "Go ahead, we're ready."

Boy disappeared. A heartbeat passed. Then two. Then Lia's world exploded in a blinding light. Her brain felt as though it was being pulled out of her skull. A red, deafening pain roared through her head, sparks going off all over her vision, burning holes in her thoughts. She was sure this was the end—that she would die or go insane. And then there was a stillness, a calm, and she opened her eyes back in the skyscraper, Scott's face swimming into focus above her.

"How do you feel?" he asked.

"Like I've been turned inside out and back again," Lia managed. Beside her, Bethany's sleeping figure moved slightly, a quiver that grew into a spasm. Before long, she was shaking uncontrollably, her eyes still firmly shut. Gendry leaned over her, muttering to himself, adjusting his instruments. Lia pushed up to her elbows and watched, anxious, while Scott paced up and down, looking at his watch.

"We don't have time for this."

Gendry rushed from one computer screen to another. "I should be able to stabilise her. I just need a moment ..."

"You don't *have* a moment." Scott gestured to the numerous tubes that connected Lia up to her own bank of equipment. "Leave the girl. Disconnect this shit. We're leaving now."

Gendry, to his credit, ignored him.

"Gendry!" Irate, Scott examined one of the tubes that ran into Lia's arm.

"Don't touch that!" Gendry rushed over to pull his hand

away. "Are you insane? That's the drug for the severance procedure. It needs to be properly drained or some of it could enter her bloodstream."

Lia looked down at the little plastic tube, tucked beneath the skin of her inner elbow. "You were really going to kill me?"

"Not kill you. Free you. Gendry, for fuck's sake. We need to go!"

"You're really afraid of him, aren't you?" Lia said.

"Dacre? Yes, I'm afraid of him. The man's insane." Scott glanced anxiously towards the door.

"Takes one to know one, I suppose."

"All right," said Gendry, breathing hard. Bethany was still trembling, although not so violently. "All right, I've done what I can for her." He turned to one of Lia's machines. "I'm going to start draining the drug, okay?"

"Quickly!" Scott snapped.

"It takes as long as it takes," Gendry replied, irritably. "Stay as still as you can, Lia."

Gendry fiddled with the machine, as Lia lay very still. Every now and again, he darted over to the other couch to check on Bethany. Gradually, Lia became convinced that he was not doing much at all with her machine; that the business about draining the drug was merely a way of stalling until he could be sure Bethany was okay. Lia warmed to him a little for that. Unfortunately, Scott seemed to have similar suspicions, as he moved in to examine Gendry's actions more closely.

To distract him, Lia blurted, "You know, I met Bethany's sister in the DreamScape. She's extremely worried. The poor girl's been searching for Bethany for weeks."

"I know," Scott replied curtly. "Gendry told me all about

her. Interesting you don't mention that she was travelling with Dacre."

Lia glanced at Gendry, who gave her a look urging her to continue. "She was," Lia said. "That's true."

"And how is our miserable friend? Did the two of you get a chance to … catch up?"

Lia looked down for a moment, feeling ashamed of herself—Scott was her husband, after all, despite all his behaviour, and she had never pegged herself as the type to be unfaithful. What would her parents think? Esmé? Marianne? And then something kindled in her. Defiance? Perhaps. Or perhaps more simply a strong sense of who she was—truly was, with all the layers she'd developed to please other people stripped away. That was who she was with Erik. Who she'd been when choreographing her ballet. Her own, raw self. She looked Scott full in the eye.

"When I get out of here," she said, "—and I *will* get out of here—we're over. Do you understand? I'm filing for divorce."

Scott didn't react. At least, not on the surface. He didn't move or speak, but Lia saw something flicker in his eyes—that same cold fury she'd seen on previous occasions when the conversation had turned to Erik. And then, as on those other occasions, he pushed it back down inside himself and shook his head, indulging her with a smile far worse than any furious outburst.

"I think you're mistaken, Li. I guess the experience of being in the Scape for the first time was a lot for you to deal with. You don't know what you're saying."

"I know perfectly well what I'm saying." Lia was determined to stand her ground. In the corner of her vision, she was aware of Gendry back at Bethany's beside. Was the girl stirring?

Scott moved over to Lia's couch and sat beside her. He put a hand on the small of her back, saying, "Listen, we'll go home, all right? Take some time to think about this. When you've heard all I have to say, I'm sure you'll ..."

"I think we've all heard enough of your shit, Hypnos."

Erik. Lia looked up to see him and Wren enter through a fire escape near the back of the room, followed by three teenagers. Scott reached for a radio on a nearby table.

"You can call for back up if you want," Erik said. "But it won't do you much good. Kazuo here has hacked the building's security systems. The elevators have been disabled. The doors are locked down." He walked right up to Scott and put a hand on his shoulder. "Time to accept defeat, old friend."

"Bethany!" Ignoring the stand-off developing between Erik and Scott, Wren pushed past them to her sister's side. "What's happening?" she asked Gendry anxiously. "Is she all right?"

"I'm trying to wake her," Gendry explained. "It's a delicate process, but she's stable now. We just need to give her time to come round, and then we can see how bad the damage is."

"The damage?" The colour drained from Wren's face.

"Could be nothing," Gendry said. "But there's a good chance that after so much time in the DreamScape, she will have sustained some kind of brain damage regardless of how carefully I've extracted her."

Wren took hold of Bethany's hand, leaning in close to her face. "Bethany? It's me, Wren. Can you hear me?"

Lia turned her attention back to Erik and Scott.

"You can't see the truth, can you?" Scott was saying, his

lip curling with barely suppressed fury. "Or maybe you just can't accept it. All this time, all you've ever done is to undermine me, but it doesn't matter. This is the future of humanity." He indicated the machines around Lia and Bethany. "You can't stop progress."

"You think I give a shit about your insane theories?" Erik glanced at Lia. "You want to end up like Gade? Be my fucking guest. I just want you to leave Lia out of it."

"She's my wife. I'll do what the hell I like with her."

"I'm not your property," Lia snapped. "And you," she added, turning to Erik. "You're not much better. You could've stopped all this a long time ago, couldn't you? But you were happy to let him carry on destroying people like poor Bethany until you knew I was involved."

Erik at least had the grace to look sheepish. "Not happy," he said. "I tried ..."

"Not hard enough, it seems."

"So, everything you said in there ...?"

"Was absolutely true. And I owe you an apology, too, for the way I left you. But I've got a lot of thinking to do, and I need to do it on my own. For the time being, at least," she added, more gently, cut to the core by the look on Erik's face. She held out her arm, where the tube designed to carry the severance chemical into her bloodstream was still embedded beneath her skin. "Gendry, would you please?"

"Move a muscle, Gendry, and I'll snap your goddamn neck." Scott turned to Lia. "You think I'm just going to let you walk out of here with him? After everything we've been through?"

"You can't stop me, Scott."

Scott's face contorted as though he was struggling with an intense inner battle. "No," he said, at last. "No, I won't have it." He approached the machine and started typing. "I am sorry, Li. I thought things would be different."

Gendry's eyes widened, and in his look of horror Lia saw her own fate reflected back at her. "No!" was all she managed, before Scott hit the enter key and a blast of pure fire shot up her arm.

44

Wren had been so focused on Bethany, trying to work out whether the flickering of her eyelids was her waking up, or just some kind of muscle spasm, that she hadn't paid much attention to the situation developing around her. When she heard Lia's cry of alarm, though, she looked up to see Lia holding her arm out, as though the tube was an insect that had just bitten her. She was breathing hard, shuddering, her face contorted with pain. Erik lunged forward—shoving Scott out of the way so hard that he stumbled and fell against the machine—and wrenched the shunt out of Lia's arm, making her scream.

"What the fuck was that?" he asked, waving the tube around. "Somebody tell me what the fuck he just did!"

"The severance drug," Gendry said quietly, looking aghast. "Scott … do you realise what you've done?"

In a flash, Erik had Gendry by the lapels. "You can fix this, right?" Behind them, Lia sunk back against the couch, gasping for air through lips that were rapidly turning blue. "Fix this!"

Gendry shook his head. "Her systems are shutting down.

It's fast acting. There's nothing … I can't stop it. I'm sorry."

Erik let go of Gendry, turning his fury like a laser beam onto Scott. "I'll fucking kill you," he spat. "You goddamn fucking piece of shit."

"Erik!"

Just as he was about to launch himself at Scott, Wren darted around Bethany's bed and grabbed his arm, wheeling him around to face Lia, who was barely able to keep her eyes open. "Don't waste your time on him."

Erik's muscles tensed beneath his leather jacket, but then he went limp, as though all the fight had drained out of him. He moved to Lia's couch and crouched beside her, taking her hand. Wren put her hands to her face and looked through her fingers, knowing she shouldn't watch, but unable to drag herself away.

There were no last words from Lia. Breathing was too much of a battle for her to manage anything else. She only clung to Erik's hand and looked up at him with a look of infinite pity in her blue eyes. He bent down to kiss her, and by the time he pulled away, she was gone.

For the longest time, nobody moved. Wren was horribly aware of the sound of her own breathing. Then she heard a stirring behind her.

"What's the matter with everyone?"

Bethany was propped up on her elbows, peering over at Lia's still form, Erik still crouched motionless beside her.

"Bethany!" Wren whispered, throwing her arms around her sister. "Are you okay? How do you feel?"

"Fine. Bit … dizzy, I guess, but fine," Bethany craned her neck to look past Wren's shoulder. "Is she … dead?"

"Shhh!"

Gendry crept over to them. "Let me take her vitals," he

said quietly, reaching for Bethany's wrist. As he went through the motions of checking Bethany's pulse and blood pressure, a scuffle broke out near the fire exit. Scott had taken advantage of everyone's distraction to make a break for the door, and had gotten as far as opening it before Kazuo had noticed and sprinted over to intercept him, Andromeda and Delphi in hot pursuit.

"Hey!" Kazuo tried to grab Scott's arm, but the actor was far stockier and stronger than the teenager and threw him aside easily. Kazuo hit the doorframe and slumped to the ground, a red gash appearing on one side of his head. Andromeda changed direction abruptly to run over to him.

"Kaz!" She crouched by his side. "Are you okay? Somebody help! I think he's really hurt."

Meanwhile, Delphi had disappeared through the door and was already clattering down the stairs in her heavy boots. Hoping Gendry would see to Kazuo, Wren went after them, but even though she ran as fast as she could, by the time she got to the stairwell it was obvious she was not going to catch them up.

"Delphi!" she shouted, stumbling her way down the stairs. "Delphi, don't go after him! He'll only hurt you too!"

Wren heard a thud and a scream beneath her and doubled her speed, jumping a few steps at a time, passing Delphi, who had fallen on the stairs. By the time Wren got to the bottom of the stairwell and burst out into the street, Scott was nowhere to be seen.

Slowly, she climbed her way back up to where Delphi sat holding her ankle.

"I tried," Delphi gasped. "I tried, I was almost close enough to touch him, but then I slipped." She rubbed her leg. "Fuck, it really hurts. I didn't want to let him get away,

Wren."

"It's all right." Wren pulled her up. "Come on."

They hobbled back upstairs together, to find Gendry patching up a dazed-looking Kazuo, while Andromeda hovered anxiously by his side. Bethany sat on her bed, pale, and thinner than she should have been, but looking well enough that Wren breathed a sigh of relief. Erik, however, still hadn't moved. Wren helped Delphi sit down and went over to him.

"Erik?"

He turned to her, slowly, still holding Lia's hand. She looked peaceful and strangely alive, her lips pink and her cheeks rosy, as though she might wake up again at any moment.

"Did you catch him?" he asked, in a blank voice.

"No. I'm sorry." Wren knelt down beside him.

Erik shook his head. "It doesn't matter, does it?"

"He'll get what's coming to him, eventually," Wren replied.

Erik turned back to Lia and said nothing.

Wren put a hand on his shoulder. "Look, I'll call Kent. He'll come over, won't he? And I guess he'll be able to get in touch with Lia's family, and ..." She trailed off, not knowing what else to say. After a moment, during which Erik didn't respond, she got to her feet again. As she was walking away, she heard him say, barely in a whisper, "Thanks, Wren."

"Poor guy," Bethany said, as Wren returned to her. "They just got back together, too, you know."

"I know."

"I guess he'll have some good material for his next album, though?"

"Bethany! That's really …" Wren rolled her eyes. "You're lucky I'm so pleased to see you, or I'd give you hell for that. Come here," Wren took her phone from her pocket. "I think I know someone who'll be just as happy to see you."

When Harper answered the video call, she was already in her dressing gown. She seemed surprised to see Wren. "What d'you want? It's late. Alfie's sleeping."

"You're not going to ask me how I am, after I ran away from you in London?"

"It's your life, Wren. You'll do what you want, I suppose. But you really upset Jared, you know. He got in a lot of trouble because of you."

"All right, all right. Can we not talk about Jared now? I've got someone here who wants to speak to you." Wren turned the camera to face her sister.

"Bethany!" Harper's eyes immediately lit up. "Jared? Jared! Come and see. It's Bethany! She's awake! How are you, hen? Are you okay? How did you wake up? They told me you wouldn't, you know. I knew they were wrong."

Bethany grinned and nodded her way through all the questions, until Jared's head appeared in the frame, and then her expression darkened.

"Well, well," he said, with a forced jollity that made twisted Wren's stomach. "You girls have just made your mam's day, haven't you?" He leaned forward, squinting at the room behind them. "Where are you? That's not the hospital."

"No," said Wren. "It's the specialist unit you signed Bethany out to."

"How did they wake her up?" Harper asked.

"Tell me where you are, I'll come and get you," Jared

said, at the same time.

Bethany shot a pleading look at Wren. "Don't," she whispered.

"Don't worry, I don't intend to," Wren replied, fixing Jared with a firm stare. "She's not coming home any more than I am. From now on, Bethany's staying with me, far away from both of you."

"Wren!" Harper wailed, her eyes already brimming. "I just got my little girl back and now you want to take her away from me again? Why would you do that?"

"Oh, come on, Mum. You can visit. But not him." Wren handed the phone to Bethany. "You guys catch up all you want. I need to see how the others are doing."

She hopped off the couch and went over to where Andromeda and Gendry were talking quietly together, Kazuo and Delphi sitting on the floor nearby.

"How's Kaz?" Wren asked, when she reached them.

"A little concussed," said Gendry, "but he'll be fine."

"How about you, Delph?"

"I just twisted my ankle. No big deal." Delphi looked at Erik, who hadn't moved. "This is shit for him, isn't it?" she sighed. "What can we do?"

"Not much, I don't think." Wren sank to the floor beside her friend, feeling suddenly exhausted. "It's so fucking unfair, isn't it?"

Erik finally unfolded himself and stood, placing Lia's hand very carefully on her stomach. He walked over to them, moving like a sleepwalker.

"I'll try and get hold of Kent now," Wren said, hurriedly getting up again. "Do you want to go outside, maybe? Andromeda can sit with you a minute, if you want?"

Erik shook his head. "Don't worry about it, Wren. Take

care of your sister. I'm going to call Lia's family." He headed for the fire exit, but Wren went after him.

"Erik, hold on. I … I'm not sure you should be on your own right now. Let me come with you."

Erik managed a faint smile. "You know me too well already. No, I promise I won't go far. I'll make my calls and then …" he broke off, running a trembling hand through his hair.

"Keep putting one foot in front of the other," Wren said, echoing his words from when they were in Gade's void.

"Right." Erik cast a last lingering glance at Lia. "Right." And with that, he disappeared through the door.

45

One Year Later

Sunday morning. Wren hopped onto the cable car, squeezing into the smallest of spaces among the tourists, clinging to an ice-cold pole with her gloved hand. The air was chill and clear as they trundled down to San Francisco Bay, the sun a burning white hole in the ocean-blue sky. At the terminus, Wren breezed past the tourists, heading for her favourite spot on the bleachers.

A dark figure sat alone, hunched over a smouldering cigarette. If Wren'd had any doubt who he was, the huddle of black-clad girls standing a respectful distance away, daring one another to approach him, would have been enough of a clue. Wren strode straight over, feeling the glares of the Dravens like knives in her back, and slapped Erik on the shoulder.

"I thought you'd given those up." She sat down beside him.

Erik looked at his cigarette, smoke billowing into the air

in tight curls.

"Fuck's sake, you've got to let me have something. No drugs, no Scaping, no alcohol—I mean, no spirits, any-way—I gotta admit to a beer now and again, but that's nothing, is it?"

"Yeah." Wren laughed. "Only beer—that makes you pretty much tee-total, right?"

"Yeah, and now you're getting at me about the fucking cigarettes." Erik took another drag. "Come on. A guy's gotta have a vice."

"You're just afraid you're going to ruin your rep if any-one sees you drinking tonic water and lime."

Erik looked straight at her for the first time since she'd arrived. His green eyes were clearer than Wren had ever seen them, and so more piercing than ever.

"Not very rock and roll, is it?"

Wren leaned back on her hands, shaking her head, and looked out at the sea. "I give up," she said. "How are you, anyway?"

Erik's expression darkened. "Still alive."

"I mean, that's good, right?"

There was a long pause, and then Wren said, "I've been meaning to thank you. For paying for Bethany's visa. She's doing great here. The school's fantastic."

Erik nodded, gazing out to sea. "I'm glad. You don't need to thank me. Fact is, I don't know what the fuck to do with my money now that I'm not burning it all on Scaping and drugs. It's amazing how much I've saved."

Wren laughed. "Come on, I'm sure you can think of something. I saw your show. I think it could've used a few more insanely expensive pyrotechnics. Or, have you con-sidered buying a yacht? Yeah, that's what you need. A jet-black yacht. The Dravens would love it."

"You think you're fucking funny, don't you?"

"Oh, lighten up!" Wren elbowed him, then laughed again. "Sorry, forgot who I was talking to. Forgive me."

Erik managed something near to a smile, but soon fell to brooding again. Wren felt his black mood beginning to seep into her own mind, too.

"Still no sign of Scott," she said, at length.

"Not that I've heard about. Guess he's hiding in Russia, or something." Erik shook his head. "Let him hide. I don't want to waste another second thinking about that piece of shit."

"And you really haven't been back to the DreamScape since ..."

Erik glared at a Draven who'd worked up the courage to approach him, and she backed off hastily.

"I promised Lia I'd give it all up." He shrugged. "I meant it. I can't take responsibility for a world bigger than the Earth. Not anymore. Last I heard Gendry had taken control of the whole place. I think he 'liberated' all of the lost souls."

"You mean killed them?"

Erik took a drag of his cigarette. "I guess they were already dead," he said. "He was helping them, I think, in his way. I don't think he's a bad person, he was just taken in by Scott's bullshit. Did you ever tell Andromeda about her boyfriend?"

"No. I feel bad, but ... Well, she's happy with Kazuo. She's moved on."

"So, you've come round to my way of thinking?" Erik's lip curled into a slight smile which disappeared almost instantly. "You know, there are times," he said, "usually at 3 a.m. when I can't sleep, when I think, if we'd just let Scott do what he wanted, Lia would still be here, in some form at least."

"You saw what happened to Gade. I wouldn't wish that life on anyone."

"No, and she would've hated it. She didn't belong there, not at all." He looked down. "Still, I think about it."

"Try not to." Wren cast desperately around for a change of subject. "I saw some pictures of you at the première of Lia's ballet."

Erik's eyes brightened. "Hey, yeah, that was something. That was something, Wren. You should go and see it sometime. Tomas and Marianne took the lead parts, in Lia's honour, and I thought they did a pretty good job. I mean, Marianne did okay, but she was nothing to what Lia would've been in that role. Lia would've been sublime."

"I'll bet. Did you speak to them after?"

"Tomas, yes. Marianne, not really. She still hates my guts." Erik laughed. "Some things never change. Still, I'm grateful to her for doing it, although I know she didn't do it for me. To see it all up there on the stage, Lia's own work … Yeah, that was something."

He looked wistfully out toward the Golden Gate Bridge, which, for once, was not obscured by fog. Wren leaned her head on his shoulder.

"You'll be okay, you know," she said. "I think you'll be okay."

Erik stubbed his cigarette out on the bleacher. "Those Dravens'll have your eyes out if we hang around here much longer, kid," he said, getting to his feet. "Anyway, I want to talk to you about that artwork you sent me. I'm thinking of a commission for our new album cover. Wanna get a drink?”

Wren grinned. “Wow, tonic and lime it is, then? I thought you’d never ask.”

She got up, and Erik slung a casual arm around her shoulders as they headed back up towards the city. At the top of the bleachers Wren paused for a moment, looking back out to the bay, and turned her face up to the sun, feeling its strong, solid warmth on her skin. Now, finally, she was truly awake.

ABOUT THE AUTHOR

Antonia Rachel Ward is an author of horror and speculative fiction, based in Cambridgeshire, UK. Her short stories and poetry have been published by Blackspot Books, Brigid's Gate Press, and the British Science Fiction Association, among others. She has published two novellas, *Marionette* and *Attack of the Killer Tumbleweeds*. *DreamScape* is her first novel.

She is also the founder and editor-in-chief of Ghost Orchid Press.

Attack
of the
KILLER
TUMBLEWEEDS
ANTONIA
Rachel
Ward

ANTONIARACHELWARD.COM